REFLECTION

Lynn Yvonne Moon

Reflection
Book 1 of Journey's Travels
by Lynn Yvonne Moon

Second Edition

ISBN 978-1-953278-17-3 Hard Back
ISBN 978-1-953278-18-0 Soft Back
ISBN 978-1-953278-19-7 E-Book

This is a work of fiction. The characters are both actual and fictitious. With the exception of verified historical events and persons, all incidents, descriptions, dialogue and opinions expressed are the products of the author's imagination and are not to be construed as real.

Published by:

INDIGNOR TREEHOUSE

An imprint of Indignor House

Chesapeake, VA 23322
www.indignorhouse.com

Front cover design: Indignor House

This book is dedicated to
those who seek the truth
and will not settle for the lies.

"The most dangerous thing you can do is
educate people. Because when people
become educated, you cannot control
them, you cannot frighten them."

— Jordan Maxwell

1
SWEET GOODBYES

MY MOM, my best friend, my life … I don't have her anymore. Now I'm a stranger even to myself. Without my mom, I have no one to talk to, no one to confide in. How am I to go on without her? I'm only sixteen and I still need her in my life — not just in my fading memories. I should run to her room. Maybe she'll be on her bed reading her favorite book. Maybe I can show everyone just how wrong they were, how they lied to me. It's just that … I know she won't be there.

I pull my dark curls away for the hundredth time. When did I last brush my hair? Last week when Mom yelled at me and told me to take pride in my appearance? Or was it just this morning when my aunt ordered me to *clean up my act*? I don't remember and it doesn't matter anyway. Nothing seems to matter anymore.

"Journey?" My aunt's voice echoes through my pain and jars me back to reality.

"I can't do this," I whisper to the stranger in the mirror who wears a sad face with dark curls that flow past her shoulders. My eyes stare at the old and faded jeans with the holes in the knees. I don't recognize this person, and I definitely don't want *her* judging *me*.

"Journey?" The soft voice comes again. "Are you in here, sweetheart? You okay?" Aunt Deborah stands at my bedroom door. Tears stain her cheeks.

To look directly at her hurts too much, so I gaze at the girl in my mirror. I hate them both because I'll never be okay again.

My aunt darts across the room and slams the window shut with a loud bang. "You'll catch your death. It's freezing outside."

I sigh. "The cold feels good right now." It's the only thing I can think of to say.

"Journey, I know how painful this is for you. I can hardly handle it myself, but life goes on, dear. We all must go on."

Aunt Deborah slaps her hands together as she glances around my now empty room. Her eyes betray her for she's trying so very hard to look happy. There's just too much anger inside me right now to care. Could it be that maybe she can't deal with my mother's recent death? As she stands there with tears rolling down her bright red cheeks, maybe I do feel a little sorry for her. After all, she did just lose a sister. But … I lost a mother.

She looks at me for a few brief moments before adding, "You really should change your clothes and put on a little makeup. You're pale and haven't eaten for days." Her gaze lowers.

All I can think about is how impossible it is for me to look any different than I feel — miserable. "Makeup?" I bite the corner of my lip. "Life might go on whether I like it or not. But don't expect me to paint happiness on my face!" I glare at her. "And who would I be fixing myself up for? *Him*?"

I can't help but think how different she looks from my mom. Being her only sister, you'd think they'd be more alike.

Aunt Deborah places her hands on my shoulders and tries to smile as another tear runs down her cheek. She starts to say something but stops. After a few silent moments, she whispers in my ear. "That *him* is your father, whether you like it or not. And he's going to be here any minute. Pull yourself together. You're really taking this a little too far." She must have realized that I didn't agree because she says the only thing that could change my mind. "If not for you, then for Makayah."

She leaves me alone with the girl in the mirror, and I cringe as I watch another tear fall.

Too far?

A wave of guilt and sadness rolls through me. My mom is dead and I'm taking it too far? 'That *him* is your *father.*' I have to laugh at that one. Some father *he* turned out to be. I've not seen him, in what … five … six years? It's as if he simply fell off the face of the Earth. It hurt when he left. I was determined to get over him, but my mom and sister cried for months when he disappeared.

"He's working," my mom would say, defending him.

The truth was he just didn't care about us. Nope, when my dad divorced my mom, he also divorced me and my little sister. I continue to study the face that stares at me. All I can think about is being left alone with *him*. I want my mom.

I flinch ever so slightly as I watch, from the corner of my eye, my little sister. With her head hung low and her eyes swollen and red, she wraps her arms around herself and stares blankly up at me.

"Hey," Makayah says softly.

Her pain is so intense that it flows off her in waves. My heart aches and I don't know how to help. I used to know how to make her smile. This time, I don't.

"Hey," I say as she plops down on my bed.

I turn to her but to face her means I also must face the truth, and I'm not sure if I'm ready.

"Do you think Dad's changed?" Makayah asks. Being ten doesn't help when it comes to understanding everything life throws at you. I sit next to her. She wears the dark, strong features of our father — brown hair and dark bushy eyebrows.

As always, my heart melts.

"Look," I say, pulling her bangs to one side and exposing her amber eyes — the only feature we share.

"I can't tell you whether Dad will be the same as we remember. I just think that we don't really know him anymore … if we ever did."

"I can't believe Mom's gone." Makayah cries and I hug her. The fact that I can't do anything to ease her pain makes my stomach hurt.

"Girls?" Aunt Deborah yells. "Your father's here."

"Let's get this over with." Still holding Makayah's hand, I stand and glance around my room for the last time. The closet and drawers are empty and my stuffed, old friends sit abandoned on my bed. My walls are stripped of my memories. I leave, pulling Makayah behind me. Time seems to slow with every step we take down that long, cold hallway.

From the landing I can hear his voice, and it feels like a punch in my gut. I've missed him. I have to admit to that. My heart skips as Makayah cries harder.

"Daddy!" She runs down the rest of the stairs. "Daddy!"

He catches her as she flings herself off the last step. He grabs hold and his eyes soften. "Hi, baby girl." He buries his face into her thick wavy hair. "I have missed you."

I watch for what seems like forever before he slowly raises his eyes to meet mine. My pain echoes from somewhere inside my darkness. I can't hold my feelings inside the walls I call my skin any longer. I run to him. As soon as he grabs me, I cry. It's not easy to explain, but I somehow feel safe in his presence. Maybe, just maybe, I might be able to live after all, as long as he's there.

Without saying a word, he guides us toward the waiting taxi. I see that our bags are no longer sitting by the front door. I'm glad because every time I looked at our luggage everything became too real. I follow his lead without thinking.

My aunt stands quietly by the car crying into a white, embroidered handkerchief. She gives us both a quick hug and kiss. No words are spoken for my aunt's tears say it all.

The drive to the airport feels more like a release from the past than the start of a future. The only other time I left home was to visit my father in Colorado and that was a long time ago. As the world flashes by the taxi's window, I lean against my father and rest my head on his arm. Tears roll down my cheeks.

On my father's leg rests Makayah's little hand. The loneliness I feel mirrors those five little fingers — alone on a vast empty stretch of a cold highway. Perhaps I will be okay but I'm not sure if I will ever be totally happy again.

2
DECISIONS

THE CABIN, nestled deep in the mountains, provided us a quiet place to heal.

"It's a great place to work out your feelings," Dad had said when I asked why he brought us here.

I still don't remember the plane ride. I just woke up in my new room with a slight headache. I guess Aunt Deborah was right after all and the stress had finally caught up with me. When my mom died, I thought I would die too. However my dad was right, this is a great place to put one's thoughts in order.

My father, George Gordon, knew that my sister and I needed some alone time. So here we are in this cabin next to a large blue lake that reflects the bright blue sky. Our closest neighbor lives many miles away. Therefore, all we have to entertain ourselves with are the songs of the birds and the crisp cool breeze.

Two huge mountains surround our cabin with jagged ridges and tall pines. I don't recognize either of them, which isn't saying much. They're covered in snow now, but down here by the lake the air is warm. All I need is a light sweatshirt to walk along the water. I love staring up at the puffy white clouds.

A trail of dirt with crushed rock covers the ground from the cabin to the lake. Near the end, a bed of beautiful roses kiss the water giving the place a little color. They're in full bloom right now, and I enjoy their sweet aroma.

I watch from the front porch as my dad and Makayah stroll along the lake. My heart yearns for his attention, then again, I want to yell at him — make him hurt just like he made us hurt.

My dad's a bioengineer working for some tech company here in Colorado. He's assigned to a highly classified project. He and my mom had decided he could concentrate more if we were not with him. They met at college where they both studied biology. They're the brains of the family, not me, for they attended Oxford. I'll be lucky to graduate from a local community college someday.

They always seemed happy but for some reason they divorced. We only heard from him at Christmas and birthdays. It probably would have been nice to have a father around, but eventually I got used to being alone. My mom and sister, they never did. Many nights I could hear one or the other crying. Not me though. I may not be as smart, but I am strong. I may be angry that Dad left, however, I will never cry for a man.

Maybe it would be a good gesture if I joined them. After all, my father was the one who said I needed to talk more about my feelings and be more sociable.

The stairs creak as I hop onto the last step. I start out toward the lake when an old truck rolls to a stop next to Dad's car. I don't remember hearing an engine, but I'm not very observant. The truck surprises me. Over the last couple of months, we've not had even one visitor. A tall man, maybe in his fifties, smiles and waves as he steps out of his ugly yellow truck.

"Hello. You must be Miss Journey."

I'm not sure what to say or do. The funny-looking man just popped out of an ugly canary-yellow truck. It's a little discomforting having a stranger treat me as though he's known me for years. It's important to be polite, so I nod, acknowledging him.

"Is your father home?" he asks as he nods to the right and grins.

I point in the direction of the lake, and he grins and nods to the right again. I watch as he walks to where my dad and sister are throwing pebbles into the water. The man is wearing what looks like an old bathrobe that's weaved with different colors of ribbons and beads. His red and brown embroidered sandals flap against his feet. His overall look reminds me of a hippie from my grandparents' era. His hair is long, white and straight. Very straight. It waves in the wind as he walks.

Makayah runs up to me. "Who's that?"

"Don't know." I sit on the bottom step.

Dad and the stranger talk until Makayah runs down to eavesdrop. Dad must be introducing her to the stranger because she's bouncing up and down. They're heading in my direction when my father points at me and waves. I wave back. Politeness is the least I can offer. For some reason, the stranger makes me nervous.

"Journey?" my father hollers. "Journey Elizabeth!"

Great. I really *hate* meeting new people. I always have. The stranger is tall, in fact, too tall. He has to be way over six feet, maybe closer to seven. His walk is almost a limp but not quite. I shrug off my odd feelings and walk to my father. I'm trying to be friendly.

"This is Abeytu," Dad says.

"Hi, A-bee-to-you." I don't mean to stumble over his name but it's hard to pronounce.

"A-bay-too," Abeytu says slowly, "and we have met. Journey was polite enough to guide me to you. I must apologize, but you *are* your mother all over again, Miss Journey. Just as beautiful."

"Thanks." I lower my gaze. I'm sure he can see the hurt in my eyes as he stands there staring at me. The compliment hurts.

"I am sorry, I should not have said ..." As he starts to say something else, Dad gives him an empathetic pat on the back.

My heart stops. I'm angry at my father for not sticking up for me. He could say something like *Back off ... Her mother's dead ... Give the girl a break.* Of course, that will never happen and ... this stranger meant no harm.

"Let us go inside," Dad says. "How about a cold beer, my friend?"

"Certainly." Abeytu lowers his head and tilts it to the right — as if he's trying to nod.

Man, if this guy isn't weird. I sit on the porch swing and listen through the front windows. Everything seems normal enough, yet something is also quite wrong. I've never seen a man wear a bathrobe in public. Plus, his mannerisms are all off. There's just something not right about this guy.

Makayah darts out with two cans of soda and yells that she'll be back in a few minutes. She tosses one to me. I catch the cold drink and shrug my shoulders as I watch her sprint to the lake. It's a comfort to know that she's coping better than me. She's already combed all the trails around the cabin. I, however, prefer to stay closer to home. I haven't even walked all the way around the lake yet.

I look at the soda. It has a funny label just like everything else around here. Maybe the stuff sold on the West Coast is labeled differently from the stuff on the East Coast. I pop the top, take a sip and strain to hear their conversation.

"You must say something to her soon," Abeytu says to my dad.

I take another sip. It's weird, this soda tastes a little sour.

"Not yet," Dad answers as he glances in my direction.

I turn and stare at the lake pretending to be looking for Makayah. When I turn around, Abeytu is shaking his head and frowning.

"You will not be able to hide things much longer, my friend. The skies will betray you." Abeytu pats my father's shoulder and adds, "She will be fine, George, give her some credit. After all she is an Elder."

An elder? An elder what? Elder sister? What a strange thing to say about me.

"She will not be fine, it is too soon!" Dad huffs as he throws his beer bottle into the trash. He yanks another from the refrigerator.

"Lectures start in less than two masikas, and they will expect her to attend. She needs time to prepare. It is not right to leave her in the dark like this." His statement seems more like an order than a suggestion. With a look close to hatred, he takes another small sip of his drink.

That's when I notice something. Abeytu is not enjoying his beer. In fact, he's loathing it.

My dad's patience must be wearing for he yells. "She just lost the only woman she called *'mother,'* Abeytu! How can they expect her to attend before she even had a chance to fully heal?"

Abeytu sets his beer on the counter and nods. His voice is firm but caring. "Journey will begin lectures in a few masikas. Classification is a requirement, not an option. Whether you agree or not, George, you must speak to her ... tonight. Do not make this harder on either of you. The unexpected is never pleasant." Abeytu pauses before adding, "She has been through enough disappointment already. Do not add to her pain because of your fears."

George sighs and frowns.

Abeytu turns and with that weird little limp walks toward me. I smile for his head just barely grazes the top of the doorframe. When I glance down, I see that his bathrobe brushes along the tops of his sandals.

Feeling brave, I speak to him. "You didn't like that beer, did you? If you don't like the taste, why drink it?"

His warm amber eyes blink. "It is only proper to partake when invited. We must always show respect while in another's home. Please excuse me, Miss Journey, I have pressing duties elsewhere." He nods to the left and limps toward his bright yellow truck.

A cool breeze ruffles my hair and I cringe. It reminds me of that stranger I saw in my mirror several months ago. To pull myself away from the painful memory, I rub the back of my neck and watch as Abeytu limps away. His truck strains to make it back up the hill. For an old beater, it's awfully quiet. I listen but still can't hear the engine.

Maybe the wind is blowing the sound in the other direction, or maybe the mountains are absorbing the noise. My dad stands in the doorway and looks at me. Instead of feeling warm and secure, my heart hardens a little because I just don't wish to talk right now.

"We need to talk," he says.

"Are you a mind reader?"

"Excuse me?" He has a puzzled look.

I smile and shake my head. "Nothing." Although I want to know what's going on, I also do not want to know. Indecision and avoidance — two of my major flaws.

"May I?" he asks, pointing to the empty seat next to me.

I reluctantly nod. As he sits, I turn away. There's nothing to do but swing. I stare at my soda and wish I were someplace else. At the same time, the moment is oddly special — a contradiction, just like my life.

Dad hooks his fingers through mine and his dark eyes make me want to yell at him. "Journey," he begins, "I need you to see something. Walk with me?"

"Walk where?" I stare at him. My furrowed brows are all for show. Even though I'm angry, I still love him more than anything in the world.

"It is important," he says. "I know you are hurting and I would like to help you feel better … if you would let me."

I want to rip his eyes out and scream at him. Tell him how terrible he was for leaving us. I can't cry in front of him. He does not deserve my tears.

"There is so much I need to say to you. I just do not know the correct words. I will promise you this … I will never leave you or your sister again."

He looks sincere, yet something keeps telling me not to let my guard down. I shake my head. If I talk now, I'll only break down and cry. He takes a stronger grip of my hand and stands. As usual, my heart melts. He's winning and I'm furious. I jump up even though my mind's protesting with every heartbeat.

Dad whistles for my sister who runs to him. She's happy living in her own little world. He's giving her the security she needs. I'm grateful for that, although, I don't know if I will ever forgive him.

The three of us follow a small trail that runs through the trees and up the ridge behind our cabin. Foliage of various colors and the sounds of small animals scurrying about almost soothe my nerves … a little. Ferns as tall as my five-foot six body tower above me.

"I don't remember Colorado having plants like these." I trail my hand through their fronds as we walk. The trees also seem taller than I remember — too big. Nothing looks familiar. I feel lost as my fear swells — my personal internal alarm system. Sometimes I have the tendency to overreact and this just might be one of those times.

"Why did you leave us?" The question escapes more forcefully than I intended, which surprises even me. I push my concerns aside as I allow my anger to consume me. The substitution of anger for fear is another one of my faults and this seems like a good time to use it.

Dad stops and stares at me with an understanding-gaze that is somewhat magical. I instantly regret my outburst and wish I would learn to keep my mouth shut once in a while.

"Dad, I …" I stop and search for the right words. I wish not to mess things up any more than I already have. Maybe I can fix it before he says something I don't want to hear.

"Baby," he says, holding both of my arms. "Nothing could have taken me from you if I had the choice. It was not up to me. You will never know how much I did not want to leave. My wife …"

"Your wife?" I yell. "You mean *my* mother?"

"Your … mother … my … wife," he repeats, stuttering.

"You divorced her! Remember?"

"We never divorced." His eyes look sincere and now I'm confused. "I am sorry for leaving you behind. Your mother and

I … we … your mother is my life, my reason to get out of bed every morning."

He aches for her as much I do. The damage was done to us both. Warm arms hug me and I lean in close. I cry as my fear and anger slowly melts together.

"I love your mother and I always will."

His tears seem real and make me cry harder. If they never divorced, then I need to know more. Why did he leave us? Why didn't he come back? I have so many questions that my head aches. We watch as Makayah runs on ahead. What's left of the afternoon sun barely reaches us now. We stand in the dense shade and I shiver. George rubs my arms to warm me. "Come, before it gets too cold."

We continue up the stone steps and the trail is becoming steeper. I'm not happy about our little walk anymore. In fact, it's no walk — it's a hike.

"How much farther?" I'm panting and sweating. I hate to sweat.

"Not much, honest."

When we reach the top, I turn and gasp. The view is spectacular. The pristine lake reflects the dark blue of the afternoon sky, and the mountains on both sides glisten with snow.

"This is beautiful," I say, the past momentarily forgotten. "Thanks for bringing me here, Dad."

"That is not what I need you to see, Journey," he says as he comes closer.

He gently puts his hands on my shoulders and guides me to where Makayah is staring out over the edge. My eyes widen as I try to understand what I'm seeing.

"W-w-what?" I stammer.

With a soft hug, he adds, "Welcome to your legacy, sweetheart."

"Dad?" my voice cracks as I try to speak. "Where are we … exactly?"

"We are home, baby," he says with a strange sense of pride. "We are home."

As far as I can see, a valley of most spectacular colors and shades spreads out below. I'm held within its hypnotic trance. Huge trees with branches that seem to reach out for miles send ripples of dread and confusion all through me. What I'm looking at cannot be real.

"How high are we?"

"Oh, I am not sure … twenty miles?" he says as though it's nothing unusual.

"Dad … we'd be dead!" I snap. "The atmosphere is only breathable for the first ten miles or so. I'm no scientist, but —"

"You are correct, Journey. On Earth only the first few miles are breathable." He holds me firmly.

"What do you mean by … on Earth?" My hands shake as my mind tries to comprehend.

"Look up, baby."

Do I dare? I slowly glance into the darkening sky and almost collapse in disbelief. High above the colorful horizon, three moons are just cresting over a distant mountain range. One is so large that I could imagine touching it. The other two are smaller — one a deep blue and the other a mixture of yellow and orange swirls. This cannot be real.

"Dad? Are those … moons?" I point to the spheres. My stomach tightens as the reality of the situation closes in around me.

"Only the smaller ones. That big, green and yellow one," he points, "is our *sister* world. We only face each other for a short time." His enthusiasm grows with every word. It's almost as though he's exposing a deep dark secret that he could never share before. "That blue one over there," he points again. "Is our moon and the smaller yellowish one belongs to … Journey."

I stare at him for the longest time. "To *me?*"

He chuckles. "That planet is named Journey, and we are standing on Traveler. Twins that need each other's strength to exist. Our moon is Makayah, which means happiness … and yes, it is your sister's name. Makayah is a moon of crystal-clear water with a few islands along the equator. The yellow moon is Aakesh, or Lord of the Sky. It belongs to us ... to Traveler." He smiles. "Without the moons, neither planet would sustain life."

"Dad ... I don't understand." My voice trembles. "How did we get here?"

"The valley behind us belongs to me ... you ... us," he is ignoring my question, "passed down through your family for generations."

"So, I'm not ... *human*?" The thought resurrects my feelings of never really belonging. I'm reminded of that stranger staring at me from my bedroom mirror.

"You are human," he says, chuckling. "We are all human. Your mother is ... well ... um ... well, *I* was born on Earth."

"Dad?" I say, feeling weaker in the knees. "Please, where are we?"

"This is enough for tonight, sweetheart. Let us just enjoy the skies together. We only get a glimpse of our sister world for a little while. Is it not enough to know that you are no longer on Earth? That you are here, with me?"

This at least explains that ugly, yellow truck!

3
CONFESSIONS

"WHY DON'T you tell me about the guy with the yellow truck?" I sit to a breakfast of cereal and cold milk. It's obvious that my father doesn't care to explain how we got here or exactly where here is, but I have to ask something. After all, how many times does one fall asleep on one planet and wake up on another?

Dad laughs. "Bright colors are important to the people of these worlds. Pure energy and a wonderful sensation to experience."

"I don't know about all that, but Abeytu needs to trade in that truck! It's the ugliest thing I've ever seen. And what was he talking about yesterday? I know it has something to do with me. I'm an *elder*? What's that?"

"Oh, so it is all about *you*, huh?" Dad ruffles my hair, and I push his hand away. "Abeytu is helping me now that you two are here. He knew you would realize sooner or later you were not where you thought you were. What with the Wanderers being here and all."

"What's a Wanderer?" I ask, taking another bite of cereal.

"We call those who worship our sister planet the Wanderers because they travel our world to share the strength they receive from the bond. Through their songs and words of wisdom they spread the will to live … makes it easier for us to cope with life's little problems."

"Oh, right, okay," I reply. Dad smiles when I slurp on a spoonful of soggy cereal. I think my father has finally lost his mind. "Where did this cereal come from? Come to think of it, all this stuff is the same as I remember back home. If we're *really* not on Earth, why am I eating Earth food? The boxes look different but it's still the same."

Dad grins as he answers. "We bought what would taste familiar to you." His smile seems staged.

I study his features and decide that I inherited my dark hair from him. My mom had long reddish blonde hair that showed only a hint of a curl. She was short, a few inches over five feet, and her eyes were a light brown. I was taller than her, and my father is way over six feet. His hair is dark, almost black and curly, just like mine. His eyes are a dark brown that sparkle when he's happy. I remember how my mom's eyes would light up whenever she spoke of him. She always said we looked like our father, but I think I look more like her. It's Makayah who's my father's identical twin.

"Eat up," he says as he places the milk back into the refrigerator. "We are running into town this morning for some Martian groceries."

"Town?" I've come to accept that we're not on Earth. But to experience a new planet first-hand, now this is going to be great! "Really? A town? I get to see an *alien* town?"

"Yes, and you are going to love it." He chuckles as he dries a dish before placing it on the shelf. "It is time you see things for yourself."

Screaming and laughing, Makayah runs into the kitchen. She can hardly talk. "Quick, come outside, Journey. You've got to see this!"

I glance at my father for a hint. He just laughs and says, "The Wanderers must have arrived."

I follow Makayah outside. The view that greets me takes my breath away. Standing near the lake are many people wearing white-hooded robes with their hands raised to the heavens. Wanting a closer look, I step into the yard. Curious about what they're reaching for, I turn around. The sister planet hovers directly above our cabin and fills the sky. Their soft chanting saturates the air with a calming vibration that feels overwhelming. I sense a need to be closer to them — to become a part of them.

"The Wanderers?" I ask, looking at my father.

Dad takes our hands and guides us down the path. We stop just in front of the roses. The longer I stand there, the more light-headed I feel.

"Look at the trees," Dad whispers.

My eyes widen as I watch the long branches stretch far into the sky. An invisible force seems to be pulling on everything, guiding them toward the sister planet. I study the amazing sight as the Wanderers' soothing song reverberates around the lake.

"They are paying respect to the force that binds us." My father's eyes are alive with a strange type of yearning.

Even though I can't understand a word, their song consumes me. The sister planet seems so close and I'm mesmerized. I can't resist the urge to reach up and feel what the Wanderers are feeling. As my fingers aim for our sister world, I sense a strong tug.

Jerking my hands back, I gasp. "What was that?" I whisper to my father.

"It is the gravitational link between our worlds," he says softly. "Your mother's blood flows through you, so your body reacts."

"And they're here because?" I nod toward the hooded chanters.

"This land is considered sacred." He gently guides us away from the Wanderers. When we reach our cabin, we sit on the stairs.

"Can I go back to the lake, Daddy?" Makayah asks. "I promise not to bother 'em?" I'm sure she's feeling the same way I am and her excitement thrills even me.

"Yes, baby," he replies, letting go of her hand.

"Dad, how can we *own* sacred land?" I ask. "Isn't that reserved for … oh I don't know … spiritual-type people or something? How can anyone own it? Doesn't sacred land belong to God?"

"You will find out anyway. I might as well just tell you." He sighs. "You are royalty, Journey."

"You're a king?" I ask, shaking my head. "Ah man, this place just keeps getting weirder and weirder."

"No, I am *not* a king. But *you* are from royal descent. Your great, great grandmother is a queen and her husband is a statesman."

"*Is?* They're still alive?"

He doesn't answer.

"You never told me any of this before. What else do I not know about me … about us?"

"This is just as hard for me as it is for you. I never thought in a million years that Rachael … I mean, your mother, would die so young." His gaze falls to the ground as he mentions her name. "I love you with all my heart. It almost killed me to leave you and come here, but I had no choice."

"No choice? No choice? Mother cried every night after you left. We missed you so much, Dad. Why? Mom would never have left you." I cry and it feels good to tell him how I truly feel.

As my angry words flow to the water, a Wanderer stops singing. He slowly walks over to us. The man has a handsome but aged face. He lowers his hood and allows it to drop down his back. His wavy golden hair is the same as Abeytu's, very fine, almost like corn silk. He studies me with his hypnotizing amber eyes.

"Destiny and fate are not something we have control over, Miss Journey." His voice has a rhythmic tune that touches my heart.

How could he possibly know who I am?

"To mourn or reject an unpleasant episode of life does not automatically quench the thirst that swells within our heart. Lingering within our despair and longing for what we have lost only adds to our pain and confusion. Come, Miss Journey, and stand by me. Your heart is in need."

The Wanderer holds out his hands and I can't seem to resist. Deep down, I know I have a choice. But I actually *want* to hold his hands and that's not like me. As we touch, I feel an instant surge of relief. We walk toward the lake and when we stop, he holds out my arms and raises them toward the huge sphere hanging above us. As my fingers reach up, all my pain and anger are pulled from my body. I can feel these negative sensations flow through my fingertips. It is wonderful to have all this pent-up emotion leave me at once. I never realized how much rage was actually inside me. After a few moments, he gently pushes my arms down and gazes into my eyes.

"Better?" he asks with a twinkle in his eyes.

I nod.

"Do not be so harsh or judge your father's actions. Quick and rash decisions set us up for ultimate failure."

I nod again.

"Your father loves you. There are reasons he lived here and why his family could not. It is important that you have patience and learn all there is to know before you pass judgment."

My tears flow and I want to yell at my father. Instead, I turn and reach out to the sister planet for liberation. The gratification is instantaneous, and I'm feeling more like myself. How can this stranger know so much about me and my family?

The man raises his arms again and says, "Give *thanks* to the Most Holy who bind us to our sister-world. Let us feel the love in our hearts. For with love, we conquer every challenge. Love is what holds us to our future and what allows us to forgive our past. It is what makes us who we are and gives meaning to every living thing."

The whole time he's talking, the beautiful singing continues to flow around me. As I gaze at the sister world, I say thank you to the spirits for the release and ask — no — beg them to never leave me. During my short prayer, I again feel something take hold of my fingertips. With shock and confusion, I pull my arms away and rub my hands together for nothing real had actually touched me.

"Ahh, Convergence," the man says. "That is good. The spirits hear your plea." He is smiling.

"Con-what?"

"Convergence. You were touched by the spirits, just now. You felt it, yes?"

I don't respond. I don't know what to say. Something did touch me, but I can't explain it. My dad is smiling. Silently, the man rejoins the others. Whether it's God or gravity, I'm not sure. But at that moment, they are one and the same to me.

4
INTO TOWN

ONCE YOU get to know him, Abeytu is quite fun to be around in a strange ritualistic sort of way. He's such a tall and bulky man that it's almost comical.

"Good morning," Abeytu says with a huge smile. He's always wearing a huge smile, now that I think about it.

I smile back and try not to smirk as I stare at his sandaled feet. His toes are huge, much larger than an ordinary man's toes. Then again, what do I know about *ordinary* anything anymore?

"Good morning to you, Abeytu." I say his name slowly, so I get the pronunciation right the first time. "You're coming with us?"

"Yes, your father invited me."

I decide to pry into his life a little. Being brave, I say, "Do you have any relatives here?"

"Yes … and no," he answers. "Some are here and others live at a distance. I must be close to my work." He takes a seat on the porch swing and stares at me.

"And what do you do exactly … for work I mean?"

"In your world, you would probably call me a researcher." He glances into the cabin. "Are you excited about visiting the town?"

"Oh yes, I want to know everything about this place, and my life or what my life's supposed to be."

"There is a lot for you to learn," he replies as Makayah bounces out of the cabin happy as always.

"Hi, Abeytu," she says, giving him a hug. She really likes the man.

"Hi, Princess, are we ready to go?"

"Yep, Daddy says for us to wait in the car," she answers, hopping off the porch.

"I guess we should wait in the car then." Abeytu stands.

Dad walks out of the cabin and takes in a deep breath of fresh air. "Wonderful morning," he says, staring out at the lake. "Should be a nice day after all, my friend."

"Yes, it should," Abeytu replies.

The drive into town is interesting. Buildings similar to Earth's line the streets, and people fill the sidewalks wearing what looks like — bathrobes — long colorful bathrobes. I giggle.

"What is so funny, Journey?" Dad glances back at me and winks. "Everything is not that much different from home is it?"

"Not much different?" I ask, trying to absorb everything I'm seeing. "Everyone is wearing *bathrobes* … and in public!"

Dad laughs. "When the Wanderers visit us, many enjoy wearing their tribal clothing. They are wearing robes, Journey, not bathrobes."

"They still look funny to me," I say, staring out the window.

"Do you think I look funny?" Abeytu asks from the front seat.

"Now that you mention it." I feel a little embarrassed for speaking so boldly. "Why don't you wear jeans or something more normal?"

"It is our custom. Times are changing and some of the younger ones, those close to your age, are wearing less formal attire. For me, I do not wish to let go of the past." Abeytu sounds a little sad.

The sights outside hold my attention. The streets are paved and the cars are slowly passing or parked along the streets. Then it hits me.

"Hey! We're in a car. They drive cars here?"

"Of course, we are in a car," Dad replies. "Where do you think people of Earth got the idea?"

"What?" I'm not really grasping what he's insinuating.

"People all over the universe have to move around in some fashion. Cars and trains are most common throughout the galaxies. The only difference is what makes them go. For example, we use a form of nuclear power. We never have to charge a battery or refill a tank."

Universe? My mind repeats my father's words. Galaxies? Not wanting to feel even more stupid, I sigh and say, "Of course. But what if you crash? Wouldn't it cause a nuclear explosion or something?"

"As I said, something similar to nuclear power."

"What were you thinking?" Makayah asks, pinching her fingers together and waving them in front of my face. "Maybe hover-cars or tiny little spaceships?"

"Very funny." I slap away her hand. Everything I see reminds me of a small Earth town from the fifties. I love it all. "Okay, where's the Wal-Mart?"

"Stores are family owned," Abeytu explains. "You will find no ... what do you call them ... chain stores? Our people work to live, unlike on Earth where people live to work. We are only concerned about making enough to survive comfortably."

"You are right, Abeytu," Dad adds. "People from Earth seem to only care about how much they can make for as little amount of effort possible."

"Where are we going first?" I ask, hoping my question will stop my dad's lectures on finances. Once he gets started on a subject, getting him to stop is quite difficult.

"The market," he replies. "We need groceries." He turns into a small driveway that's between two brick buildings.

"This is so cool." My mind twirls with the possibilities as my anticipation soars.

He parks behind a small store and as I step out of the car, a thin young girl of about ten or eleven with bluish green skin and amber eyes walks past. She's wearing jeans and an orange T-shirt with something written on it that I can't read, but I recognize the Nike logo. Her hair is a brownish-red and pulled into a ponytail. A thin leather strap is attached to her hair that drapes down her back. She smiles and says *'hi'* as she passes. Makayah waves before darting into the store. I, however, can't move.

"Uh, Dad?"

Hugging me around my shoulders he explains, "Do not be alarmed. She is from our sister world, and her race is called Swetaachata. Her people and ours now share both worlds."

"Oh?" I follow him, not knowing what else to say.

Walking into the small market, eagerness consumes me. The store has all kinds of fresh food that I've never seen or tasted, and all within my reach. I grab several of everything that doesn't look familiar and toss them into our cart. Dad watches as though he's experiencing it all for the first time. There are strawberries that have blue and yellow stripes. I doubt if they're called strawberries, but that's what they look like to me. I'm staring at them when my dad plops one into my mouth. A wonderful flavor I can never put into words explodes across my tongue. The juice runs down my throat and I instantly want more.

"These are great, what are they?" I wipe the juice off my chin with the back of my hand.

"Ovarfleash, they are the fruit of the Most Holy," he answers. "An old story tells of a war that was once fought over these little things."

"Did Mom ever come in here?" I ask, stealing another one.

"Yes, she does and your mother loves these," he says with a tenderness that warms my heart. "She can eat them for hours, and then spends the rest of the afternoon in the bathroom."

"Dad." I slap him on the arm. "More information than I need."

"It is the truth. She loves these." He picks up a little brown berry and hands it to me. "Here, try one."

Although he still speaks of my mom in the present, my heart tightens as I remember her. But my emotions are rescued as my mind drifts over the new flavors of the little brown fruit. This berry is just as juicy and sweet as the other one and I love it.

"What is this?" I ask, trying to ignore his statement about my mother.

"Now that is a Chachafleash," he explains. "It is from a valley on Journey. Very popular here."

"I'm liking it on this world more and more." I grin as I shove another Chachafleash into my mouth.

As I pick out those I believe to be ripe, I notice a young man searching through what looks like orange bananas with black stripes from a large wicker basket. I don't mean to stare, but he is gorgeous. His skin is a light bluish green just like the girl from outside. He isn't overly shiny but his skin does reflect the light as if he'd just applied a light film of oil or lotion. His hair is a dark reddish brown with blonde and red highlights. Several strands are braided with a leather strap that is decorated with a few colorful beads. Some of his hair is pulled into a ponytail with the rest falling loosely down his back to his waist. He's also wearing jeans.

George glances over at the boy and grins. "What a surprise, I do believe that is Takodaovi."

Doesn't anyone have a normal name around here?

"Takodaovi?" Dad waves when the boy turns around.

His face is amazing! I can't take my eyes off him. He stands almost as tall as my father with broad shoulders and lean muscles. His eyes are huge, and I'm surprised to see that they're the same color as mine — amber. I'm mesmerized by his lips for they are a deep shade of pink.

"Sir?" Takodaovi says. "How very nice to see you again, my lord." He nods in the same strange way Abeytu did the other day.

"I would like you to meet my daughter, Journey. Journey, this is Takodaovi. His father is a co-worker and very dear friend."

I can't talk and I can't breathe. All I can do is hope he doesn't notice the juice dribbling down my chin and all over my brand-new yellow top. Takodaovi doesn't smile right away because he's staring at me. Probably wondering what's wrong with me.

"Pleasure to meet you, Miss Journey."

That voice! I'm melting from the inside. I have this urge to grab him and never let go. Dad stares at me, quizzically.

"Journey? Are you all right?" Dad asks with honest concern.

"Uh huh," I mumble, but I can't talk. I can only make a crooked little grin and pray that I can soon find a hole or something to crawl into. *Have I just fallen in love at first sight with an alien from another galaxy?*

With Dad holding back a laugh and looking very amused, he says something that changes my life forever. "Takodaovi, Journey will be starting classes later this month. Could I impose and ask if you would be so kind as to show her around the campus for me? I could drop her off at your cabin, or you can pick her up at ours. I think it would be easier on her if she is familiar with the place before classes begin."

Now I know I'm going to faint, and when I do, I will hit the floor and my head will split into two pieces and roll into different directions. I grab onto the fruit stand for support.

I can't go anywhere with this guy. He's just too drop-dead gorgeous!

"I would be honored, sir," Takodaovi replies without hesitation.

"Journey?" Dad asks with his eyes narrowed. "Are you sure you are okay?"

Mustering all my courage and with a half-eaten berry still in my mouth, I whimper a small, "Yes."

"Miss Journey, I am free tomorrow. Perhaps I could escort you then and introduce you to our governors?"

I giggle. I'm thinking this guy could take me anywhere he wants. I nod and wipe the juice from my chin. I'm probably just smearing it all over my face. My dad and Takodaovi say their goodbyes. I stand there gawking like an idiot. I have never felt so stupid.

"Maybe you had one too many berries?" Dad suggests with concern. "Perhaps you are allergic or something?"

Yeah, maybe I'm allergic. Allergic to Takodaovi.

As I'm trying to recoup from the most embarrassing moment of my life, Makayah runs up to us. "Journey." Makayah laughs. "You have red stuff all over your face, and I think you've ruined your new shirt."

"Come, little one." Abeytu pulls her away as he glances at me with pity. "Let us see what is in the cereal section. Perhaps we can find you something good."

The rest of the day flies by in a blur because all I can think about is *him*. My father keeps looking at me like I have totally lost it, and perhaps I have. I can't concentrate on anything he's telling me. It isn't until we return to the cabin that I start to feel a little more like myself. All the while, I cannot get Takodaovi out of my mind. Earlier in the week, I saw a computer in my father's study. With curiosity getting the better of me, I decide to snoop. I have to find out more about these blue people. After a dinner of fresh fish and potatoes, I decide to ask Dad.

"Dinner was great, Journey." Dad compliments me as he helps me clear the counter.

"Daddy, can I watch TV?" Makayah asks as she gulps down the rest of her milk.

"A little." Dad studies me as he sits the dishes next to the sink.

Now is the perfect time, I tell myself, because he's preoccupied with Makayah. "Dad? Do we have internet on this planet?"

He places the last dish on the counter. "Yes. You can use my laptop until I pick one up for you. The system is set to English so you should not have any problems. Just click the icon that looks like a small television. The rest is pretty much like the Internet you are used to back home. Let me know if you have any problems. You cooked, so I will take care of these dishes."

"Cool, thanks." I aim straight for his office.

As usual, Dad is right. The Internet is just like at home. My only issue is that I can't spell what I want to look up. I glance around George's study and see several books on a shelf that catch my attention. I'm lucky, the first book I grab is just the one I need. It's titled, *History of the Swetaachata People*. I skim through the pages. There are pictures of people who resemble Takodaovi and the girl from the parking lot. The writing is not English, so I can't read the captions.

"They are an interesting culture, Journey. Want me to tell you about them?"

I jump and almost drop the book. I didn't hear Dad sneak up on me. "Sure."

I must sound a little too eager because he chuckles. "It is a beautiful evening. Let us sit outside."

The fresh air reminds me of rosemary and pine, and the sister planet and moons are hovering just above the treetops. The late afternoon sun is reflecting off Journey and keeping the evening in a layer of heavy twilight. Standing around the lake, the Wanderers are still softly chanting their prayers of respect. Everything is perfect.

"Do they ever eat or sleep?" I ask, as we sit on the porch swing.

"They must because they are just as human as we are."

The chanting is soothing, not too loud, not too soft, just right. Perhaps I'm finally settling into my new life. I miss my mom something terrible, but if I have to be somewhere, here is where I want to be.

"Let me think … how do I start." Dad's thinking out loud. "Most of this you will learn in class. I can tell you what I know. The Swetaachatas are from our sister world Journey. You were named after her because your mother loves her so much. We spent many nights sleeping outside beneath her. Your mom can gaze upon her for hours."

Dad pauses as if remembering a precious memory. I smile. I really wish I could have had them both at the same time. Now I feel cheated out of something special.

"The Swetaachata are tribal. Their numbers must be in the millions by now. We made contact about a thousand generations ago. In fact, a long time before Earth was even colonized."

"Earth was colonized?" I repeat, confused.

"Yes. We will leave that little bit of history for your professors." He laughed. "The Swetaachata are a proud people. Education is almost a religion to them. They do not put a face on their god like we do. They consider God as their maker and provider, not someone to worship as we do on Earth."

"Do they pray to our planet like the Wanderers do to theirs?" I ask.

"As a matter of fact, they do. When our ancestors first met the Swetaachata, they discovered that our beliefs were almost identical. We both prayed to our sister world as it passed. Our skin color is a factor of our environment — or so the scientists tell us. We can survive on Journey as they can survive here. Something in Journey's atmosphere causes a change in the child while growing inside the mother."

"Are you telling me that if Mom carried me on Journey that …?"

"That you would have been a different color? Yes, that is why she lived here during her pregnancy. She thought you should resemble us as much as possible."

"Interesting." I have so many questions I don't know where to start.

"As we traded between our worlds," Dad continues, "we learned about each other and how similar we were. We also learned about our differences."

"Differences?" I ask.

"We have a two-chambered heart where they have three or four. Our bodies use a liver to purify our blood, and they have a different organ for that."

"Can we mate with them?" I ask, blushing.

He laughs at my question. "No, Journey, it is forbidden."

"Forbidden? Why?"

"Unions were tried but no child survived. After many generations of broken hearts, the council decided to prohibit unions or marriages between our people." I must have given him a strange look because my father adds, "It is better this way. It guarantees that our races remain pure."

"I'm a crossbreed? I'm half Earthling, and ..." I realize I have no idea what my mother called herself. "What *is* my other half?"

"Fornaxian. These planets are in the Fornax galaxy. Your ancestors, who colonized this world, came from somewhere unknown. We have no way of knowing if life still exists there. We have found some ruins on planets in nearby solar systems but we cannot verify if our theories are correct. The teachings only go back so far and beyond that there are no written records. Even the Swetaachata have limited teachings in regard to their origin. The people here are as the people of Earth, naive about where they come from. As do we, they must rely on their religions or ancient carvings for what truths they can find."

"Can't you dig up something?"

"There is nothing to dig up. The ruins were abandoned long ago and nothing was left behind — no writings, no drawings. The ruins on Earth were staged, so to speak. They were created to leave hidden messages for future generations. The ruins here are empty."

"No pyramids?" I ask.

Dad laughs a little. "No pyramids."

"Would you like some tea?" I have a need to touch something normal and familiar.

"I have some great Passifloral tea, you will love it. It is a flower from Journey's moon."

We walk inside. Makayah is lying upside down on the couch with her head resting on the floor. She's watching the television, which is a large flat screen.

"What are you doing?" I ask as I stop to check on her.

"They say we have to watch it this way," she answers as she chews on her popcorn.

"You're going to choke. You need to sit up to eat that stuff."

"No, I don't," she argues.

Shaking my head, I sit next to her to see what's on. It's a bunch of kids dancing and singing and running around a large complex that resembles a zoo, however, they are inside not outside. Monkey-looking animals are hanging upside down from a tree branch and dancing. It doesn't look very interesting, so I give her a pat on the leg and join my father in the kitchen. He hands me a cup of hot tea.

Our cabin is just right, comfortable and cozy. The front faces the lake and is all glass. A small parlor with a fireplace is to the right when you enter. The porch swing is just outside the large windows. Across from the fireplace is the kitchen with a bar and four chairs. Behind the parlor is the den, our bedrooms and my father's study. We live very much the same as we did in the mountains of North Carolina.

The furnishings are simple, and I can sense my mom's presence everywhere. A painting of a fox and bear drinking from a stream hangs over the fireplace. I know that it belonged to her because she loved animals. A day after he took me on our little walk, I snooped in his bedroom and found that mom's clothes are still hanging in his closet. It's sad.

"Dad?" I ask, trying to find the right words. "Why *did* you leave us on Earth? Why weren't we raised here?"

He doesn't answer. Instead, he walks into his study and returns carrying a brown album with both mine and Makayah's baby pictures on the cover. I've never seen it before. Every page is filled with pictures of either him or my mother, or of me and my sister together. The pictures are endless, and I cry.

5

INTRODUCTIONS

THIS MORNING, Takodaovi is wearing jeans and a long sleeve shirt, and he captures my heart by being just as beautiful as the previous day. Makayah gives him a quick hug before running into the house. If only I could be more like her with all that self-confidence.

Deciding that everyone on this planet wears jeans, I wear mine. Since it's a little chilly this morning, I add my dark-brown sweater to the mix. Instead of tennis shoes, I pull on my tall brown boots with the one-inch heels. The perfect match. My hair, being hopeless as ever, is pulled back into a ponytail. As always, several strands pop out curling tightly about my face. Having dark eyebrows and thick eyelashes, makeup is never required. However, I did decide on a little lip-gloss to brighten my face.

"Good morning," Takodaovi says as he enters the cabin.

"Want some breakfast?" Makayah asks. "We bought some great cereal yesterday at the store."

"No, thank you," he replies. "I ate before I left."

"I thought it only polite to accept what's offered?" I say standing on the front porch. I was hiding under a tree and he obviously didn't see me. I can't believe how forward I'm acting after yesterday's stupidity.

"Yes, you are correct, Miss Journey. Perhaps I should accept some cereal," Takodaovi says as he nods to the left.

I sigh. "You don't have to eat. I'm only kidding. One of my dad's friends … well, he hates beer but he forced himself to drink it just to please my father. I thought it odd that's all."

"So, she does speak." Dad yells from the kitchen.

I laugh and Takodaovi smiles. "Yes, I speak. It's just that —"

"You are shy?" Takodaovi suggests.

"Yes, shy." It's almost as if Takodaovi is protecting me and it feels good.

"You are prettier without the juice on your face," he adds, with a cute grin.

Shaking my head, I shrug. *I guess I deserve that one.*

"You two stay safe today." Dad calls from the kitchen.

"I will have her home in a few hours, sir." Takodaovi nods to the right.

I give my father a kiss on the cheek. "Love you, Dad."

I guess the change in my attitude is a little unexpected because it even takes me by surprise. I'm just really happy right now.

Takodaovi has, what can only be called, a covered jeep. It's kind of cool, but its neon-green color is not.

"Nice color," I muse as he opens the passenger door.

Luckily, he doesn't catch my sarcasm for he replies with, "Thank you." And again, he nods.

When he scoots in behind the wheel, I have to ask, "Why does everyone nod when they answer a question?" Takodaovi looks puzzled so I clarify. "You and my dad's friend nod. You did it just now when you said thank you. You nodded your head like this." I demonstrate for him.

"If you nod to the right, you are in … agreement. If you nod to the left, you are … how do you say … apologizing? Saying you are sorry." He hesitates a few moments as though he's thinking of the best way to explain it. "I believe that is a good example."

"Oh, okay. Where are we going today, Takodaovi?" I do not wish to dominate the conversation. Takodavoi's accent is almost a melody, and I want to hear his voice, not mine.

"May I ask a favor, Miss Journey?" Takodaovi asks as he starts the vehicle.

"Of course, anything."

"Would you please call me Takoda?"

"Certainly, Takoda," I try out the nickname. That he even asked me makes me feel special. "And … call me Journey … no miss necessary."

We start down the mountain road with big smiles on our faces. Instead of turning right onto the main road, we head in the opposite direction. I've never been this way before.

"I am honored that your father asked me to show you around. We do not call it school but it is what comforts you." Takoda glances at me and my stomach tightens.

I'm still nervous around him and do not wish to make an idiot out of myself.

He parks at a small station where long silver train-looking vehicles are hovering over tracks. I can just barely make out what looks like a thick dull strip of metal embedded in the ground. I look under one of the trains. Nothing but air is holding it in place.

"Where are we?" I ask knowing the answer as soon as I ask, which again makes me feel stupid.

"We live far from the campus. We must ride the trains."

"Floating?"

"Magnets. Our roads do not travel everywhere, Miss Journey."

I sigh. "Journey … please, just Journey."

He nods to the right, which makes me feel a little better.

The station is empty except for one other person. I see no attendants. Everything must be purchased from a vending machine. Takoda buys two tickets and two drinks. We sit on a bench to sip and wait.

"Are you happy living with your father?" His question comes from out of nowhere.

Before I reply I take a sip of the drink. Something very bitter hits my tongue. I cough and almost spit it out. Takoda frowns and the look on his face frightens me. I'm not making a good impression on this guy.

"My apologies, Miss Journey. Have you not tasted this before?"

"No … what is it?"

"Everyone loves it." He reaches for my can. "May I find you something else?"

After thinking about it for only a second, I hug the can to my chest. It's better if I can fit in. "No, I think I like it." I lie. "I was just expecting something sweeter, that's all."

He smiles. "Next time I will warn you first."

"Okay and yes, I'm happy here. As happy as I can be. I mean … I never thought I would lose my mom."

With a sincere gaze, Takoda's eyes sparkle. "We never expect to lose our parents when we are so young. I had not heard of your mother's passing. May I ask how she died?"

His soft voice seems so warm that I believe he really does care. Takoda is just so sweet I want to tell him everything about me.

"She was sick for a long time, a blood disease. It wasn't easy for her … or us."

"I feel as you feel, Journey. My mother died when I was young." His eyes echo my emotions.

Sharing our grief makes me feel closer to him. "What happened to her?"

"She died giving life to my younger sister," he says as our train comes to a silent stop just a few feet from us. No sound, not even a hum or a vibration. "It is nice having someone who understands." He stands and reaches for my hand. "This is our ride."

I take his hand into mine. The touch sends ripples throughout my body, and the sensation exhilarates me. Never in my life have I felt like this, and I never want to let go. I can tell he's feeling it too because he stops and looks into my eyes. We stare at each other for what seems like forever, although it's only a few seconds. But within those few seconds, it's as if our minds have merged. I sense his breathing and beating heart as my internal rhythm suddenly syncs with his.

Together we board the train to find seats. We pick ones next to a window. We sit in silence as the train pulls out of the station. I'm too afraid to speak. I don't want to ruin the special moment we just shared.

As the train flies down the track at a tremendous speed, I try to see the countryside. I can't see much of anything except for a big blur. With nothing else to do, I sit back and empty my mind. The train makes two stops before we arrive at our destination.

Our campus is a hectic place with lots of students coming and going. Since the school is not yet in session, everyone is wearing colorful clothing and blue jeans. The girls are gorgeous, with their long red hair and delicate features. The boys are even more god-like, with their long hair decorated with various colorful straps of leather. I see several students who look like me but most are Swetaachata. I hear laughter and talking. Everyone seems to be friends with everyone else.

Maybe I have a chance to make some friends. Back home, I didn't have many. Most girls were into heavy makeup and skimpy clothes. That's just not me. Feeling only a little out of place, I follow Takoda through the crowd. Every now and then someone calls out his name and waves. It's obvious he's popular, and despite our shared moment, I'm worried that he is way out of my league.

"Not much farther, Miss Journey. This way," he urges.

Walking slightly behind Takoda, I feel like a puppy following my new master. I just hope I don't look like one. As we leave the small courtyard, the campus spreads out before me. Large buildings, a mixture of gothic castles and modern skyscrapers, nestle quietly between two huge mountains. Rolling green lawns surround and hug each building. In the center, a small lake, decorated by flowering trees, reminds me of a postcard I once saw.

"Wow," is all I can whisper.

Takoda chuckles and tightens his grip. He guides me down the walk and toward the first building. The warm sun's hitting my face and I'm enjoying his hand in mine. My dad had told me that holding hands didn't mean anything. However, there's no reason I can't pretend.

"Takoda!" A high-pitched screech echoes out from under a nearby tree. It's a Swetaachata girl who was talking to several young women who are nothing less than blue goddesses.

Takoda grunts and squeezes my hand tighter. "This is not what I need right now."

He seems to be happy seeing everyone after their short break. But the look on his face gives away his true feelings. He doesn't like this person.

She's tall and slender with dark red hair. Her skin is a bluish green just like Takoda's. Her hair's thick and she wears it straight. She walks toward us and her beads make a tingling sound that would have been pleasant on another individual. The scowl that's plastered across her face takes away from her beauty. I dislike her immediately.

"What is it you want, Anneeta?" he asks, glaring at her.

Anneeta fixates on me with a hateful stare. Her chest is puffed out and her hips are swayed to one side. It's unlike what I've experienced so far on this peaceful world. Anneeta definitely has a problem and I know immediately what it is — it's me.

"Perhaps I should leave you two alone?" I say, trying to pull my hand away but Takoda's grip tightens.

"Anneeta," he says, a little louder this time. "What exactly do you want?"

She hesitates. Her gaze never once leaves my face.

"If you have nothing pressing, we must be going. We have much to do."

We take a step and Anneeta blocks our way.

"I have not heard from you in many dzanas, Takoda." Now her gaze falls to the ground and her shoulders drop. "Why not?"

He answers her more gently than I would have. "I told you, Anneeta. I will not union with *you*. We have no relationship."

"Who is this?" She points at me.

"This is Miss Journey, she is the daughter of —"

"I know *who* she is, but I cannot believe she is here with you! Or better yet why are *you* here with *her*?" She's so loud that it's as if she wants everyone on campus to hear.

"That is none of your concern and you are being rude, Anneeta. Your attitude is not appropriate. Take leave of us." Takoda's serious and his grip tightens even more. If she doesn't leave soon, my hand may not survive. "Now, Anneeta!" His words have such conviction that they make *me* want to leave.

"I will not accept this, Takoda. I will be your nubere alicui, not her!" Tears form in her eyes and her voice trembles. "It was foretold in the writings, remember?"

"Look," I say, feeling completely out of place. "Takoda and I just met, and my dad asked him to show me around —"

"I care not what you have to say!" Anneeta screams so loud that I take a step back. "Your words mean nothing to me. I do not see you."

This is definitely not a good way to start my education. I glance around to see if anyone is watching, but no one is. In fact, it's as if everyone suddenly disappeared into thin air.

"Enough, Anneeta!" Takoda yells. "What a shameful display of disrespect for our statesman's daughter. Select your words carefully. Do not say something you will come to regret. I demand that you let us pass."

Takoda isn't backing down, and I want to leave. I want to run away. Ever so cautiously, I slip behind Takoda trying to hide the best I can. Unfortunately, he's still refusing to release my hand.

Several men wearing uniforms run up to us. They must be the campus police. "Excuse me," an officer says. "What is the problem here?"

Anneeta replies in a language I don't understand. She gawks sternly at the officer as though she's now challenging *him* to invade her space.

"Miss, would you come with us please?" The officer's orders are stern and he grabs hold of her arm. "Do not make this more difficult than it has to be."

Anneeta gives me the death stare before glancing at Takoda. She makes a strange motion that touches my heart. Anneeta strokes her cheek with her knuckles then opens her hand to Takoda. He stands there staring at it. His lack of response obviously hurts and she cries. She walks away with the officers. As soon as she's out of earshot, Takoda relaxes his grip, which is a good thing because I think the blood has stopped flowing to my fingers.

"Okay, what was that all about?" I ask.

Takoda notices that people are staring at us. With the warm sun calming our nerves, we again start our walk toward the first building. I can't resist looking over my shoulder. Anneeta is nowhere in sight. I just know I have not seen the last of her, and I know she'll definitely not make my life here an easy one.

"We were to be unioned," he says, pulling me from my thoughts.

"You mean married?"

"I believe that is how you understand it," he replies. "I saw what she is like on the inside. Her heart is not good."

"I see." I want to know more but I'm hesitant to intrude.

We stop under the shade of a large tree and he continues to explain. "A good heart is important to me. If a heart is sad, then life with that person would not be happy and filled with sorrow. I want a happy life."

"She said it was written. Are your marriages pre-arranged or something?"

"Yes and no. She is talking about the Oracles who predict what will be. Their writings do not always come to pass." Takoda smiles and it's nice watching his face brighten again. "Come, let me show you around. After all, this is why we are here."

The first building we enter is some kind of a student center with offices and a cafeteria. There's a bookstore in the middle, and I can look straight up through the building to the glass ceiling many floors above. Hanging vines drape toward the floor as the trees reach up to meet them.

"This is Administration." He says, pulling me around the lobby. "You sign up for your classes here, buy your books and other supplies over there. There is a place to sit and eat too. The gym and swimming pool are on the second level. The higher floors house the library, our philosophy and healing classes."

We stand for a few seconds so I can adjust to my new surroundings. Students and teachers are walking around shopping or eating. Some are just talking or sitting. People seem content.

"What do you think?" he asks.

"Wow."

"We really need to work on your vocabulary," he adds. "Come and let me show you the other buildings."

By the time we finish strolling through the campus, eat lunch and walk the grounds a second time, it's time to leave. I discover Takoda's easy to talk to, and he actually listens to what I have to say. He tells me about his family and how it saddens him that his little sister will never know their mother. He explains how my father used to work with his father at the assembly center. I tell him about Earth and how funny it is that people here seem to love blue jeans so much. A new fad, apparently.

I find it odd he never mentions his home planet of Journey. It's okay though because I just want to know about him.

"I wish to be your friend," he says as we ride the train home. "You have a good heart. I enjoy my time with you. Will you please be my friend?"

"I thought we were already friends?" I'm surprised he thought he had to ask. Then I remember I'm not on Earth anymore and quickly add, "Yes, Takoda, I will be your friend." We sit together the rest of the way home holding hands. When we finally walk back to his jeep, I ask, "Will Anneeta be okay with us being friends? Am I safe being your friend?"

"You have no worries from Anneeta. You are the daughter of a Council member and it would be very bad for her if she does not show you the respect you are owed."

Although I understand, his answer doesn't make me feel any better. *Kickboxing*, I say to myself. *I must learn kickboxing.* Do they even offer a class for that here? I will have to check once I'm officially enrolled.

6
TUTORIAL

THE MORNING sun woke me early. It's my first day of school and the mystery of it all only adds to my excitement. Dad will be taking me this morning, and I'm a little anxious to see if I will run into Takoda.

We really seemed to hit it off, and it would be easier to make it through the day with someone to talk to — or hide behind. As my anticipation grows, my heart also sinks as I think about Anneeta. I shrug. Even if she makes my first day a nightmare, there isn't much I can do about it now.

I pull the uniform that Abeytu dropped off for me out of my closet. Black isn't exactly my color, but I'm stuck with it. The outfit's not bad, not really. The slacks are tight fitting and flare a little at the ankles. The jacket reminds me of an elevator man's uniform with gold buttons down the left side, not in the middle. We're to wear a lightweight, dark-blue turtleneck, which is very soft and comfortable. There's even a cute little hat that reminds me of an old English army beret with the school logo on it.

Standing in front of my mirror, I feel a little awkward. I look good for the outfit compliments my rather thin frame. We picked up some black boots when we went into town the other day, and I'm zipping them up when my dad enters my room.

"Ready for the big day, sweetheart?" he asks.

"Do I have a choice?" I reply. "This uniform is comfortable."

"I think the clothing here is better than back home," he says with a chuckle. "And six more uniforms will be delivered sometime today. You will not survive with just one."

I nod and smile as we head for the kitchen. Makayah's just finishing her breakfast. I smile as I admire her red school jumper and plaid knee-socks. The outfit matches her spunky personality.

"Good morning." Abeytu greets us from the front door.

"Good morning, Abeytu, my friend." Dad pours himself a cup of coffee. "Would you like some?"

"Don't accept it unless you like Earth coffee," I warn with a smile. "Where we come from, it is not an insult if you say 'No, thank you.'"

He nods with a smile. Abeytu seems to have a good sense of humor. "Earth coffee is good, Miss Journey." Dad hands him a cup and he *coos* out a long-drawn-out sigh as he takes a sip, "Mmm......, very good, thank you."

I laugh because I know his moan of delight is just for me.

"You are welcome," my father replies. "It looks like Makayah is ready to go. Right, Sport?"

"Yep," Makayah answers, jumping up from the table and giving Abeytu a hug. "Let's go, Abeytu. Bye, Dad. See yah, Journey."

"I guess we are off then," Abeytu says, nodding.

"Perhaps we should be going too," Dad says.

After I finish my toast and juice, I grab my bookbag. "Are we taking the train?"

"Yes," he replies. "And we need to get a move on. Ready?"

"Ready as I'll ever be." I follow him out of the cabin and into the cool and crisp morning air.

Our ride to the campus is uneventful, and I'm soon registered for classes and saying goodbye to my dad. I reassure him I know my way home and he kisses me on my cheek. I watch him as he walks away. It feels good to be alone but also a little scary.

Although I've always thought that uniforms were for geeks, I think I'm going to like wearing one. Everyone all dressed up makes the classes seem more official. My guide escorts me to my first class, which is at the back of the campus. Although the buildings are made from large stones and are huge, the classrooms look just like any other classroom back on Earth. Swetaachata Culture is on the fifth floor, and the group is small with only fifteen students, which is a good thing. I'm already intimidated enough.

Math is next, then philosophy and right before lunch is Ancient History. These classes were much larger, about forty students in each. When I enter Ancient History, I accidentally bump into the person in front of me, and when she turns around my heart stops. It's Anneeta.

"Excuse me," I say, trying to evade her while desperately searching for some place to hide. She refuses to budge, and I have nowhere to go.

"There is no excuse for you." She snickers. If looks could kill, I would be several feet under right now. In fact, I should have fallen straight through this planet.

Out of defense and not knowing what else to do, I lower my head and wish that my first class each morning was kickboxing. Like a complete idiot, I just stand there holding up the students trying to get into the classroom. My worst nightmare is coming true — I'm causing a scene on my first day.

"Please, Anneeta. I really am sorry for bumping into you." I look behind me for some kind of support. No one seems very anxious to help. She's taller than me and I'm frightened. Before I can say I'm sorry again, an arm wraps around my waist and a strong bluish green hand shoves Anneeta away.

"The lady apologized to you, Anneeta. Get out of her way or I will report you to the authorities." Takoda is almost yelling at her as he escorts me into the classroom.

Thank God, I'm saved at last.

"Want to sit with me, my friend?" His warm smile is what I really need at this exact moment.

"Yes, most definitely." I know I'm smiling no matter how hard I try not to.

"Good. Lunch is next so we can sit together," he adds, as he glares over his shoulder at Anneeta. When he looks back, he whispers, "Having a friend is a good thing."

"Yes, it is." I now glance at Anneeta and feel as though I've accomplished something. But I'm sure the only thing I've accomplished is inviting an early death upon myself. It's great to be with Takoda again. Therefore, I don't really care.

The class is interesting, and I take lots of notes. Throughout the whole time, I keep feeling the heat bouncing off the back of my head as Anneeta continues to stare at me.

"I think I'm doomed," I say, as we shove our tablets into our packs.

Glancing over at Anneeta and then back at his pack, he laughs.

"It's not funny." I'm whimpering now. "She's going to cream me."

"She looks worse than she really is," he explains, as we walk out the door and head toward the cafeteria. "She is actually quite harmless."

Not believing a word he says, I accept the fact that my life is officially over.

Fresh fruit and a bread roll compose my lunch, but Takoda has a plate full of just about everything. We talk about our lives from pets to kid sisters. Unfortunately, the lunch hour passes all too quickly. Every second is wonderful, and I never want it to end. It does and Takoda's soon escorting me to my next class, which is Swetaachata Literature with Professor Limpwitch.

"I never had a class with her. What do you have after this?"

I read over my class roster. "General Science with Professor Trippett."

"She is really nice. I will be waiting for you when your class ends, and we can ride home together. Is that acceptable?"

"Acceptable." I watch him walk away. It feels good having him in my life. I enter my classroom and a young girl says *hello* from the front row.

"Hi," I reply.

"You're Takoda's friend."

It really isn't a question but I answer anyway. "We just met a few days ago." I'm a little worried that she may be a friend of Anneeta's.

"My name's Tryanna," she says. "With a *y* not an *e*. You can sit here if you want."

"Sure." I decide taking a seat next to her is probably safe.

"I can't believe Takoda is your friend," she says. "He was Anneeta's little pet for quite a while."

"I know. Anneeta doesn't like me." I drop my backpack onto the floor next to the chair.

"Anneeta doesn't like herself." Tryanna giggles. "I don't believe many around here do. We all avoid her like the plague. She's double trouble."

"Don't I know it," I state as the teacher enters the room and begins unloading her material.

"I heard that Takoda dumped her," she explains and then asks, "you're not from around here are you?"

I shake my head. "I'm from Earth."

"So am I, what part?" she asks. "I mean, from where?"

"North Carolina."

"Really? Too cool. I'm from Utah. My dad's a scientist. He's on some kind of a research exchange program. So here we are!"

I instantly like Tryanna. "My dad's from …" and that's when it dawns on me. *I have no idea where my father's from.* "My mom's from here. So, here *we* are. My name's Journey by the way."

"What subject do you have next?" she asks as she pulls out her tablet.

"General Science with Professor Trippett." I mimic her by pulling out my tablet.

"So do I! We could walk together if you want."

I agree because it would probably be a good idea to keep witnesses around for the next time I run into Anneeta.

Swetaachata Literature is a breeze because I love to read and I'm anxious to experience the new stories. Homework will not be a chore for this class. Science is a little more difficult but I tolerate it. Before I know it, the time is gone and Takoda is waiting for me as promised with a huge smile. Although I never thought it possible, Takoda is even more handsome in his school uniform.

"Hey there," he says, leaning against a pole and looking edible.

"Ready?" I ask.

"Always," he answers, melting my heart with his warm voice. "What are you doing this weekend? Want to spend it with me? I wish to show you around. It would not be good publicity if a Council's daughter were to get lost."

"I don't know what my dad has planned. If he hasn't booked me, I'm yours."

Takoda's eyes brighten, and I wish I hadn't said that. I feel stupid again.

After school, Takoda wishes to take me somewhere special and suggests I call my dad. Takoda's phone is similar to the ones I'm used to but it's also different. The symbols are foreign, so he has to initiate the call. Once I get the okay from my father, Takoda allows me to play with his phone a little.

"You should have one," he says.

"I guess I'm behind everyone else and it shows."

"I would be in the same situation if I suddenly found myself on your world."

"I'll see about getting one." I hand him back his phone. "Where are we going?" I ask, enjoying the scenery.

"You will see."

Mountains are all around us with trees so huge that a skyscraper would look like a two-story house next to them.

"Tell me about this planet," I say, breaking the silence.

"What do you want to know?"

"Is it larger than Earth?"

"Much larger. This world is about the size of your gas giant Jupiter. That is the closest comparison I can think of."

"Excuse me?" My parents are, or were, scientists. Makayah and I grew up knowing more about our solar system and general science than most. But a planet as large as Jupiter? Impossible.

"Did you see the crossing the other day?"

"Yes, but …"

"Journey is very far away. It is as far as Mars is from Earth. If you were to take an Earth ship and leave here today, you would not land on Journey for about three months. Does that help you get an idea of the size?"

"Yes, I believe so."

Having the distance between our planets explained in a way I can understand is a good thing. No wonder the pull was so strong that I could feel it through my fingertips. It's all making a lot more sense now. I still have one very important question that I ask cautiously.

"How in the world did I get here?"

"Travel is through an energy beam. It is the only way we can travel long distances. Otherwise, we take the chance of crashing into the destination instead of landing on it."

"I experienced a pull the other day. Is that the reason the rock cliffs are so tall?"

"Is that something your father explained to you?"

"Nope, guessed it on my own. Are you proud of me?" I ask with a grin.

"Very."

Takoda turns off the highway and onto a dirt road. The ride's no longer smooth. Holes and fallen branches are everywhere and we're bouncing around in our seats.

"My father said your vehicles don't run on gasoline."

"No, they do not. Our vehicles use … I guess you would call it nuclear. On top are the solar cells." He pats the ceiling of his jeep.

"Makes sense. I haven't heard an engine since I got here."

"We gather energy from our suns."

"Suns?" I ask now more confused than ever. "There's more than one?"

"Our system is binary … two suns. Single star systems are rare. Earth and its single sun is unique. You will not see our second sun for about an Earth year. Both are not visible at the same time. Our smaller sun rotates around the center one.

"I knew I'd find this place interesting," I add, as we come to a stop.

Takoda helps me out of the jeep, and we walk hand in hand down a dirt path. My heart skips a beat with every step. Even if he doesn't feel the same way I do, we are friends and that is worth everything to me. We come upon a huge, broken-down structure that's made of stone. It's very old and moss is growing in the crevasses.

"Wow, what was this place?" I touch the rock wall tenderly.

"Your dad told me you were interested in our history, so I thought I would bring you here. These are the closest ruins to us. Perhaps I will get a chance to take you to the other ones someday. Come, let us explore."

Vines and trees are everywhere, working to reclaim the space for themselves. It's kind of sad to see the hard work of others fall to nothing. I feel like I'm walking through a jungle with huge trees, long vines and colorful flowers.

Tree roots jet up from the dirt and break through the brick walls. Some are larger than a house. Much of the structure is still intact, and we climb up the crumbled steps and crawl through empty windows. There's enough remaining that I'm able to use my imagination to envision how magnificent it once was.

"This is great!" I'm enjoying every minute of our exploring.

"I am glad you like it."

"You never answered me about what this place used to be?"

"Not sure. My father said it belonged to one of the royal families. It has been abandoned for a long time. There are smaller buildings over there." He points. "Most have fallen. This building was the largest and most complete."

"Nice."

We continue exploring the ruins until we come to a pedestal with an intricate carving. Unlike Egyptian, the writing is more like letters than pictures.

"Can you read this?"

"No," Takoda says, running his fingers along the carvings.

"I wonder what it says."

"Not sure."

"There's a way to capture this," I say. "Next time we're here, we should bring paper and a piece of coal or a big crayon. We'll put the paper up and rub the crayon over it and get a copy." Takoda gives me a look of confusion so I add, "I've done it loads of times on other things. Maybe my dad can read it for us one day."

"I doubt it," he says, studying the writings. "The ancient language has long been forgotten. There is no way to translate."

"Honest?" I ask. "With all the books and technology around here, your people never thought to document your original language?"

"Many generations ago, there was a devastating war that almost destroyed our worlds. That is why we are so against violence. Almost all of our ancient teachings were burnt. Many innocent lives were lost. There is a gravesite not far from here. We should go sometime. You may find it interesting."

"I bet I would." I think of the Arlington cemetery back on Earth. "Thanks for bringing me, Takoda, this is really great."

"You are welcome, my friend." He reaches out and takes my hand in his.

Before either of us can speak again, lightning flashes and a deep rumble echoes through the forest.

"We better get going," he says, pulling me from the ruins.

The ride home sucks because the rain's heavy and the winds are strong. Takoda's jeep bounces all over the road, and my nerves are a wreck by the time he comes to a stop in front of my cabin.

"Here you are. May I walk you to your door?" he asks.

"Don't you dare!" I protest. "No reason for both of us to get drenched."

I grab my backpack and I'm about to dart into the rain when my jeep door opens and Dad's standing there holding a huge umbrella.

"Perfect timing. Thanks, Dad." I laugh.

"Good day to you, sir," Takoda says.

"Nice to see you too. Drive home safely," Dad cautions.

"Yes, sir. I will." Takoda smiles and that tells me he had a great time. "May I pick you up in the morning for school? And would you like to explore the countryside with me this weekend?" he asks more to my dad than to me.

"May I?" I beg.

"Of course, see you in the morning, Takodaovi." My father shuts the jeep's door and ends my wonderful day.

With puddles everywhere, we walk strategically through the yard as we aim for the cabin. Another bright light and deep rumble make us hurry. Standing on the porch, my father shakes the umbrella, and we both wave as Takoda drives away. The coolness swirls around us, and I shiver. We retreat into the warm and dry cabin.

"You two seem to be hitting it off."

I smile. "Can you call him Takoda? He's my friend and that's what he prefers to be called."

Dad nods.

"And we understand about the no co-mingling between our races."

"Oh really?" He whispers under his breath as I enter my room to change.

7

NOT FORGOTTEN

I MADE it through the first week of classes. As I wait for Takoda, the morning is fresh and makes me feel special. Crackling rocks soon announce his jeep's arrival. I'm smiling when he jogs over to greet me. His hair is not in braids this morning. Instead, tantalizing reddish-brown hair with golden highlights fall loosely past his waist. Takoda has a sensuality about him that's hard to ignore. As he moves, my world now moves with him.

"Ready?" he asks, with his beautiful smile. Standing close, I take the time to study his face. Long, thick eyelashes highlight his light golden-brown eyes with a yellow tint — amber. His skin is a light bluish green, but there's a pattern to it. I nod instead of speaking and concern fills his eyes.

"Anything wrong?" he asks.

"No." I sigh and shake my head. Everything is just too perfect. I can't take my eyes off him. He's wearing form-fitting jeans. A red button-down shirt with a black tee that hugs his chest, allowing his muscles to show through. A golden bird hangs from a delicate chain around his neck. It takes all my strength not to jump into his arms and make an absolute fool out of myself. "Let me catch my breath, okay?"

"I do not understand." He looks at me, confused.

"Takoda, you just look very handsome today," I say, trying not to stutter.

"Well, Journey, you are very pleasing to my eyes as well. Your eyes and your hair …"

"My hair? My hair is, and always will be, a mess," I argue. "It does whatever it wants. Sometimes I can't even get a comb through it. And I'm too skinny, and my face is too fat, my eyebrows are too bushy, and…"

He takes my hand and places it over my heart. "You are special right here. What you look like on the outside has no meaning. What is on the inside is pleasing, because I am looking at you, Journey."

"Oh great, I'm ugly but I'm so nice it doesn't matter?" I ask half joking.

"That is not what I mean. The most beautiful woman in any world cannot compare to the beauty that begins deep inside. Your beauty radiates throughout your existence. You are more than what is on the outside. In my eyes, I never want to stop admiring you. It is difficult to say goodbye when it is time to part. You are my friend, and you will forever be my friend." His eyes are soft and his smile warm. "In this life and in our next, you will always be a part of me. Do you understand?"

I can't stop smiling. "I think so."

"Come, let us take leave. We have a long day ahead of us," he says as he escorts me to his jeep.

My father stands on the porch drinking his coffee and waves. Everything is too perfect. When will it all come crashing down? I so pray that my place is with my father. It's obvious now why my mother fell for him. He is very caring and loving.

"Seat belts on … motor on … and we are off," Takoda announces as he waves at my father.

The drive is long and I enjoy every minute. Tall cliffs decorated with large trees line the road. Waterfalls peek out between the mountain ridges. We discuss our classes and share our personal lives, what we want out of life, and where we hope to end up some day. After an hour or so on the highway, he turns onto a small two-lane road.

"Not many people live out here, do they?" I ask.

Takoda shakes his head. "Most live in the cities. There are some farms up here, fruit trees mostly. The few who are here are families like ours who want to live away from others."

"It's beautiful."

A huge, intricately carved arch greets us at the end of the road. He parks in a small circular lot. The walk is calming. Our talk is enjoyable and I doubt if we'll ever run out of things to say. Takoda opens a small wrought-iron gate and after climbing several steps, we stop just before the top of a small ridge.

Before we step down the other side, Takoda takes my hand and asks, "Are you ready to meet your ancestors?"

"I guess so," I reply, feeling puzzled.

"If not, we can come back another day."

"Don't be silly." I walk off heading for the stairs in my own stubborn way. "We're here so let's —!"

My heart stops. My knees buckle, and now I'm afraid I'll fall down the stairs. My emotions overwhelm me. Takoda's strong arms hold me steady.

"Takoda," I whisper. "Please explain?"

"A war, Journey. As I said many died."

"Many?" I repeat. "There has to be hundreds of thousands of graves down there."

"Try millions," he replies with a tenderness that's full of understanding and acceptance.

My eyes fill with tears. "My God," I whisper as I descend the stairs into a cemetery that looks more like a sea of white ovals. As far as I can see gravestones of different sizes cover every inch of the valley floor. The long staircase takes a while to descend. When I step onto the thick green grass, my heart pounds. It's hard to grasp the magnitude of what lays before me. "All these people?" I whisper as tears run down my face.

"And not one fought in the war. These are all civilians."

I turn to him and stare into his beautiful eyes trying to comprehend. But I can't, there are just too many graves.

"Everyone was just killed? Murdered? Children too?"

"Unfortunate, but true. Whole families," he explains.

Takoda holds my hand as we continue our walk through the ghostly graveyard. The words etched into the stones are in another language and he translates for me. The death simply goes on and on. I want to hug this world and make everything better. I kneel and lay my face against the cool grass. It's hard to imagine anyone doing something this terrible to another. They just wiped them off the planet as if their lives were meaningless. I cry for the longest time with Takoda sitting at my side waiting patiently. I'm related to some of these long-forgotten souls, and I can feel their suffering and their fears as they watched their loved ones perish.

With my head resting on Takoda's leg, I ask softly, "How did it happen? Was it quick?"

"I am sure they suffered. High-level energy beams, as hot as a sun, exploded everything they touched. Many died instantly. Those farther away were burnt and died after a long illness and much suffering. The assault lasted many days." As he talks, Takoda strokes my head. "We retaliated as quickly as we could. Our satellites have mirrors and we tried to direct their beams into space. Not long after, we placed more mirrors to protect us from future attacks."

A major revelation flashes through my mind and I bolt up. My words come out a little stronger than I anticipate. "Both planets? I'm sorry I thought that Journey and Traveler were at war with each other? Now I'm thinking it's something else. Journey and Traveler fought them off together?"

"You are correct. They came from another system that has two habitable planets. One belongs to a race we call the Tarkadians. They attacked our worlds at the same time."

"Is there another graveyard like this on Journey?"

Takoda nods and I can see that he's holding back his tears. "Many more died on Journey than here on Traveler. We lost a moon during that war too."

"A whole moon?"

I would have never thought that could be possible. I imagine huge beams of light streaming toward me faster than anything possible. I can feel the intense heat as they get closer and closer. The thought makes me cringe, and I hug my arms. The sky overhead is now a beautiful blue with small puffy white clouds scattered about. But the day these people died I know it didn't look like this at all. Instead, it was dark and sinister with fire streaking through the sky. The odor of burning flesh must have filled the air.

"My God," is all I can muster.

"The Most Holy was with us that day. It could have been worse, but we were able to get the mirrors activated before they did more damage. If our satellites had been destroyed first, our twin planets would not be here today."

"I just had a terrible thought," I say, with a strong fear rising from the pit of my stomach. "Are those Tarkadians still out there? Do they still hate us? Do they still want us dead?"

"Very much. They are still out there, and they would wish to wipe us out. When we travel outside our system where there are no mirrors to protect us, we must be alert to the possibility of their presence. Their technology is not quite as advanced as ours. We at least have that advantage."

"But why? What did we ever do to them?"

"What makes you think we did anything to them? Some simply enjoy for the sport of killing. They are afraid of anything they do not understand, and others, well others just want what is not theirs. There is never any reason as to why one life would destroy another.

It is sad but something we must learn from, not something to imitate. This is our past and our honor, and we must respect what we cannot change. It is our responsibility to understand what happened and to ensure it never happens again."

"Does our military stay on top of these Tarkadians?"

Takoda chuckles. "They do what they can, yes. Our *guardians* are out there protecting us right now. They patrol the heavens and report anything suspicious to the Elders. Something we did not have to do before all this happened. We have learned."

As we stroll through the graves, Takoda talks and I listen. I learn about the strong and highly advanced military shared by both planets, which Takoda calls the guardians. I learn about the people who discovered they could accomplish more as a team than as separate players, and that large spaceships are searching our solar system at this very moment for invaders. I discover that our telescopes are pointed toward Tarkadia to watch what those evil things are planning next.

It's a creepy feeling knowing that another race of people wants to kill us. This is a problem I never had to face on Earth. We had to worry about our neighbors bombing us sometimes, but not some *thing* coming from another solar system to do it. It's a lot to take in. I do my best to understand and to learn. As we walk around a bend in the valley, a large white marble building with carved columns is nestled within a group of trees. It reminds me of the temples found in Italy or Greece.

Takoda pulls on one of the large double doors that's intricately carved with the outline of male and female bodies inlaid with golden wraps of cloth. It creaks and moans as though protesting at being disturbed. We try to be quiet as we enter but our footfalls echo off the marble slabs. The lights flicker and brighten the chamber. The walls are over twenty feet high and divide the place into sections that depict the history of the war. Some of the walls display interactive movies that document the horror. It's very humbling. I close my eyes and listen to the stillness. I can almost hear my ancestors crying out to me.

"Are you all right?" he asks.

"Yes," I answer. Although, I'm not sure. Somehow I feel different.

Takoda hugs me and we stand quietly together. My heart's crying but my mind's yelling out in protest. It's hard to comprehend how many children had their futures ripped away, their short lives ending with such pain.

"It's not right," I whisper.

He doesn't say anything right away but after a few moments of silence, Takoda speaks softly. "No, it is not. There is nothing we can do, Journey. The damage has already been done. We can only pay our respects and remember those we have lost."

We drive home in silence. Every now and then Takoda glances over at me, but I can only stare out the window. These Tarkadians must be terrible people who live on an ugly and dark planet — if they are people at all. It's the only explanation that makes any sense. They must be devils, demons.

When we arrive home, Dad is standing outside. "Have a good day?" he asks, giving me a hug and a kiss on the cheek.

"An interesting one for sure," I reply, glancing at Takoda.

"Oh? What did you two do?"

"I took her to the cemetery, sir," Takoda answers. "Perhaps I should not have."

"I'm fine, Takoda, really," I add, defending his choice. "It's just a shock. Earth has its faults, but to wipe out that many people in only a few minutes."

"It is a lot to take in," my dad says, hugging me tighter. "I have been there and it was hard for me. I would ask you to dinner, Takoda, but I know your father is expecting you."

"Yes, I must be going," Takoda says with a grin. "Tomorrow morning? Train … together?"

"I'll see you in the morning," I reply.

I hug him around the waist and rest my cheek against his chest. He smells good and I don't want to let go. Dad's watching so I don't linger. Takoda hugs me back and kisses me on top of my head.

"Until tomorrow," he says and he's gone again.

I stand outside with my father for a little while and we talk about the war. He doesn't tell me anything that I hadn't already read in the visitor center.

As I sleep that night, my dreams are of chaos and fighting, which wake me after a few brief hours. I lay in my bed and try to think about Takoda.

8
THE ASSIGNMENT

TIME PASSES and classes seem to be getting easier, but more importantly, they're becoming enjoyable. Some days it seems like I can't hear enough from my professors to satisfy my curiosity about this new and exciting world. The worst class and also the best is Ancient History. It has nothing to do with the fact that Takoda sits right next to me. It's interesting because the class includes lectures about the Wanderers, those I watched paying homage to our sister planet in my own front yard.

The Wanderers are a religious sect but religious in an unusual way. Their acknowledgment of God is more of a sensation than an actual belief. The Wanderers teach us that the Holy Ones created our people so we could experience the sensations that radiate between our worlds. Our soul, it is taught, is actually made up of this magnetic stuff. It's this stuff that enables us to feel the tug as the sister planet passes overhead. When we die, our souls merge with the stream of the magnetism, and this merging of the souls is what they worship.

The week of the crossing is called Convergence, and it's at this time when the soul blends with the Most Holy, and a person becomes one with the twin planets. I didn't think this was too strange because back home everyone talks about merging as one with the universe.

The downside of Ancient History is that Anneeta, who sits behind me, burns a hole in the back of my head with her eyes. Takoda tries to comfort me, but her gaze gives me the chills. On this particular day, our professor drops two small packets in front of me.

"What's this?" I ask, pulling my hair from my face and glancing up at him.

"You will see," he says as he moves on to the next table.

The packets are loaded with material that looks like some type of advertisement for a rustic getaway vacation. The pictures are remarkable, and the landscapes are exotic. They must have held my attention because I didn't notice Takoda taking his seat next to me.

"What are you reading?" Takoda asks, dropping his book bag next to his chair on the floor.

I glance at him and smile as I hand him his packet. "This one's yours. It's some kind of travel brochure. Professor Graysonian handed them to me a few minutes ago."

"I know what this is." Takoda's eyes widen. "My father told me about it. I did not believe him. I thought he was joking. I cannot believe we go this term."

"What is this for?" I ask.

"Excuse me," the professor says to the class. "Calm down now, please. I know this is exciting but please."

The class slowly stops talking and everyone turns to listen. I'm at a complete loss as to what's going on.

"Journey, since you are new, let me explain the packets," Professor Graysonian says directly to me.

His one-on-one attention makes me a little self-conscious. I glance at Anneeta who's still glaring at me. I sigh and turn my attention back to the instructor.

"Mythos term is the period before Skopocit. During Mythos you are to explore as much about *you* as possible." The professor points his finger at me. "It is your time to discover who you are before you come of age. During this term you will actually be teaching yourself by successfully completing the Trials." Professor Graysonian paces around the room. "This term is to allow you to awaken your inner self, to discover who you are and who you will eventually become."

I snicker but Takoda looks serious.

"Now, if you open your packets, you will see several different places from which to choose." As he explains, he stops to talk to a couple of the students.

"Okay, what's all this?" I whisper to Takoda.

"It is as he said. We get to go away, Journey." He smiles and winks.

I frown. "I don't want to go away."

"Shh," Takoda adds, "we can go together. We get to choose a partner."

"And what is that supposed to mean, exactly?" I'm not sure whether to be happy or apprehensive.

"Have you read over your packet?"

"Not really."

"Class, you must read all the literature before you decide on a Trial," the professor says as he walks down the aisle.

I still didn't get it. Later, while riding the train with Takoda, I thumb through the material again.

"I think we should choose Kronian, *Searching for the Voyage*," Takoda says. "We would be exploring ancient ruins. I enjoyed our time at the ruins the other day and would like to visit more. These are supposed to be big."

"That sounds pretty cool, but I'll have to ask my dad about this. I'm sure he knows all about it," I say, trying to convince myself that everything will turn out fine.

"Are you two planning something special ... like your honeymoon or something?" Anneeta asks, as she sneers at us from a few feet away.

Intimidated, I turn my head toward Takoda and try to ignore her. As always there is no ignoring Anneeta.

"Takoda, I really do not believe your father would approve of you partnering with *her*. *You* were promised to Trial with *me* and you will not be traveling with *her*."

"Fine," he says, which takes me by surprise and drops a huge knot in the pit of my stomach. Until he continues with, "Wait for me at the train station. I will pick you up." He says it so sarcastically that I know he's not serious. He doesn't even look up at her, he just keeps flipping through his packet.

"This is not over, Takoda! She will not be your Trial partner. I will put in a complaint with the authorities." Anneeta threatens with a stare that should have buried us both, but this time she finally crossed that line.

Takoda jumps up so quickly that my packet falls and the pages scatter across the floor. He stares at her with a finality that frightens even me.

"You have no say on what I do, where I go, or who I go with. We are not together. We were never together. You are not what I want, you never were." His voice is deep and demanding of respect. "Who I decide to travel with is up to me. I do not need to ask for your permission or get your approval."

As I pick up the pages, Takoda sits and stares out the window.

Anneeta stays only a few moments longer before she says directly to me while pointing her finger into the middle of my face, "This is not over, Gayoid."

"That is enough!" Takoda yells, jumping up and grabbing her arm.

Anneeta stares at me one last time, yanks her arm out of Takoda's grip, and storms down the aisle.

"I'm doomed." I'm trying to put the pages back into the correct order but my hands won't quit shaking. "My life is over."

"You are not doomed," he whispers with a slight grin. "However, I would keep my distance."

"You don't have to worry about that." The train is slowing down. "I guess we're here."

"Come, let us return home," he suggests, taking my hand into his.

Standing in my yard, I'm hating having to say goodbye to Takoda. He holds me close, and I inhale his essence.

"Takoda? What is a Gayoid?"

"Forget about it," he says, kissing my forehead.

As he walks away, I again feel lost. I glance at the lake and wish that the Wanderers were still here. I need release from the fear that's gripping me from deep inside. I could definitely use some peace right now.

Makayah runs out of the cabin with her hands full of bread. As she runs past and toward the honking geese, or what I think are geese, she yells out a short *'hi'* but doesn't stop to talk. Feeling alone and dejected, I decide it's time to share my packet with my father.

"I remember your mother talking about her Trial," he says gazing up into the nothingness of our ceiling as though watching a movie only he can see or hear.

"Can we get back to mine please?" I push the packet toward him. "What does it mean when someone calls you a Gayoid?"

Dad pauses. His eyes widen and a large frown slowly grows across his face. "It is a very bad name for someone who is not blue. Where did you hear that word?"

"A girl from school called me a Gayoid today on the train," I answer. "What does it mean?"

"First, never use that curse word. Others will frown upon you if you do. It comes from an ancient one … Gaia. She ruled our people for many generations. She was like us. The word means people of her descendants."

"I see," I say. Now I understand why Takoda was so mad at Anneeta. I shrug it off. Prejudice is something I'm used to. I remember how some people were treated on Earth just because of their skin color. I look back at the pamphlets and smile. "What is this *trial thing* anyway?" I ask, not really sure if I want to know. "And … do I have to go?"

"Of course, you must go. It will be a great experience." He flips through the pages. "This voyage allows you to learn who you are and what you are capable of accomplishing."

"Takoda wants us to go together," I say, staring at a picture of a beautiful landscape and avoiding my father's prying eyes.

"Some go on Trial in groups and some with just a friend," he says, softly. "How do you feel about going with Takoda?"

"I don't really feel one way or the other," I answer, a little louder than I intended. "I have no idea what this Trial stuff is all about."

My dad pushes the papers aside and turns his attention to me. He takes my hands into his and says softly, "Journey, what happens is simple. You choose a place, which is here on Traveler. It may not be on this continent, but here all the same."

"I just thought of something," I say, gazing into my father's beautiful dark brown eyes. "Are there oceans on this planet like on Earth?"

"Huge oceans, Journey." It's obvious that my father wants me to be curious about this world, my *home world*, because he smiles. "There is so much for you to learn that there is no way I can tell you everything. You have much to discover, my daughter." His enthusiasm radiates from his eyes.

"I guess there are lots of cities and continents and mountains?" I ask, pausing to think about what the rest of the planet might look like. I'd only been to our cabin, the small town, and my school.

"This will give you a chance to see more of your world. Be excited about whatever you choose, and I will support you in your decision."

"What happens when I get there?"

"You will be given a task to complete. Nothing terrible, usually something exciting," he adds. "It is safe. This will help you to grow."

"If you say so," I reply. As long as Anneeta is a long way away, I will probably survive. "Where did Mom go when she was my age?"

"Her experience was with a group of other girls who were her closest friends. *The Grand Cave Junction* was their choice, and she was tasked to locate a small electronic device. It took weeks, but they finally found it."

"Weeks?" I ask now wondering how long I'll be out in the wilds of this unknown world.

"You will not know what your challenge will be until you choose your destination and your partners. They always wait until the last minute to give you your task. I will not lie to you, it was not easy for her. However, she did learn many things about herself."

My phone rings and I jump. We both laugh as he answers. "Peace be with you, Takoda," he says.

It's strange how they answer phones around here. I still don't see anything wrong with a simple *'Hello,'* but I'm constantly reminded that things are different.

"Yes, just one moment." Dad looks over at me. "It is for you."

My hands shake as I take the phone. "Peace be with you."

"Good evening, Journey," Takoda answers, which makes my heart leap.

"What's up?" I ask, trying to sound as calm as possible.

"Have you picked a destination?" he asks with excitement in his voice.

"Not really, have you?"

"My father said that the *Ruins of the Wicked Lady* would be perfect for us." As he talks, I flip through the pages until I come to that place. Nestled under a large cliff is a city built from huge stones. There are more floors than I can count, and large tree roots have broken through many of the walls. It's quite beautiful in a rustic and forbidden sort of way.

"Ah," my father comments with a chuckle. "The wicked lady caves. Yes, a great place to explore."

I take in a deep breath and sigh as I reply, "It's pretty wicked looking. I guess it'll be okay."

Now I don't know which to fear most — the wicked lady under the cliff or the wicked lady at my school. Either way, one of them will do me in for sure.

9

THE CREATURES

AS WE pick out the destination, our bond seems to be strengthening. It's almost as though he can read my mind and feel what I'm feeling. Anneeta is just as cold and hateful as ever, and I ignore her the best I can. She is making Ancient History almost unbearable. After all these weeks, I'm sure her gaze has burnt an everlasting impression into the back of my head.

"I wish she wouldn't do that," I whisper to Takoda.

He glances over his shoulder then turns to me. Takoda shakes his head and chuckles. "Maybe it will not leave too big of a scar."

His comment takes me by surprise because he knows what I'm thinking. *How does he do that?* There are even times when he finishes my sentences for me.

"Let us share choices," Professor Graysonian announces, dragging me from my thoughts and back into the present. "Near the back … Anneeta, you are first."

His statement takes her by surprise. She stutters and hesitates as she tries to answer his question. "Um, well," she says.

I keep my eyes on my clasped hands. It feels good just knowing she's been caught off guard. I giggle.

"Shanta and I decided on the *Crystal Watering Pool*," she explains with a little more conviction in her voice, which disappoints me.

"Excellent!" Professor Graysonian says clapping his hands together and making a loud noise that echoes around the room. "A beautiful challenge and you will learn much about yourselves." He walks to the next table. "Bylia, what about you?" he asks the blonde girl sitting in front of Anneeta.

"I am going with Deenea and we picked the *Crossings of the Moons*," she says, blushing.

"Another excellent choice. Many different paths to take with that journey. And speaking of journeys, what about you two?" Professor Graysonian stares at Takoda and me.

I become speechless, but Takoda speaks up. "We are going together and we have decided on the *Ruins of the Wicked Lady*." He says it with so much pride that I know my face is blushing a bright pink.

"That is a difficult one," Professor Graysonian replies with eyes wide and a large frown. "I have never had any students choose that one before. You will be the first. In fact, I do not believe anyone has taken that challenge in many generations."

My heart skips a few beats because I don't like the way he emphasized the words *difficult* or *generations*.

"Difficult?" I ask.

"Yes, it is rumored that those ruins are protected by an ancient race of creatures called the Nomaddas. I am surprised, very surprised, you would pick that particular challenge."

"Yeah, me too," I whisper into my now shaking hands.

With a raised eyebrow, the professor asks cautiously, "And may I ask what made you decide on this challenge?"

"Journey and I love to explore ancient sites," Takoda replies. "We thought it would be fun to explore our land … together."

"I see. And do you agree with this choice, Journey?"

I glance at my teacher and try to smile. "Yeah, sure."

I'm pretty sure that my answer is not very convincing because he stands there with a look of concern for a few moments.

"Okay then, let us get back to work. I would like to go over what happens next."

As he continues explaining, my head reels and my imagination runs wild through all the negative possibilities. Now, aside from Anneeta to worry about, I have monsters in my future. I don't pay much attention to the class after that little excitement. All I want to know about are the wild creatures called the Nomaddas, and if I will become their next meal. I can see it now, running away from a huge monkey-looking animal with extra-large sharp teeth, and then it drools all over my body and …

"Journey?" Takoda asks, holding his bag and smiling. "Journey? Let us go."

Class is over and the room is empty except for us.

"I'm sorry," I say as I grab my things.

Takoda pauses just outside the classroom and looks at me. His eyes are tender and his smile sincere. "We will be fine, Journey. I am sure he was just trying to frighten us."

"I hope you're right. I don't have a real good feeling about this."

"Come," he says, taking my hand into his. "Let us get something to eat."

As we touch, I understand that I would follow him anywhere. Nothing seems to matter when I'm with him.

The rest of the day flies by. Even the ride home seems shorter than usual. The more I try to grip how I'm feeling about this Trial thing, the faster time seems to speed up.

@

I'm standing at the train station with a very large backpack crammed to the splitting point with all the necessary items I need — sleeping bag, water, snacks, a change of clothing, and a few small items like a toothbrush. It seems a little odd to bring a toothbrush when I know I will be some *thing's* dinner. I stare in despair at my over-stuffed bag and pray I haven't forgotten to pack my courage. After a quick hug from my sister and father, Takoda and I are, once again, on the train and sailing at an incomprehensible speed. As the outside world blurs past, I'm dizzy and feeling uncomfortable.

"We receive our instructions when we arrive," he explains, with more enthusiasm than I can muster.

My only comfort is to nibble on my lip until it hurts. I need something to keep me grounded and pain seems like the only thing that will work.

"Journey, we will have a great time," he says, shaking my leg.

"All I can imagine are those creatures wanting me for their dinner."

"How can you think such a thing? You do not even know what they look like or if they exist."

He looks way too serious and I laugh. Then we both laugh and he hugs me. We use the time to study the material that our instructor gave us. I really want to enjoy this private time with Takoda but my imagination keeps me seeing a big hairy monster drooling over my dead body.

"The train's slowing," I say, glancing out the window at the darkening skies.

"We must be there," he announces not taking his eyes off the paperwork.

"Oh, goodie," I say, fearing the outside darkness.

It's as if the world knows of my fate and is casting me into the blackest of voids where there is no return. Takoda grabs our packs. The air outside is cool and misty. We walk onto the platform and three men in uniform are looking at us. One of them approaches with a serious expression. Takoda nods to the right and hands him our papers. After the officer reviews them, he signs the forms and hands them back. The officer turns to the others who nod. As they walk over to us, my stomach hurts and I feel like I need a bathroom.

"Your instructions, sir," one of the other officers says as he hands Takoda a large envelope. It's about an inch thick and looks heavy.

"Thank you." Takoda nods as he takes custody of the packet. "Will you be accompanying us?"

"No, we take our leave here. A vehicle is parked by the road. Keys are in the packet. We wish you luck and safe passage."

Takoda smiles and nods to the right.

"You might get a few miles before it is too dark to continue," the third officer suggests. He frowns and glances down at the ground. "I recommend you leave as soon as possible."

"Good luck," the first officer says. "May the Most Holy watch over you as you travel."

The men board the train leaving us alone on the dark and gloomy platform.

"We had better get going." Takoda hands me my backpack.

We walk down the dark road and toward a waiting vehicle. The night is cool and a thick mist hangs heavily in the air. My hair and face feel drenched. It's as though we're walking through a veil of light water.

"I'm wet," I say when I spot the vehicle.

A covered black jeep waits for us on the dirt road that fades deeply into the darkening shadows. It reminds me of an armored car that's used on Earth to transport money between banks.

"This doesn't look promising." I moan, as Takoda drops the tailgate and tosses in our bags. He slams the door and turns to me.

"Journey." Takoda sighs. "The next few days are not meant as a punishment. We are supposed to look forward to this day. This is an exciting time for us. You will learn much about yourself."

I really wish I could share in his enthusiasm, but I'm just plain scared.

"Come, time to go," he says, as he helps me into the passenger seat.

The vehicle starts right up, and I decide that at least we have a method of escape when the time comes, if nothing else. We ride in silence for what seems like a very long time before he pulls off the road and into a small clearing. Someone had removed several trees and placed the trunks along the edge of the forest creating a little camping area. It's dark and I cannot see a thing.

"We will sleep here for the night," he suggests.

I sigh and follow him to the back of the jeep to help with our bags.

We use the headlights to set up the tent and search for fallen tree limbs for a fire. It's not long before I'm warming my hands and resting my back against an old log.

"Hungry?" Takoda asks, as he uses a stick to stir the fire.

"A little." I glance into the darkness. "This place is creepy."

"You are afraid," he says softly. "Everything seems unsafe to you. Darkness is not dangerous, Journey. You should only be afraid of what may be hidden in the shadows. And right now, there is nothing there."

I smile and bite my lip a little harder. "Right …" I wish I could trust what he says.

The officers left a small cooler in the back of the vehicle that's loaded with food. That evening we eat bread and cheese for dinner. As the fire slowly dies, Takoda motions for me to get into my sleeping bag. He zips up the tent and then zips up his bag after making sure I'm comfortable and warm inside mine. We stare at each other for a while before he turns off the light that's illuminating the tent from above our heads. The night's quiet, almost too quiet. We listen to the insects and small animals that are scurrying around outside. The longer I stare into the blackness the more I want to be closer to Takoda.

It's not long before he asks, "Want to talk a little?"

"Sure," I answer with relief. There's no way I'm going to fall asleep. "I'm really glad you are my friend, Takoda. Thank you for bringing me."

"And me to you," he replies, scooting a little closer.

"May I ask you something?"

"Anything." His soft reply makes my stomach tighten. I just love listening to his voice.

"My father told me it's forbidden for your kind and mine to marry — I mean to union. He said something about the children. That the children didn't turn out right or something like that. Do you know what he meant by that?"

Takoda doesn't laugh at my question, which I appreciate. I just can't understand why anyone would forbid one person from being with another.

"Many generations ago," he says, "they allowed unions between our people. And yes, the children were born damaged. The pain it caused created harsh feelings between us, which did more harm than the prohibiting of the unions. Laws were passed probably to protect us from ourselves."

"What was wrong with the children?"

"There are no written records. Our ancestors wished to erase the bad memories. Council laws were amended after Gaia's death."

"That's weird. I would think they would want you to know what happened so no one would be tempted to marry — I mean union."

"Maybe," he says. "Or spare us from the horrors."

"It still seems a little odd. What if two people wanted to marry but not have kids? Would that be okay?"

"Prohibited," he says.

"I don't think that would work on Earth. I guess we are more stubborn than people here. Interracial marriages were prohibited for a long time on my planet but eventually we realized those laws were there for no other reason than to make one race feel more important than the other. It was a stupid law on my planet and it's a stupid law here."

"No one has challenged the laws since they were passed," he explains.

"How long ago was that?"

"A while — generations actually," he sighs.

"How many?"

"Maybe a dozen or so," he says. "Maybe more."

"Who was Gaia?" That name keeps popping up in different conversations.

"She was the original ruler of your people."

"Oh?" I have no idea what he's talking about and decide to wait until I return home to question my father.

Takoda continues to talk about his people. He explains the strange laws that were passed and that are still heavily enforced. His voice is soothing and relaxing and before long, I fall asleep. My dreams are of my mother. Feelings of warmth and security surround me, and I wake feeling much more confident. We pack up and cover the campfire with dirt. When we're satisfied that we've left nothing behind but a few footprints, we head deeper into the dark and gloomy forest. We drive for hours before he stops and turns off the motor.

"I need a break," he says, exiting the vehicle.

I grab the toilet paper and a small shovel and find a quiet spot. It's disgusting but for now this will have to do. As I'm heading back, a loud screech echoes through the forest and makes me jump. My hands are shaking so much it's difficult for me to hold onto the shovel and paper.

"Takoda!" I scream. "Takoda, where are you?"

A dark shadow crosses my path. I freeze. I can't move. I can't yell. That odd scream echoes again through the forest, and I want to find some place to hide … anywhere. But here I am, out in the open and totally exposed. I urge my feet to move and they remain glued to the ground.

"Takoda," I whisper. I aim for the jeep and climb into the passenger seat.

Takoda jumps in just as I close my door.

"That was not good." I sigh not knowing what else to say. "Do you think those screams were from the Nomaddas?"

"No," he answers.

I shake my head and frown. "Are you sure?"

"Yes, those were pigguisers. Now *they* are dangerous." He is driving and keeping his eyes on the road.

"Okay, I give up, what's a pigguiser?"

"Let me think … imagine an Earth gorilla, a big one."

"Okay," I reply not sure if I want to hear more.

"Then make it the color of your skin and give it long shaggy hair, sharp teeth, and big nasty red eyes. Oh, and don't forget the real nasty disposition. That should just about do it."

"They sound dangerous." I glare at him.

"You could say that, yes." Takoda slows and reaches over to take my hand. "I will keep you safe, Journey."

"I would appreciate that," I reply, gripping his hand a little firmer. "And so would my dad."

I promise myself that if I ever get out of this little adventure alive, I will never go camping again.

10
ILLUSORY MINDS

WE TRAVEL for what seems like forever. Headlights are required to see where we're going. The road's thinning and the trees seem to be encroaching upon us. As we round a sharp curve, Takoda slams on the brakes and stares blankly out the front window. His hands are shaking and he's panting.

"What is it?" I whisper.

He doesn't reply but continues to sit and stare.

"Why did we stop?"

"No more road," he says, staring straight ahead.

"What do you mean no more road? Where did the road go?"

Takoda touches my chin and turns my head toward the headlights. I stare into the darkness as he flips off the lights. My eyes slowly adjust and my heart falls. It's hard to comprehend what I'm staring at because there's nothing there.

"What in the world?" I ask, as he opens his door and steps out. I open mine but wait and listen for any animals that may be nearby. All is quiet except for the insects buzzing around me. I stand next to Takoda and stare out at the nothingness.

"Oh my …" I can't finish my sentence.

Only a few feet in front of the jeep there's nothing but a vast empty space. I take a few steps and strain to see. As my eyes continue to adjust, I can just make out a faint impression of a valley far below. A long way down.

"You can say that again," Takoda states, trying to catch his breath. "No one said that the road just ended like this. We could have died."

"How did you know to stop?" I'm surprised he didn't drive us off the cliff.

"I do not know. Something told me to stop and to stop now. Look, my hands are still shaking."

"I guess we walk from here."

"Seems that way," he says still staring into the emptiness.

"Right or left?" I ask not seeing a trail to follow.

"Down."

"Down? How can we go down?"

"The ruins are under a cliff ... remember the pictures?" He turns back to the jeep. "I think I know where we need to go."

"I don't think I can do this," I whisper.

Takoda sighs and rubs his face. "We will be fine. We love exploring and these ruins will be beyond anything we have ever imagined. And Journey ..." he stares into my eyes, "I will not let anything happen to you."

He locks up the vehicle, which seems a little stupid to me, and I follow Takoda down a shallow trail. The sun's gone and the stars are all that remains to light up the night sky. No Milky Way to gaze at from this planet. But the beauty of the universe is still a spectacular sight to behold.

"Wait," I say as we stand at the trail's edge.

The night is dark with only a streak of colorful stars that paint the sky as if an artist's hand had strategically placed them. The colors are of every shade and brightness. It's beautiful and takes my breath away. Takoda holds my hand and squeezes it ever so tenderly.

"Okay," I announce, "I'm ready." I squeeze his hand a little.

The trail ends about twenty feet down the cliff before opening onto a landing of dirt and rocks. It appears that another trail leads down on the other side. I can see more brush and foliage. It's cold and misty and I'm wet and tired. My temper's about to explode if I don't get some food and much-needed rest. My backpack's heavy and I'm ready to get it off my shoulders.

"We will camp here for the night," Takoda announces. "We should be safer on this ledge than in the jungle above. We will move on after the morning sun greets us."

I drop my pack and stretch out my shoulders. It's pretty where we're standing. The landing's about fifty feet wide. To our backs, the tall rock wall is draped in vines and other small shrubs. A sheer cliff drops away forever only a few feet in front of us.

It doesn't take Takoda long to set up our tent and have dinner simmering over a hot fire. The aroma is comforting and I relax a little. We eat hot vegetable stew, warm bread, and fresh fruit. As my stomach fills, my tension eases even more. After dinner, I unroll my sleeping bag and stretch out under the stars. Takoda follows me and soon we're lying together only a few feet from the warm fire. He holds my hand and neither of us say a word. I wonder what it would be like to have a boyfriend who truly cares about me — someone as handsome and wonderful as Takoda. But here, on this planet, holding hands is only a gesture of friendship, not love.

"Do you miss your home world?" I ask.

"Sometimes," he replies.

"What's it like?" I really want to know.

"It is very different. My world is similar to Earth only larger. Only certain rays of light penetrate through our dense clouds. We see no browns or reds."

I look closely at Takoda. Until this moment, I took his color for granted, it's what he is. Now I see that his skin is very smooth and shiny and quite beautiful. My hand trembles as I rub my fingers lightly over his colorful blue and green arm. He smiles at me, and we stare into each other's eyes for the longest time.

"You're so beautiful," I say. "I could really get used to having you around all the time."

Takoda's expression changes. An almost guilty look appears on his face and surprises me. He glances at our hands and tightens his grip.

"Journey, I enjoy being with you too. But the laws …"

I stand in protest and walk toward the cliff. "On my planet we've learned to overcome our prejudices, we've moved on and if two people want to be together nothing else matters."

"Why do you think it was so acceptable that we could come together? No one questioned our motives." He walks over to me. "It is safe because of the laws. We, you and me, can never be more than just friends. No matter how much we both may want more."

"Maybe not here," I whisper, walking back to my sleeping bag.

I yank it up from the ground and climb into the tent. The call of the wild is suddenly deafening. At least it's taking my mind off the horrible laws that I believe are stupid and are keeping me from my desires.

@

Morning arrives and I awake to a layer of frozen dew and a cool breeze. I pull on my heavy sweatshirt and my thickest socks. By the time I'm dressed and finished rolling up my sleeping bag, I'm fuming. Who do these bureaucrats think they are deciding who I can have feelings for? These laws are stupid and I will not tolerate them.

My family has supposedly been royalty for generations, and therefore it should be up to *me* to decide and no one else. I take in a deep breath and let it out slowly. Taking a firm stance gives me the feeling that I'm taking a little control over my life. The morning sun is waiting for me and it's time to greet the day.

"Good morning." Takoda says with a smile and a steaming cup of coffee. It almost tastes like Earth coffee and helps to wake me up, so I call it coffee.

"Thank you," I say, taking a sip.

I'm still angry because I believe if a person really cares for someone they do not give up just because others tell them to. Why can't he fight back? Perhaps he doesn't feel the same way as I do, and if that's the case, then that's something I don't want to know.

"It will only take a few minutes to pack," Takoda says, pulling the tent apart. "Your breakfast is next to the fire. Enjoy it. We cannot take the cooler with us. We can take only what we can carry."

What looks like fried potatoes mixed with another red vegetable is waiting for me along with a piece of toast smeared with a yummy fruit jelly. The flavor's amazing and I enjoy every bite. I had not realized how hungry I was until I started eating. When I finish, I wipe off my dish. Takoda has hooked the pots to the back of his pack. I giggle.

We stand by the cliff for a few moments before he touches my hand. "Are you ready?"

I nod and we descend the trail leaving behind our little safe haven. The nodding to the right seems to come more naturally to me now.

As I walk, every little sound makes me glance over my shoulder for those creatures — the Nomaddas. I'm ready to run as soon as it's necessary. But I'm walking down a path that's no wider than my body. Therefore, there's really nowhere to run.

A heavy mist hovers over the valley as bright as a white fluffy blanket lying across a large bed. We can see nothing below the fog and have no idea what awaits us at the bottom. The trail ends just as our feet hit the top of the misty blanket. Takoda grabs onto a piece of wood that is sticking out of the ground and climbs out and over and into the misty fog. As his head falls below the cloud, I regretfully understand that it's necessary to climb down a ladder. It's now my turn and my hands are wet and shaking uncontrollably.

The ladder feels slippery and I wonder how far I will fall before I hit the bottom. I grab on as tight as I can and climb down the bamboo ladder. There is a thin rope wrapped around each rung. Without that rope, the ladder would have been a death trap. My legs burn after what seems like we've climbed forever. To keep sane, I start counting the rungs. I count just past five hundred before I hear Takoda announce that he's reached the bottom. I have my eyes closed for the last hundred steps or so, and finally I feel Takoda's strong hands grab hold of my hips. He gently lowers me to the barren stone floor. I turn and gasp as my eyes adjust to the dimmer light.

I'm standing on a landing that overlooks a huge green valley. A river curves through it like a snake that's wandering off into the distance. Large vines drape from above and cover everything. The ancient brick walls seem to be holding their own, for now at least. Large birds caw from a distance and small animals run into the closest bush.

"Wow," I say, smiling at Takoda.

"I knew you would come around once we arrived. Come and look." He takes my hand and guides me to a brick wall that's about four feet high.

As far as my eyes can see is a huge ancient city. The city's at least twenty stories high and I cannot tell how far it extends around the other side of the cliff. Every opening is intricately carved with strange animals or people posing in odd ways. Demonic faces stare down upon us from above as if daring us to continue on our journey. The entryways and columns are huge, as if the ancient city used to house giants.

"The Nomaddas," I whisper.

"If this entryway was built for them, then we are in trouble."

Takoda takes another quick look around as I stand under the entryway. I pause in either revelation or fear. The arch is over ten feet above our heads and extends down into the vast emptiness below. The whole city's built from a grayish stone that's now mostly covered in dark green moss. Plants clinging to life in any way they can send their roots deeply between the stones. Some bricks are small, but the majority are huge, way too large for one person to simply pick up and move about. Some of the archway is carved directly out of rocks that make up the actual cliff. It's an amazing work of craftsmanship. Nothing on Earth could compare to this magnificent old city.

"Shall we go in?" Takoda asks as he squeezes my hand.

"This is why we came here, right?"

The stairs are wide, at least ten or more people can stand side-by-side and walk down together and not bump into each other. The farther we descend, the darker it gets and eventually we can't see anything. We don our helmets and turn on the lights. We can't look directly at each other, or we'd blind ourselves, so we have to focus on the direction of our descent. As we near the bottom, the stairs open up and a vast amphitheater awaits us. I stop and glance over the railing.

"What is wrong?" Takoda asks.

"I just want to see what's out there." My eyes slowly adjust and I can barely make out a huge area filled with balconies all on a different level. Intertwining stairways are everywhere. Thin faint rays of sunlight fall from above and cast eerie shadows. I gasp.

"How many people do you think used to live here?" I ask.

"Must have been millions at one time."

"I wonder where everyone went."

"I have no idea." His voice cracks as he speaks and I realize he's just as surprised as I am. "I never knew this place was so huge."

"I wish we could turn on the lights," I say more as a joke than anything serious.

"That is not a bad idea," he declares.

"Oh, like there's a light switch around here somewhere." I laugh.

"Journey, a place like this could never be supported with just burning fires. There has to be a method of lighting. We just have to find it."

"And where do you suggest we look?" I muse. "A broom closet?"

"In an area that would be similar to a basement."

"Great, then we *are* looking for a broom closet."

I smirk and leave him standing alone as I count the stairs to the bottom. I'm on stair three hundred and sixty when my foot finally steps onto a solid brick floor that is carved with a geometric pattern that reminds me of bubbles attached to bubbles. I twirl to see the whole design. As I twirl, a loud high-pitched scream echoes through the chamber and chills me to the bone. I drop to the floor and freeze. Takoda's soon by my side and he clicks off our lights. We remain motionless in the darkness and listen as more high-pitched screams continue.

"It's a warning system," I whisper.

"A what?"

"They saw our lights and those screams are a warning to whatever they are that we're here."

"Follow me," he says, pulling on my hand.

Follow me? How in the world can he see where he's going? We walk, or more like it, crawl to an entryway that leads away from the vast cavern of balconies and stairs.

"The broom closet, I suppose?"

"Excuse me?" he replies as we dart into the long hallway.

"How did you see this in the dark?" I whisper, turning on my light.

"I noticed it before that thing screamed."

The hallway leads us down various corridors with locked wooden doors on both sides. We continue to walk with our lights dim in order to not attract too much attention. After about an hour, we eventually enter a large room that's barren except for one wall along the far back. I'm shocked at what I'm seeing. Could it really be what I think it is?

"Electricity?" I surmise.

"I believe so. If I can figure out how this thing works, I might get it started," he replies, dropping his backpack to the floor. "Keep an ear out for anything that might be looking for us."

I stand guard with my helmet light off. All's quiet and that's fine with me. My legs feel swollen from all the stairs and I sit on the floor. With my back resting against the wall, I allow my imagination to take me to wherever it wants.

I imagine Takoda and me together as husband and wife. I see a little boy who looks like him and a little girl that looks like me. My life has taken me to an unexplained height of happiness. I'm living on a strange and wonderful world, with strange and wonderful people. And one thing I know for sure, I'm hopelessly in love with Takoda. Whenever he's around, my life has meaning, a purpose. I feel alive when Takoda takes my hand into his. I long for him to touch me in a gentle and warm way, but I know that Takoda and I can never truly be as one.

A deep rumbling echoes through the chamber and the floor vibrates, rousing me from my thoughts. The room lights as though it's daylight. I squint and my eyes try to focus. I glance around and there's no light structure anywhere. *Where is the light coming from?* I jump to my feet. Takoda turns to me with a huge smile.

"You did it!" I yell.

"I did it!" he yells back surprised at his own accomplishment.

We jump into each other's arms, and he twirls me as we celebrate his victory. We study the room. This place must be a central area for the electricity. The room's huge, just like everything else around here. Human-sized tables and chairs made from stone line the wall on one side and the electrical panel lines the other.

"How do you suppose this works?" I ask.

"I am not really sure." He shakes his head. "If I had to guess, I would say it is thermal, pulling the heat from underground. I do not believe it is nuclear because of the noise. I had to pull on those long chains and when I did, the floor vibrated. I probably opened a chamber somewhere that turned everything on. After that, it was as simple as flipping on the lights. Let us flip the rest of the switches and see what happens. Listen, can you hear the generators working?"

"So, that's what that rumble is. I was wondering about that."

Takoda continues to flip switches and I help. Otherwise, who knows how long we would be in this room. We proceed slowly and constantly watch the gauges. The ancient writings were in a basic language Takoda could read, and he was able to gather enough information to understand how the switches were organized. As long as the gauges did not enter the yellow, everything was fine.

We flip a few switches and then wait, if the pointer stays in the green, we move on. Finally, we flip the last few switches and when everything seems to be working, we stand back and admire our work. When he's satisfied that we haven't done any harm to the city, we grab our packs and walk up the long hallway to the center archway. It seems that the ancient people built their city inside a huge natural crevice that falls miles into this world and extends just as far above our heads. The gap between the two sides must be miles apart with homes or businesses built into the sides of both cliffs. It's a visionary wonder. Something that should have been impossible to create but it's here.

"I don't hear any more screaming or warning signals," I say as we admire the view.

"All is quiet," he adds, holding my hand. "Maybe the lights are scaring them off? Which way first?"

Perhaps Takoda is correct, maybe we will be safe with the lights on. After all, when I was a little girl bright lights did chase away the monsters.

"Let us walk and see where it takes us." Takoda's drawing on his small electronic tablet. "A map."

I glance over his shoulder.

"Would not do to get lost, would it?" he asks.

"No, it wouldn't." I agree as we head off down another flight of stairs.

As we walk, we admire the carvings on the walls. When we find ancient writings, we stop so Takoda can read them to me. We eventually come to an enclosed garden with a fountain in the center. The water's flowing and Takoda assumes that with the electricity on, other equipment must have started up automatically, such as the water and sewer systems.

There is a plaque on a wall near the fountain and Takoda reads it out loud:

> *The purpose of life hides from us.*
> *Just as our time of death is a secret,*
> *so is the time of our birth.*
> *In this garden, I surrender my love.*
> *As the waters of time flow,*
> *so will my desire for you.*
> *Living is a rebirth and ever changing.*
> *And my love for you is ever growing,*
> *never ending.*

"Beautiful," I whisper, staring into the tumbling water. "He must have really loved her. I bet he built this home for her and this fountain was a symbol of his love and devotion."

Takoda stands by my side as we watch the water. There's nothing to say. I'm in love with him but I cannot show it. I can be nothing other than a friend.

"Let us camp here," Takoda suggests. "We both seem to like it."

"Question?" I ask, turning to him. "How do we know what time it is?"

"I have my timekeeper." He shows me something that looks like a wristwatch. "This will tell us what time it is, and it is almost time for dinner. We forgot about lunch. We have been so busy."

After dinner, I sit with my back against Takoda's knees. We make up stories about who lived in what balconies and what businesses were where. We try to figure out how the people lived and why they would have left such a beautiful city behind.

"Takoda?" I ask. "How can I find out what month and day it is back on Earth? I know we don't have months and years here, but I remember someone telling me that you are taught how to calculate Earth's dates and times?"

"If I remember my studies correctly, it would be …" He calculates the numbers in his head. I watch as his beautiful eyes close and his mouth moves silently. It's all I can do not to kiss him. "December."

"Oh?" I stand and walk over to the brick railing. I glance up and the remains of a long-deceased plant rest on a ledge just above my head. I laugh and glance out into the space separating us from the other side.

"What is it?" he asks, joining me.

"What day would it be?"

"The 24th or the 25th, why?"

I explain our holiday of Christmas and the tradition of the mistletoe. I explain that back on Earth, men would steal a kiss from the woman they desired. It didn't even matter if she was married because the kiss was allowed under the plant. In fact, it was mandatory. Thus, everyone avoided mistletoe at all costs.

He laughs and the wonderful sound of his voice fills the air. I turn and gaze into the nothingness wishing things could be different between us.

"A legal kiss," he whispers. "Fascinating."

"It's stupid, I know. Just a custom. I wish I were back home with a stupid Christmas tree and all the lights."

Takoda remains silent for a few moments. He gently turns me to face him and smiles. He says softly, "A legal kiss is okay then?" And … he kisses me.

His lips are soft and warm and fill my heart with a desire I've never felt before. I reach my arms around him and hug him close. Then as quickly as it came, it's over. Takoda pulls back and smiles. I don't know what just happened but his eyes speak to me. Takoda longs for me.

I lean into him and again I feel his warm lips against mine. I never want him to stop. I now know that he wants me just as much as I want him. When he pulls back this time, he doesn't pull back as far.

He stares into my eyes and whispers, "May the Most Holy forgive me, but … Journey Elizabeth Gordon … I love you."

11
CHAMBERS

IT'S OUR first day in the ruins and I'm excited in more ways than I can count. My growling stomach tells me it's time to get up and do something. Takoda is not lying beside me, which means he's probably making breakfast.

"Good morning," he says, handing me a hot drink.

"Morning," I say, staring into the vast cavern just off the balcony. I'm not sure how to act around Takoda. He said he loved me last night but is he regretting it today?

"Journey?" Arms wrap around my shoulders and a soft kiss is planted on my neck. "I love you. Nothing has changed since last night."

I turn and stare into his wonderful large eyes. "I wouldn't want it any other way."

Warm lips touch mine and I melt into his strong embrace. At the same time, my hot drink falls from my hand and splatters across the rock floor.

"Ah man!"

Takoda shakes his head. "This is exactly why I love you so much — unpredictable."

Breakfast includes warm bread and fresh fruit. I gobble it up. I clean up the mess as Takoda packs us a small bag of munchies and other little trinkets.

I tie my shoes and one of the laces snap. "Drats!"

"What is wrong?" he asks.

"String broke." I hold it up.

"Your shoes are pretty worn."

"I know," I say, frowning.

The idea of throwing them away is something I can't think about. Not now. They were the last pair I bought with my mother.

"Here," he says, pulling something from his larger pack. "Will this work?" Takoda hands me a long strand of leather.

"Yes, thank you."

"I was going to make you a draping," he replies. "I think you need it now more."

"I could call it a shoe draping," I say, smiling.

We leave our modest home to explore the ruins. Streets carved from the rock, smoothed by thousands of feet over many generations, spread out for miles in all directions. Not knowing where anything is, we blindly pick a path.

Empty merchant shops line the streets. Their windows long since shattered and their doors crumbled from years of neglect. The only way we know they were once stores is by the ancient writings carved above the entryways.

Several hours into our walk, we come across a complex with many levels and rooms. Carvings of twin women, inlaid with gold, decorate the hall's extra-large doors. Tall statues of men are guarding each corner. A geometric pattern adorns the floor and ceiling. Many of the rooms house counters made from wood and rock.

"What is this place?" I ask.

"I think it may have been the Council's center," he replies.

We enter the central chamber and I'm blown away. "Wow!" Ceilings tower above our heads, and a circular staircase follows the wall up to the second floor. "Let's see what's up there!"

Halfway up, I stop to peek over the railing. The geometric design on the floor glares back at us.

"Do you see what I see?" Takoda asks.

"Yes!" I say, not believing it. "Looks like a strand of … DNA!"

"Yes, it does," he replies.

"Why would someone put a strand of DNA on the floor?"

"Have no idea," he replies.

We continue to the top landing and enter another vast chamber filled with partitions, desks, shelves and counters. Different types of equipment line the counters and shelves.

"We've hit pay dirt!" I yell. "Look at all this stuff! What is it?"

"Medical equipment?" Takoda shakes his head. He picks up a microscope and examines it.

"What's it doing up here? Look, slides." I hold a glass slide between my fingers.

"You should not touch." He takes it from me and places it back on the table. "You do not know what is on it."

"What difference would it make?"

"Please," he says. "Until we know what this is or was, do not touch the slides."

"Okay." I search the other tables. Beakers of some unknown fluid are scattered around the room. I find something that looks electronic. "I see no plugs or cords. How do they turn them on?"

Takoda tries to lift the odd contraption but it's too heavy. After examining the apparatus, he shrugs. "There are little holes here. Big enough for a vial. Maybe a blood analyzer?" He glances around and sighs. "Reminds me of a laboratory."

"Could have been one." I too look around.

"Many generations ago a plague killed millions. Maybe this is where they conducted their research."

"Then not touching things is a very good idea," I say, nodding.

We continue exploring and find nothing else of importance. We eat a small lunch at the foot of a large statue before exploring another hallway. Takoda marks where we are on his map. We enter another large complex that's decorated with ornate carvings. We investigate.

Walls are covered in murals and statues of people posed in different ways. The entry is a large, ornate arch and the room is oval. Rows upon rows of benches carved from the rock adorn the center. Directly in the middle are stairs that flow down and end on a round platform.

"A theater?" he asks as we descend the stairs.

"Maybe they sat on those seats up there and the actors played out their stories down here. I wonder where the actors came out?"

"A door," Takoda points, "dressing rooms perhaps?"

"This place is amazing," I climb back up and sit on a bench. I look down at Takoda and wave.

"They had everything they needed." Takoda's voice echoes up through the large hole. I can even hear him breathing.

"It's something to admire."

We spend the rest of the day walking the halls and exploring rooms. By the time we return to our camp, we're exhausted. After a meal of warm bread and raw vegetables, we crash on our sleeping bags. Takoda wraps his arms around me and we kiss. His lips are warm and inviting.

"I want to be with you forever," he whispers.

I relax into his embrace and as sleep finds me, my last thoughts are of spending the rest of my life with him.

12

PARTNERS FOREVER

THAT NIGHT, we sleep peacefully in each other's arms. It feels right. Nothing has ever felt so natural. The next morning, we make a decision — for the next few days, this camp will be our home. The days are for exploring, and the nights are for us. However, we respect that forbidden hidden line that separates us.

The ruins are exciting and I can't seem to get enough of them. I want to see and experience everything. As we explore the empty halls, we carry only a small bag with absolute necessities such as water, a snack or two and his tablet. The streets are well lit and the shops line both sides. I pretend to be shopping for clothes as Takoda pretends to be shopping for books.

Most of the homes are on top of the shops. Some of the rooms still have items but most are empty. Luckily, we see no creatures.

One afternoon just after lunch, we enter a room with crystal-clear water and sparkling rocks for a floor.

"A swimming pool?" I step to the edge and gasp. "It has a crystal bottom."

"This room is a bathhouse," Takoda says, pulling off his shirt. "We cannot allow this go to waste."

Wearing just our undergarments, we jump in. That afternoon, we splash and kiss the day away. It is wonderfully refreshing to be clean.

"Journey?" Takoda asks, as I sit on the edge of the pool allowing a fresh breeze to dry me.

"Yeah." I wring the water from my hair.

"On Earth … when someone like me wants to date someone like you, how does that work?" He's treading water and splashes a few drops at me.

"Nothing special. You would ask me to go out with you. Then we'd go to a movie or something and hold hands and eventually we'd kiss. I'd tell everyone that you're my boyfriend, and you'd tell everyone that I'm your girlfriend."

"That is all?" he asks with a scurrility that makes me a little nervous.

"Okay, what are you getting at?"

He pulls himself onto the ledge next to me. I watch as the water runs down his muscular bluish body and drips from his braided hair. My stomach leaps into my throat and I almost choke.

"Are you okay?"

"Yes," I lie and stare into the clear water.

"On our worlds, it is different. We are chosen for a union."

"You mean like you and Anneeta?" I look at him and frown.

Takoda places his cold hands on my face and gazes deeply into my eyes. I melt, of course, but at the same time I'm a little angry for the thought of her almost ruining my fantasy.

"My heart does not belong to Anneeta. What I feel for you, I have never felt for anyone. You make me believe that I can do anything. When I am with you, I am complete."

Tears roll down my cheeks and he kisses me. He lays me back and with his body next to mine, I can feel his heat radiating, warming me inside and out. As his warmth engulfs me, it thaws my mind and spirit.

"I love you, Journey," he whispers. "I have from the first moment I placed my eyes upon you back at the market. I loved it when you could not talk and your face turned red."

I roll my eyes and he caresses my cheek and my body trembles at his touch.

"We must talk," he says in a very serious tone. His look is somber, and I'm afraid all of this will end as quickly as it started. "I must explain something."

"What?"

"Here, things are different. When we approach manhood, we experience Kupatanna. And it can be very painful."

"Have you gone through it yet?"

"No not for several of your Earth years. If I do not have a partner chosen by then …"

I sit up and glare at him. "Then what?"

"I could die."

I sit up on my knees and brush the hair from my face. What is he talking about? Death? From going through a change of life? "Explain." There's no way I'm going to lose him, not now. If he's not sincere, then this is the cruelest joke I've ever heard, and Takoda is not prone to jokes.

"Our bodies are similar. We have most of the same organs. We breathe the same air and eat the same food. It is our reproductive system that is different. Men on your world do not change. I will change."

"Change? Change how, exactly?" I'm reminded about the novel Dr. Jekyll and Mr. Hyde.

"Nothing you can see. I will look the same. It is my body readying itself for …"

"Okay," I raise my hand, "enough said."

"I want for you to be my partner, Journey."

"Me?" I stand and take a few steps away. "How can that be? It is forbidden remember?"

Takoda stands and steps toward me. "Yes, it is forbidden … but I want you."

All kinds of crazy stuff flows through my mind. Would I have to have sex with him or something like sex? Does he even have sex?

"What would I have to do?" If his health is on the line, I may have no choice. "Exactly?"

"Just be with me." His eyes brighten with expectation.

It's almost as though he's sure I will tell him no, that I'm not interested. But I am interested. I feel protective over him and will do anything to keep him safe.

"Yes," I say with as much confidence as I can.

"Yes?"

"Yes," I repeat, gently touching his cheek.

"Journey, you will never know how much this means to me."

"I would do anything for you." I whisper, "I love you, Takoda."

He rubs my cheek and kisses me tenderly on the forehead. "I will explain more later. Thank you."

"You're welcome." *What did I just get myself into?*

That night we eat in silence. We sit close and our hips touch. It seems that Takoda wants us touching all the time. I don't mind, kinda feels good.

After dinner, I need to use the facility. The bathrooms are not next to the bedrooms or the main living areas. They are what I conclude are communal bathrooms. Large areas with running water that flows continuously. Everything here is carved directly from the rock. A slow stream falls from a small hole into a rock bowl. A constant pool to wash ourselves. Along one wall are what I believe are toilets. Water flows along the bottom and washes away the uglies.

I allow the cool running water to hit the back of my hands. I'm concerned about what I just promised — to be Takoda's partner. What will my father say when he finds out? What would the authorities do?

Takoda's lying in bed when I cross the garden. I start to crawl into my sleeping bag when I notice that he has zipped them together.

"Takoda!" I take a step back. "I'm a virgin! What are you doing?"

He laughs. "What is a virgin?"

"I've never been with a boy … like that!" I point to our bed.

"We will not … how do you say … have sex. That would get us into trouble. I can, however, love you and you can be mine — for now."

With a sigh and feeling a little presumptuous, I climb in and sink into his warm embrace. His body is hot, very hot. *Is Takoda coming down with something?*

"Explain this Kupatanna thing." I yawn.

As he talks, I'm soothed by his voice. "Kupatanna starts at the ages of eighteen to twenty Earth years. It only happens to boys. When our system is ready."

"And how old are you now?" I ask, wanting to know how long I have until I must perform — something.

"Seventeen of your Earth years," he replies.

"What happens then?"

"If we have a partner, it is easier. They pull the heat from our bodies and make our transformation less painful."

"I just hold you?"

Takoda nods.

"I can handle that." I close my eyes on the world around me and sleep pulls me away.

I awaken to a very quiet room. I glance around and immediately know that something is very wrong.

"Takoda …" I whisper.

No reply.

"Takoda!" I yell this time but still no reply.

I jump out of bed and run to the bathroom. No Takoda. I dart back to our bedroom and dress. Takoda is not in the garden. Something is wrong and I have to find him.

"Takoda!" I yell again but still no reply.

I run into the empty and dark street. The lights automatically dim when the sun goes down. No sign of Takoda anywhere.

My God, where is he?

Could the Nomaddas have gotten to him? I run. Since I forgot to take the time to put on my shoes, the tiny rocks are cutting into my feet. I don't care. All that matters is that I find Takoda.

"Takoda, where are you?" I scream out. I am close to panicking now.

The swimming pool is just a little farther. I don't know why I'm aiming for the pool, but something inside is telling me to get there. I turn the corner and slip. I scream as my hip slaps against the stone floor. Air is pushed from my lungs. I gasp. It takes me a few seconds to recover. I try to stand. I cannot. Blood is pooling around my feet and my hip is screaming out in pain.

I've really hurt myself.

As I raise myself up with my arms, I finally see him. He's rolled into a ball in the shallow end of the pool.

"Takoda!"

Takoda doesn't respond.

"Takoda, are you hurt?"

I can't move. My hip is probably broken. I scoot toward the water. Would I drown if I fall in? Do I have a choice? I push hard and roll into the water. I scream and water fills my mouth. Using my good leg, I push myself up. After coughing, I finally get a lung full of air. Using my arms and one good leg, I inch my way over to Takoda. Thank God he is in the shallow end.

Takoda is resting against the side of the pool. He glances up and I gasp. His eyes are a deep red. It is obvious that he is in a lot of pain. Without thinking, I wrap my arms around him. His body's on fire. It's almost too painful to touch him.

"My God, Takoda, it's the Kupatanna isn't it?"

Takoda looks at me with a sense of searching that I can't explain. I know he needs me but how do I help? Suddenly, his arms wrap around me and it's all I can do to not scream. The heat radiates directly from his body and into mine. I cannot think. I can barely breathe or stand on my one good leg.

We remain locked together for what seems like forever before the heat fades. As his last little bit of energy leaves me, Takoda screams. The sound that echoes through the ancient city reminds me of the screams we heard when we arrived. With Takoda's one shriek, I realize that the Swetaachatas are somehow related to the Nomaddas.

It takes all my strength to pull Takoda from the water. I struggle but eventually I manage. Panting to catch my breath, I try to figure out how in the world I'm going to get him back to our camp.

"Takoda, I need you to walk. We can't stay here." I am begging and hoping he'll respond. But he doesn't.

My feet are throbbing. With no other options … I cry. I'm deep inside a cave, with bleeding feet, and a sick partner. I have no idea how long this Kupatanna is going to take. As much as I know, it could take weeks, even months. Takoda's still running a slight fever. As he trembles in my arms, I try to get him to respond to me.

Is he dying inside my embrace?

Takoda screams again and as his cries echo through the chamber, several *things* wearing black robes appear at the entryway. More high-pitched screams echo from somewhere deep inside the ancient city. The shrieks are loud. I hold my hands over my ears as I try to balance Takoda on my legs. When the screams finally stop, I pull Takoda higher onto my lap. He's now as cold as ice and all the color has drained from his face. Instead of the vibrant blueish green, Takoda is now a dull gray.

I cry harder as the *things* slowly step closer. One of the creatures holds out its hands.

"Get away from us!" I grab tighter onto Takoda. "Go away!"

My tears flow and I can barely see. I refuse to release Takoda to wipe my eyes. My hands are locked tightly onto the man I love, and I will protect him with my life.

As the creatures inch toward us, I glare at them. I can't see their faces because of their hoods. But their hands! They are *not* human, nor are they Swetaachata. They're thin, bony and black. These must be the Nomaddas they warned us about.

My fear of becoming their dinner rings through my mind and I scream. I scream again and again.

A warm hand gently touches my shoulder and instantly I feel as if someone has given me medication. My pain and fear subside and my heart beats slow. There's no reason for me to scream anymore. Although, these monsters are here with us, I feel safe. Two new creatures enter and pick up Takoda. One lifts me. As they take us down the empty streets, I understand that they're taking us to our camp.

I am placed on our sleeping bags next to Takoda. One of the creatures tends to my feet. It cleans them, puts medicine on them, and bandages them. Another one leaves us fruit and a filled water pitcher near our bed. As they leave, another is wiping my blood from the floor.

The last one lingers for only a moment before nodding to the right. I lay in silence for hours just staring at the ceiling. I keep my hand on Takoda. It's hard to comprehend exactly what just happened. Could those creatures really be the Nomaddas? If yes, why didn't they eat us?

The longer my mind wanders through the strangeness, the sleepier I feel. Inside my dreams, I'm enjoying the pool with Takoda. We're splashing when the screaming starts. I grab Takoda to protect him from the evil creatures. The screams get louder and louder.

Opening my eyes, I realize that the screeching is not coming from my mind but from Takoda. I pull him in close. I wrap my arms around him and can feel the heat flowing from his body.

"Takoda," I whisper. "I'm here. I love you. Stay with me. Please don't die, Takoda. I don't want to live without you."

His grip tightens. Again, the waves of heat penetrate deeply into my inner core. I close my eyes and relax into his strong embrace. My mind wanders and when I open my eyes, we are no longer at our camp. Instead, we are standing next to a sea of green. The heat is gone and so is my pain.

The water is calm and the sky emits an eerie hue. It is strange that I feel so safe. Takoda takes my hand and smiles. We walk along the beach without talking. We don't have to because I can understand everything he is thinking.

Takoda takes me in his arms and kisses me so tenderly that our hearts melt into one. The love we are sharing is intense and takes my breath away. We have merged and are now one soul ... one mind. We are breathing each other's breaths. Our hearts beat as one. As our love becomes us, we become our love.

I receive a vision. I watch as Takoda grows. It starts from birth, then he is learning to walk. I see his first bike, his first day of school and so much more. I now know everything about Takoda. I even sense how he feels about Anneeta and how much he loves me. He desires me to be his mate and bear his children.

I don't want to let go. I can hear him telling me everything is okay, and I can release him now. It is so painful and I feel cold and empty without him. Takoda is regaining control of his private thoughts. My eyes burn as I try to open them. Every muscle aches and my hip explodes through the waves of agony.

"Takoda?" I whisper. "Takoda, are you okay?"

A couple of moments pass before he answers. When he speaks, my mind relaxes. "I am fine. I need water."

I struggle to sit up. My head's spinning and my stomach tightens, but I resist the urge to vomit. The only way I can reach the pitcher of water is to fall to the floor. As my knees bang against the hard rock, I hold back a scream as the pain shoots throughout my body. The water's cool and wonderful and I gulp, allowing the liquid to soothe my sore throat. It takes all of my strength to pull myself up to the bed. As I sit next to him, Takoda lays his head on my pillow. I help him take a sip. He is now cool to the touch. The fever's gone.

"Is it over?" I ask, stroking his forehead.

Takoda nods and takes a few more sips.

"That was pretty intense." I try to lean over to kiss his forehead but the pain in my hip is too forceful. I don't want to tell Takoda that I'm hurt. He has been through so much already. "Thank you for sharing that with me."

We remain in bed for the rest of the day. We gratefully eat the fruit the creatures left behind. Several times, I hop or limp to the water fountain to refill the jug. Slowly, we recuperate together. Takoda keeps a tight hold on me. Every now and then, he leans over and kisses me. He constantly whispers how much he loves me. Even though I'm in severe pain, I never want this day to end.

13
NOMADDAS

THE ALARM on Takoda's timekeeper wakes me. At first, I'm disoriented and not sure where the noise is coming from. When I recognize the beeping, I roll over and push the small button. The excruciating pain shoots up through my back. I can tell that it is morning. I make myself stand. Everything aches, especially my hip.

The bathroom looks like it's a hundred miles away. I take in a deep breath and take a step. I have to get to the bathroom. I place my weight on my good hip and slowly hop across the garden. Every leap is an agonizing nightmare. It seems like forever before I'm leaning on the basin. Splashing cold water on my face feels wonderful.

I turn and stare at the holes. I need to relieve myself. I'm not sure if I can make it that far. Tears streak my cheeks as the pain echoes throughout my body. My feet feel a little better but not my hip. I balance to take a hop when one of the creatures steps in front of me. I'm too shocked to move, scream or cry out.

The creature gently places one hand on my shoulder and the other onto my injured hip. As soon as it touches me, the throbbing stops. I still feel weak and sore but at least the intense pain no longer racks my body. After a few more moments, the Nomadda releases its grip and takes a step back.

Cautiously, I straighten and try to place my weight on my injured hip. No pain. The thing *healed* me?

"Thank you." I nod to the right.

The creature nods back.

For reasons I'll never understand, I reach out and pull off its hood. A bald and black face smiles back at me. The Nomadda looks human and frail and old at the same time. Its eyes are amber, huge and beautiful, and its nose and mouth are small. Too small for its extra-large head.

Who are these creatures and why are they here?

Perhaps they're all that remains of the forgotten race of people I was told about. I reach out and touch its cheek. Its skin feels cold and damp, almost leathery. As soon as we make contact, our minds do too, and all my questions are answered, and I give all my concentration to the images that are flashing through my head.

This creature is trying to tell me something important.

I see images of the city teeming with healthy-looking people working, playing and living out their lives. Then the world becomes dark, and I see that the people are sick and dying. The suffering is horrible. I can sense the evil that was inflicted upon this magnificent city.

After the illness died off, their offspring were born different. The sickness had actually changed their DNA. These people would never be healthy again. Over time, others feared them and eventually laws were passed that prohibited anyone making contact. Instead, they were hunted, tortured or killed. The atrocities inflicted upon them were unspeakable.

My heart aches. I have an inner desire to help. *But how?* The creature breaks our connection and steps back. I smile and it nods to the right. Without saying a word, it walks away leaving me with my thoughts.

I try to sort out the visions that were shared with me. What will I do with the knowledge? After relieving myself, I walk across the garden. The Nomaddas have again left us fresh fruit and this time, they left bread and a hot stew. As soon as I smell the food, I realize how hungry I am.

I pull out some bread and cheese and cut up the fruit. With a plate in both hands, I sit next to Takoda. He rolls onto his back and opens his eyes. His color has returned and he looks so much better.

"Food?" he whispers.

"Stew and bread," I say. "And I made tea."

"You are wonderful." He takes a bite.

We eat in silence and then rest for hours. Takoda watches as I use the fountain to rinse off the dishes. With everything tidy and neat, I pull out my phone. My father picked it up for me just before I left for this Trial. I plug in the little speakers and search for my favorite music. The fifties and sixties 'oldies but goodies' reverberate off the rock walls. The tone sounds deeper, richer. I join Takoda on the bed and he smiles. When an old strolling song, Kansas City, comes on, I jump up and dance.

"What is that sound?" he asks, rising from the bed. His strength is returning fast and he seems more like his old self.

I laugh as I swing my head around and yell, "Music — join me?"

Takoda stands and stretches. I am feeling so full of energy that it is amazing. Takoda tries to dance. It's obvious he too can't ignore the beat. We have fun just jumping around and flailing our arms. We laugh and play through a couple of songs before our energy dies and we fall onto our sleeping bags panting. He wraps his arms around me and snuggles his face deeply into my hair. We remain silent as we catch our breaths.

After a while, Takoda says, "Thank you."

"You're welcome. What do you remember about the last couple of days?"

"There are a few dark spots but I remember most of it. I do not know how I got back here. I do remember you coming to me in the pool — and our joining …" The way he is talking, it's almost as though he's feeling guilty.

"Are you feeling bad about what we shared?" I ask.

Takoda nods.

"No, don't. That was the most amazing thing I've ever experienced."

"I did not know it would be that strong."

"Are you sorry I partnered with you?"

He stares into my eyes and replies, "Never. I want to be with you forever. And somehow, we will find a way."

As I lay in his arms, I consider telling Takoda about the creatures and my hip. I'm afraid he'll be concerned about our safety and suggest moving our camp. No. I'll just wait until he's stronger before I say anything. They mean us no harm.

Later that day, Takoda's feeling even better and wants to fix dinner. Since he's looking more like himself, I don't object. As he prepares the vegetables, I sit by the fountain and talk.

"Takoda, what have you been told about the Nomaddas?"

He doesn't look up to answer but replies, "They are an ancient race and are dangerous. Why?"

"Just look at this city. It's huge and millions used to live here. Doesn't it pique your interest about what happened? Why they left?"

"We should be able to search tomorrow. Maybe we will the find hall of records. That is what our Trial is all about. Although, I would not raise your hopes. We have not found much of anything that was left behind."

His renewed interest makes me feel a little better. As we eat our dinner, I try to work out exactly how I will explain the last couple of days to him.

The next morning after breakfast, we pull out the packet that was handed to us by the officers. We thought it best to establish our bearings prior to starting our actual challenge. The packet's a booklet describing what is known about the Nomaddas. Drawings of what the creatures look like are labeled with directions on what to do if we encounter one. I laugh, because the real Nomaddas don't look anything like the renditions.

We find our challenge and look it over. We're to find the central depository and recover the records. The thought of stealing from these people doesn't feel right. But until that time comes, I think it best to keep it to myself. I don't know why, but it just feels better to keep my meetings with the Nomaddas a secret, at least for now.

We tidy the camp and head deeper into the city. Takoda continues to use his tablet as we search the ruins. With each turn and stairwell, he meticulously takes notes. Before our challenge is over, we should have a fairly decent map.

We rest under a huge arch with halls leading off in different directions. I'm tired and my hip is starting to ache a little. As I take a bite from a fruit similar to an apple, a little red-light flickers in the darkness. It's faint, but it is there. I search for it again. Nothing.

"Are you finished?" I stand and shake out my legs. "I would like to go this way, if you don't mind."

Takoda gives me a weird look but doesn't object. "That is fine."

He grabs our bags and we walk down the dark hallway.

"No lights down here. I wonder why?" I ask as I turn on my headlamp.

"This direction may not be a good idea," he says. "The creatures may live this way."

Oh my, how do I start? There's no good way to say what I need to say, so I just start talking. "I met them already, and before you say anything, just hear me out."

"You met … what?" Takoda's voice is filled with concern.

I stop walking and explain how they carried us back to camp, mended my feet, and left us food and water. When I get to the part about my hip and how the creature touched me, Takoda interrupts.

"Wait, are you telling me these things *helped* us … *healed* you?" His voice sounds more amused than concerned.

"Well, yes." I nod. "If they were going to eat us, they would have done so by now. They've had plenty of opportunities. I don't believe they want to hurt us."

"Do you know what they want?"

"I don't think they want anything. We are the intruders, not them."

"We did barge into their home."

"I think I saw something down here. I believe they want us to follow them."

Our long walk challenges my hip, but I'm not going to stop. I have to know what's at the end of this hall. We soon come to a set of stairs. We climb and when we reach the landing, I can't see very far. We are standing in a small room. It's dark and I can just barely make out something from the corner of my eyes.

"They're here," I whisper, tugging on Takoda's sleeve.

"Where?" he asks, glancing around.

"To our left. Don't move." I turn my head slowly and the light shines on several creatures wearing long black robes. They are just standing there.

"Now what?" Takoda asks.

"Not sure." As soon as I speak, I hear a creature beckon to me from inside my head. "This way." I take Takoda's hand. Just before we reach them, they turn and walk away. "I believe we're to follow."

They lead us through various halls until we come to an enormous circular room with a round table in the center and walls lined with shelves. Thousands of golden disc-shaped objects are everywhere.

"What is this place?" I ask.

"I think I know what this is." Takoda walks up to the huge circular table. He studies it for a moment before he takes a gold disc from one of the shelves.

"If I am not mistaken," he says, "this is a parallaxal viewer. I thought they were only a myth."

"A what?"

"Parallaxal viewer," he repeats. "Let us see if this works."

The gold disc slides easily into an opening on the table and instantly we're surrounded by a colorful three-dimensional video. The technology's far more advanced than anything either of our people have. I stand in amazement and watch a living documentary of the past civilization that was recorded for all time. It was all revolving around us.

"Takoda, I believe we found the archives." I sense that the creatures are standing along the far wall. I turn to them and nod to my right. "Thank you."

Takoda kneels and bows. He remains in this position until one of the creatures steps up to Takoda and touches him on the shoulder. Takoda stands. He towers over the Nomadda who is barely five feet.

"Your secret is safe with us, ancient one," Takoda states. "We are only here to learn and understand. Thank you for sharing your knowledge with us."

The creature nods and backs away. Again, they leave us a plate of fruit and a jug of water. I turn my attention to the video. People who look like me are talking, but unfortunately, they're speaking a language I don't understand.

"It is an ancient dialect," Takoda says. "I think I can translate enough to understand. I may have to play some of these over a few times."

"Better get started, 'cause there's a lot of material here."

After ejecting the disc from the reader and placing it back on the shelf, Takoda studies the other labels. I watch as his fingers brush over the various symbols and his eyes concentrate on deciphering the ancient writings.

"Here it is," he exclaims.

"Here's what?"

Takoda inserts a disc into the reader. A three-dimensional man with bright blue skin stands motionless on top of the round platform. He is wearing a white suit and his hair is long and braided with ornamental gold and silver beads. If I had to guess, I would say his age is about fiftyish. His expressions announce wisdom and knowledge.

After a brief moment, the three-dimensional man asks, "What information may I pass, Questioners?"

"This video is interactive?" I ask.

Takoda nods and speaks slowly. "We question the start and end of this city, and the whereabouts of its citizens." Takoda waits patiently for him to reply. It's obvious the computer's searching for answers, and as it does, the man remains motionless.

"I have the information you seek," the man says, only this time, he is speaking in English.

At the same time the man fades away, and I find myself gazing into the deep crevice that runs down the length of the mountain ridge.

The man's voice starts with a dissertation. "In the year of Our Lady, our people searched for a suitable place to settle. After the Draconian war, our planet, Qapadhue, could no longer sustain life. We left by twos in search of a suitable home. Many star systems would not sustain life. After four generations, we found the twin planets orbiting this binary star system. Our Elders named the twin planets, Journey and Traveler. Journey, to remind us of the long distance we endured, and Traveler to remind us that we came as visitors, not conquerors.

"Twenty-two thousand we were, ranging from newborn to elderly. Our hopes were high and our expectations great. There were large carnivores in those early years. Living in the valley was not an option. Our Elders chose these cliffs, as they were not accessible to the flesh-eating beasts."

As we listen, we learn that the people built their city in this vast cavern, believing they were safe from the wild animals that freely roamed the valleys. It took over two hundred rotations before the city was complete. This great city was named after their leader, a woman. The city was built purposely on top of a major volcanic river that runs between the two mountains. Just as Takoda had surmised, this is where their power originates.

The people lived a normal life, fell in love, married and raised children who attended school before choosing a career. Ruling was socialistic with a council of Statemen establishing the laws.

The people were happy and many generations passed before the population exceeded one hundred million. Time was labeled by generations and their accomplishments, not from circling their sun. The twin planet, Journey, was settled during the twentieth generation. It was during the one hundredth generation that everything changed.

A plague killed many and the population dwindled to only a few thousand. Both planets were stricken and people were frightened. Many believed it was the extinction of their kind. After two generations, a scientist on Journey discovered it was their Elders who created the Death Plague and released it.

This scientist didn't know what to do with the damaging information. When she told the remaining Elders, she was put to death. Unbeknownst to the Elders, the scientist had sent the information to her colleagues as insurance that her findings would not be lost. When the news of her death was announced, her colleagues were forced to release her research. The people were angry and turned on the Elders. They struggled to repopulate the city but the plague had rendered many sterile. The population dwindled on both planets and each blamed the other for their plight. The relationship was severed. Many generations passed and each world lived within their own secluded environments.

The vaccine unexpectedly extended the Elders' lives. They lived well beyond a thousand generations. The children were changed into what we see today, the Nomaddas. Over time, the people became hostile, earning the city the name *The Wicked Lady*. The Elders lived on. Eventually they left the beautiful city and their powers extended around the twin worlds. On Journey, people are blue skinned with eyes of amber. Those on Traveler kept their original brownish coloring.

Takoda and I remain a long time in that room just listening and watching. What we learn can only mean one thing ... the Council had lied to the people. Our Council is corrupt and now I'm a part of that Council.

As we sit dumbstruck on the floor, Takoda whispers, "This information is dangerous."

"I wonder how my royalty fits into this?"

"I will ask." Takoda stands. "Explain the royal lineage. Where did they originate, what kind of power do they still have?"

The man disappears and the video surrounds us again. We're told the original two captains were husband and wife and two children were born of this union. Those two children each had six and it was those original six grandchildren that became the first council. After the royal court was established, unions between the two races were forbidden. It was difficult to believe that I share the same blood with these cowards that murdered millions. Because of my ancestors, Takoda and I cannot union. I stand and approach the three-dimensional man.

"If a person born on Traveler unions with a person on Journey, will their child be born damaged?"

The man looks directly at me as I speak. It's the first time he acknowledges that I'm here. A light hits my body and I can feel a slight electrical charge. The computerized man clasps his hands together and bows his head before lowering down onto one knee.

"You are an Elder," the man says. "I submit to you, my lord. Royal blood runs through your veins."

"Yes, I know. So, answer my question," I demand.

"Yes, my lord. The union between one from Traveler and one from Journey will not result in a damaged child."

"Then why are the people told this?"

"The Council wishes to keep the bloodlines pure."

"Why?"

"Unions would alter the children's DNA."

"The plague came during the reign of the Council of Elders," I say to Takoda. "Which means that the union law came about much later." I walk around the table and try to think. "So … that can only mean that the Elders were afraid of the altered DNA … but why? How long do the Elders live in Earth years?"

"Many thousands," the man replies.

"Ah, I get it. The Elders were afraid of becoming mortal again," I state.

"Not exactly," the man says.

"Then explain it."

"Their powers would be reduced," he says.

"What powers?" I ask.

"When the vaccine altered their DNA, the inner powers of the Swetaachata were activated."

"What powers?" I repeat.

"There are too many to answer," he says.

"I can't listen to any more of this!" I yell. "I refuse to believe any of it and he's not really saying anything."

"My lord," the man adds, "you have the power to make the change. You are the one who was foretold would come."

"What?" I ask. "Foretold what?"

One of the creatures hands Takoda a reddish disc. He motions for him to slip it into the reader. When Takoda drops it in, a Swetaachata woman appears. She's sitting on a fallen tree inside a bright green forest. Her long gray hair is partly braided. She's slender with blue skin and golden eyes. As she talks, her voice is soothing.

"During the year of The Great Change, a female child will come from the royal lineage mixed with the royal blood of the ancient ones. Her powers will be the greatest of all. Her wisdom and accomplishments will attest to her courage. From her comes a new bloodline to reestablish the ancient laws. She will bring peace and prosperity to all worlds. Her mother will be of the new and her father of the old. Her convictions will be strong and her heart pure. I bless her with Rhea at her feet and Hera at her head. I pray the enlightened ones sanctify her with a long life. That her travels are safe. That her journey is fruitful."

The woman bows and fades away. When I turn, Takoda is staring at me.

"What?" I ask. "And don't start doing anything stupid."

Takoda doesn't say a word.

Creatures enter the room and kneel at my feet.

"Oh no you don't!" I yell. "Up. Get up, now!"

No one moves.

"Hello?" I scream out. "Isn't anyone listening? Get up!"

They stand but continue to bow their heads.

"Okay, this is totally not happening. Takoda, tell them I'm a nobody, please!"

Takoda's still staring at me. He almost looks cross-eyed.

"Takoda, what's wrong with you?" I grab his arm and shake him.

Finally, he says, "I bonded with an ancient?"

"This is not happening. I am nobody special. I've had enough."

I turn and stomp my feet as I run from the room. I'm heading back to camp. I need sleep and food, and I'm not going to put up with any more of this ancient royalty stuff. I run down the different hallways and stop. I have no idea where I am going.

"Drats … I'm lost."

14
QUEENIE

I'M TIRED and cold and hungry, and I'm lost, absolutely and completely lost. With no other option available, I cry. After all my temper tantrums I had as a child and my mother ignoring me, you'd think I would have learned something by now. But no, as always, I have to be stubborn and pay the price.

The hallways before me are dark. After what seems like I'm walking forever, I come to a flight of stairs that lead down. I shrug and decide to walk boldly into my ultimate demise. Nearing the bottom, I can hear familiar sounds. I enter into what can only be described as a marketplace.

Hundreds of Nomaddas are walking about living their daily lives. Mothers are holding their babies as older children run around enjoying each other's company. With my mind in denial and my body in shock, I just stand there and stare as several children run past screaming and yelling.

When three of the older children realize I'm just standing there staring at them, they run up to me. The children yell out something, and suddenly all eyes are planted firmly on me — a tall skinny white girl with long curly dark hair and bright amber eyes. No one looks very happy to have me standing there.

"Ah … hi?" I whisper, not knowing anything else to say. I wave, and of course, offer my biggest smile.

They all keep staring at me as though I just popped out of thin air. After a deep breath, I walk into the market as though this is a perfectly natural thing for me to do. As I walk, different creatures stare at me with terror written all over their faces. I wave and say 'hello', or 'hi', or 'how yah doing'.

These creatures are living their lives down here. This place is their home. The structures are not as well built as those above and are in dire need of repair. Tattered drapes cover the doors and windows. Benches are broken or cracked, and the ground is hardened clay.

They are living not just in dirt but in filth. The longer I walk through the crowd, the more I understand that these people were abandoned. Yes, they are *people* not *creatures*, and they are *my* people.

My heart reaches out to them and so does my mind. As I acknowledge this, several turn to me and smile. I can hear their thoughts as if they're speaking directly to me. A person who appears to be the size of a five-year-old runs up. I'm shocked when I see her face. She looks to be about seventy years old but she's in a little girl's body. Her face is shriveled and she has a slight hump on her back that makes her stoop. When she takes my hand, her smile lights her face.

"My Queen?" she asks, with a very high-pitched voice.

I kneel to her height and take both of her hands into mine. My heart will not allow me to say *no* to her, so I simply nod to my right.

The crowd cheers and their voices sing out from all corners of their village. Some of the older ones chant. It is the same chant of the Wanderers who were by my lake.

This can't be.

They're crowding around me and my panic swells. Just before I explode, an older woman takes my hand and guides me from the crowd. We walk together into the center of the village, and she beckons me to sit by the fire. She offers bread, fruit and water, which I gladly accept for I am starving.

We sit for a long time and I listen with pleasure to their chanting. I have no desire to leave. It's comfortable here and I'm feeling content. The chanting quells after a while and Takoda steps up to me. A few of the Nomaddas wearing their black robes stand on the other side of the fire. Then it hits me, these people are not wearing black robes but togas of various colors with beaded ropes as belts.

"You have found your people, my Queen," one of the Nomaddas standing next to Takoda says as he bows his head to the right.

"You can talk?" I ask surprised because none of them had spoken before, at least not verbally.

"Yes," he replies.

I walk over to him and ask, "Why haven't you said anything before?"

"We had to be sure, my Queen," he replies.

"They are sure now!" Takoda declares as he takes my hand into his. "You are more than you will ever know, Journey."

"Then tell me," I demand, staring at him. "What is it *exactly* that I am?"

"These are your people," he replies. "I think they want our help — your help."

"Well, they need to move away from here," I say louder than I expected. "It's filthy. Why do they stay?"

"This is where the Elders allow us to live," one of the Nomaddas replies. "If we go anywhere else in this city, we are stricken with the ancient illness."

"What?"

Several Nomaddas hand me small gifts of handmade jewelry. Some just want to touch me or stroke my hair. It feels weird to be the center of attention but I also feel a strong urge to protect them.

"I'd like to go back to our camp now," I say to Takoda. "I'm tired and I need to be alone."

As we turn to leave, the old woman rubs the back of my hand and smiles. Then she nods. I can feel a warmth spreading throughout my body. I also have a strong feeling I know this woman but that would be impossible.

"That felt weird," I whisper to Takoda.

The robed Nomaddas guide us back to our camp. We say our goodbyes. As I lay on our bed and gaze at the ceiling, I can't help but wonder about the amazing people I'd just met — my distant cousins — my legacy.

"Takoda, I need to go back to the discs. I have questions."

"I bet you do," he replies holding me. "Does the Queen object to this?"

"No, but don't call me Queen!" I giggle and melt into his warm embrace. He kisses me. It's intense and I feel the love radiate from his body as he hugs me in close.

"I love you, Queen Journey," he whispers.

I smile because I know that eventually I will change things, and Takoda and I will be together. Someday we will union and have children. Because, I have the power to make a difference.

The following morning, I find myself standing in front of the virtual man again. He looks somewhat Swetaachata but he's also different. I can't quite put my finger on it yet.

"My lord has a question?" he asks.

I don't respond, instead I study him, circle around him, and watch his every move.

"My lord requires my assistance?" he inquires again.

After a few moments I ask, "Why does my silence concern you?"

"I am here to assist. You ask no question."

"You are just a program. What difference does it make how long I take to ask a question?"

The man doesn't answer.

"Journey do not play with your toys," Takoda jokes, as he reads over the titles of some of the golden discs.

"Fine, here's your question then. Am I a direct descendant of the ancient ones who created the Death Plague?"

After a brief pause, he answers. "Yes."

"Explain the lineage."

"During generation two hundred and twenty-seven, five children were born to a union between an Elder and a female Swetaachata. The eldest daughter, child number three, did not agree to the treatment of her people. Her name was Shyanna and she unioned with a human from Earth. They begot one child, a girl, and named her Lylillea.

"Lylillea married a Swetaachata from Journey, and she is your grandmother, your mother's mother."

I turn and stare at Takoda. "How can this be? Unions are forbidden."

"Explain how they were able to violate the law," Takoda asks.

"The Royal family does not follow the laws. The Royal family is the law." The man replies with a harshness that is almost frightening.

"You mean to tell me these people created stupid laws for everyone else but not themselves? That they lied to their people, suppressed them, treated them like crap?"

"That is correct, my lord."

"Where are Shyanna and Lylillea now?" I ask with my hands shaking. "My father told me my mother's family was dead, but something tells me that's a lie too."

"Lylillea, your grandmother, lives on Traveler's moon. Your great grandmother, Shyanna, is here below in the city."

"Here? I wisht to see her. Are they healthy, are they prisoners?" I ask.

"They are healthy and free, my lord," he answers.

"Our moons are uninhabitable," Takoda says in disbelief.

"Both moons harbor life," the man says.

I can tell this is upsetting Takoda. Everything he's been taught is being proven false, and he's not taking the news very well.

"Where is my grandmother?" I ask, staring over at Takoda. "I want to see her."

"The time for reunion has not yet arrived," the 3-D man replies.

"Patience," Takoda whispers.

"That is a stupid answer. Why can't I see my grandmother? She's mine, time or no time."

The 3-D man remains silent.

"Then show me the life on these moons," I demand.

"Forbidden," the man replies.

"Forbidden, my ass," I yell out. "You either show us or I'll smash your golden little discs to dust!"

Even though he's only a virtual man, he understands death. He replies meekly, "You would not. Valuable information would be lost forever."

"You're not giving out this valuable information, so what difference would it make?" I reply, sarcastically. Then I reach my hand toward the reader.

"Stop! You do not understand. There is information I am forbidden to reveal," he adds with panic playing out in his eyes.

"I am your lord, remember?" I snap my fingers and smile.

It only takes a few seconds before the man answers, "Yes, my lord, I will comply."

The room darkens and Takoda and I find ourselves standing in a beautiful garden. We're on one of the moons. Colors that I have no name for are splattered all around me. Beautiful flowers and shrubs are everywhere. I feel like I'm standing in heaven. The 3-D's man's voice echoes through the beauty.

"We are on the moon, Aakesh — Journey's Lord of the Sky. The moon's gravity is one fifth as on Traveler. Aakesh's atmosphere is a mixture of various gases similar to Earth's. The ratios differ, which allows the plants to have a wider spectrum of color. Where there are twelve basic colors on Traveler, Aakesh has over a hundred. No oceans are on Aakesh although there are three major freshwater lakes."

The scene changes to a large body of water surrounded by vast forests and rolling hills. Strange animals run through the tall grasses or fly gracefully through the blue skies. It's difficult to believe all of this is just over our heads.

"Various animals exist on this moon," the 3-D man continues, "in the air, on the ground and under the water. The largest animal is called a hoodlevarmine and weighs several tons. No human creature is native to this moon."

A huge hoodlevarmine strolls proudly past. He has to be over twenty feet tall. He reminds me of a cross between a bear and a horse. The fur's a deep shade of red with bright golden highlights. Two large horns protrude from his head and are almost as large as the animal itself. It's amazing.

"After the fall of the city," the 3-D man says, "ancient ones escaped to the moons to rebuild their lives. It was soon discovered that Aakesh heals all who remain for more than two thousand cycles."

Small farms are scattered throughout the land, and we're flying over them as gracefully as a bird in flight. It's obvious to me that those who live on this moon do so in pure harmony with nature.

The scene shifts again, and Takoda and I find ourselves flying above a sea of dark blue with beautiful white foam tip waves.

"Makayah," the man continues, "is a water moon with three land masses. Each mass is small and a person can walk across an island in forty-five Traveler days. The plant life on Makayah is not as abundant as on Aakesh and consists mostly of large trees. No insects on Makayah therefore no flowering vegetation. Animal life is found only in the massive oceans where thousands of marine life call the small moon their home."

A few very modest farms are built on the different islands, which are near the equator. Other than these three small islands, the moon's covered by water. Huge whale-like creatures jump from the water before diving back in. We admire their beauty for only a few short moments.

"Show me the Council as they are today," I state, glancing at Takoda.

"I cannot, my lord. The information is not in my records," the man replies.

"Then show me what you have."

"I could surmise," he suggests.

"Fine, surmise! Start from the beginning … the very beginning."

A picture of about thirty people is displayed, the original ancient council of Traveler. They appear human, but they're taller, thinner and their heads are somewhat elongated. Their eyes are much larger with far less pronounced facial features.

The very first ruler of Traveler was a lady who commanded the two ships and whom the city was named after. She ruled for three generations before she passed into the afterlife. It was her twin daughters, Rhea and Hera, who ruled after her and changed the city forever. Rhea ruled the ground — the rocks, the sea, the mountains, the dirt — anything that was part of the planet. Her sister, Hera, was the ruler of the sky — the clouds, the suns, the moons, the stars, and the space that surrounds Traveler. After their deaths, they became the Holy Ones who now guard the ancient city — Traveler's ancestors. To this day, Rhea guards the underground and Hera guards the heavens. All the carvings within this city are of Rhea and Hera.

"During their rule, Rhea and Hera each had six children, and from these, each had exactly six of their own," the man says continuing his dissertation.

"These individuals made up the original Council of Elders. Only twelve remain alive today. Many died during the great plague. The vaccine extended these twelve Elder's lives for generations."

"Stop!" I yell out with my hands shaking. "Wait!"

I glare at Takoda who shakes his head. My mind flows through the possibilities and what questions I should ask.

"Show me the most recent picture of an Elder who lives near me on this planet."

I know I'm about to see a picture of my father or my mother. The picture that's displayed, however, is not of either but a tall man with long yellow hair … Abeytu …

"Oh my," I whisper.

"What is it, Journey?" Takoda asks.

"I know this man. Tell me more about this person."

"His name is —"

I finish the sentence for the virtual man. "Abeytu."

"You know of this Elder?" the man asks.

"Yes, tell me about him."

"Yes, my lord," he replies. "Abeytu is one of the original Council of Elders. He never married and never left Traveler. It was this Elder who argued against the plague and for the people. He did not wish to take the vaccine, but his brothers held him down and injected him without his consent. This Elder has honor. Abeytu remains on Traveler to ensure adherence to the laws from the royals."

"Am I related to him?"

"You are related to all the Elders, my lord. Just many generations removed."

15

ENLIGHTENMENT

WE LAY awake holding each other. I've never felt so betrayed by my family before. I need answers and my father *will* provide them once I return. As for Abeytu, I'm not sure what to do about him. No matter what, I *will* free my people and make this a wonderful place to live.

I lay quietly in Takoda's arms and feel his muscles relax. He's finally fallen asleep. I inch myself from his warm embrace. I can't sleep and need to walk and think. Walking always seems to clear my mind.

As I tie my dirty and worn tennis shoes, I can't help but remember the pictures of the filthy city below. Who would allow this to happen? The ancient city's quiet now, and I feel safe wandering the empty halls. I know I have the support of the Nomaddas and nothing will hurt me.

The lights create a soft orange hue that radiates through the ancient halls. I pass the pool and remember my intense experience with Takoda. I nod and accept the responsibility that was given to me.

The long streets are deserted, but if I listen, I can almost hear the people who once lived here. It's hard to imagine that anyone would ever want to leave. My people first had to leave their home world when it was destroyed by an evil race. Then they had to leave this beautiful city. I need more answers. How could their god, or gods, abandon them when they needed him or her the most?

I enter a home and a small drawing etched in a corner catches my attention. I kneel to get a better look. A child's drawing. Stick figures — two adults holding a child's hands. I laugh, because that's exactly how I used to draw when I was little, my mom and dad holding my hands as I stood between them. I always added a tree or the sun. No tree or sun is in this drawing. A child raised here probably never saw the sun, and no trees grow in these darkened halls.

"Farms!"

These people must grow vegetables and fruits. I knew something was missing, and it finally dawns on me what it is. Where do these people grow their food? I run back down the long hallway with my mind reeling. I forgot my flashlight and scold myself for being so stupid. I keep running anyway. The straight hallway seems to flow on forever. Finally, I'm panting in front of the virtual man.

Takoda and I left the gold disc in the machine. He seems so real we didn't have the heart to take it out and put him back to sleep.

"May I assist you, my lord?" he asks.

"Yes," I reply, glancing around making sure that I am alone. "I want to know where the people of this city grow their food. Where do they raise their farm animals?"

For some reason, I need to know everything there is about the people who lived here.

"Yes, my lord," the man replies and the room dims as the pictures again display in full color. "On the upper level are the gardens."

He explains that these people carved a huge farm along the side of the rock cliff and brought in volcanic ash and dirt to grow their vegetables and fruits. It must have been a huge undertaking carving acres and acres of land directly from the hard rock to create an area large enough for all their needs. I have to see it for myself.

"It took several generations for the land to be fully operational," he said.

"How do I get there?" I ask.

The virtual man shows me the way. It's a little farther past the stick figures that I found on the wall. If I had kept walking, I probably would have found it on my own. I thank the man and leave with my new goal for tomorrow.

Takoda's still sleeping when I return. I crawl in next to him. He turns over and I pull the sleeping bag over my shoulder. With his back to me, I twirl his braids through my fingers as sleep slowly creeps over me. As I drift away, I promise myself that even if it takes a lifetime, I will find out everything I can about my people.

I wake to the wonderful aroma of what Takoda is stirring over an open flame. He smiles as I yawn and scratch my head. My hair's a tangled mess but I don't care.

"Bugs?" he asks, taking a taste from his wooden spoon.

"I just need a good shower," I answer, sitting next to him. "Yum! That smells so good."

"You must be hungry," he replies, handing me a small bowl of the steaming stew.

"What is this? And where did the vegetables come from?"

"Our friends," he answers. He blows on a spoonful of the hot food.

"It's good." I say, taking a taste. It's too hot to eat so I set mine down while I excuse myself to freshen up. "Can I choose where we explore today?" I holler from the wash area.

"That is fine," he replies.

After I bathe in the running water and dress, I rejoin Takoda to finish my breakfast. The flavor's amazing. I can definitely taste tomato and potato, but that's all that's familiar. I'm again surprised by what Takoda can accomplish with so little.

"Okay," he says as he hoists his small pack over his shoulder. "It is your choice, which way?"

"This way." I point as we head toward the water pool. He smiles and grabs me around the waist and kisses my cheek.

"Another romp in the water?"

"No, silly." I run playfully away from him. "Well, not now anyway." I wink.

As we walk, we talk about what the virtual man had told us. Soon, we come to an ancient doorway with twisting stairs that are carved from the rock. They twist upward. It's steep and makes me a little nervous.

"It is obvious you know where we are going," he surmises.

"Not really."

"Where are we trying to go?" He stops for a few seconds to rest.

"To the gardens." I strain to hear the chirping. "Birds?"

Fresh air greets us closer to the top, and the sounds of chirping birds and other animals echo down the stairwell. The noise of life gives us the strength we need to dart to the top. We step out into a vast garden. On one side is the rock cliff that extends miles into the sky. On the other, the garden rolls out for as far as we can see.

"This is a field of vegetables," I say as birds fly overhead before dipping into the growth to emerge with something in their beaks. "Look!" I point to a small stream that winds through the field and ends in a small pond. "This garden must cover the whole city!"

Fruit trees tower above us. Row upon row of vegetables grow wildly, fighting each other for space. Takoda picks up something and tells me its name.

"That is a pelonnia," he says. "And you are correct. This field must cover the entire city."

"How much work this had to have been," I add.

We walk through the thick growth enjoying the strong aroma.

"I guess the Nomaddas live off these fruits and vegetables," Takoda says.

"I agree."

We aim for a small building far off in the distance. Being made from just rocks and tree logs, it's in relatively good shape. After living in silence for the last several days, it's a wonderful sensation listening to all the wildlife.

"What a beautiful bird." I watch as a huge red parrot-type bird flies across our path.

We reach a small grove of fruit trees and decide it's the perfect place to sit and eat our lunch. A deep grunting startles me.

"What's that?" I ask.

"Not sure," he replies.

"Maybe some farm animals are still here?"

"Maybe," he replies, glancing around nervously.

"I don't see how else an animal could have gotten up here."

The grunting grows louder when a huge pig-looking animal walks by with its snout in the dirt searching for food. It's quite big, and we freeze, hoping it won't notice us, which it doesn't.

"That looks like a hog or pig," I whisper.

"I do not know about a hog or pig, but there is obviously farm animals here."

We finish our lunch and resume our walk toward the small building. Takoda points out that several people are tilling the soil. Hoods cover their heads hiding their faces.

"Let's talk to them," I suggest.

Takoda smiles.

As we approach, one stops working and leans on their shovel. I wave and the worker waves back.

"Good day to you, my friend," Takoda says as we get closer.

The worker bows in respect.

"Hello," I add when I'm standing in front them.

The other workers stop tilling at the sound of my voice. The first worker lowers her hood. The woman looks to be in her early twenties. She's slender and wearing a colorful robe and beaded sandals. She reminds me a little of Abeytu but with darker hair, which is braided with leather and beads. She smiles but doesn't speak. Her skin is wrinkled like everyone else who lives down below but she is not black.

"My name is Journey and this is Takoda, we're here on Trial."

The young woman doesn't reply. I glance at Takoda with a look of helplessness. He nods and speaks in this beautiful language I've never heard before. Takoda speaks with such confidence that I realize he knows this language as well as he knows mine. The language includes clicks that are made deep in the back of the throat. He talks to the woman and I play with my tongue wondering how he's making the sounds. The girl replies. Takoda smiles and glances at me.

"That explains it," he says.

"Oh yeah, most definitely." I stare at him wondering if he forgot I'm from Earth.

"Oh, sorry." He chuckles. "They are the keepers of this area, and do not live below with the Nomaddas."

"I could have figured that out for myself by just watching them." I punch Takoda on the arm.

Since I can't communicate with the keepers, I explore while Takoda talks. The younger worker offers me some berries.

I take one and nod. "These are great."

I take a few more from her. The more I eat, the more I want. After eating several, my hearing fades and the light dims. It's hard to stand. I reach out for support but find nothing but the ground. Takoda's by my side. As he tries to help, my world falls dark.

The old woman from below is standing silently in front of me, her amber eyes full of sorrow and pain. I want to comfort her, but I'm not sure how.

"Where am I?" She motions for me to follow her.

My fear swells and my self-preservation mode kicks into high gear. My hands reach out to grab at anything solid but there's nothing there. I am nowhere and everywhere at the same time. She stops walking and faces me. I gasp. She's no longer old but young and beautiful. She smiles and speaks softly.

"You are seeing what you expect to see, Journey. I am here to help, nothing more."

"Who are you?"

"My name is Shyanna," she replies.

"Shyanna was my great grandmother's name," I say. "Am I dreaming?"

"As I said, I am here to help." Shyanna is still smiling. "Since this is your dream, where shall we go?"

"How old are you?" I ask.

Shyanna is a little more than five feet tall with long beautiful red hair. Her features are strong and her color reminds me of our Native Americans back home. She's wearing a smock that is beautifully decorated with beads and leather straps.

"When I looked as you see me now, I was twenty of your Earth years. A few years later I would marry and give birth to your grandmother, Lylillea."

"Where are we?" I ask again.

"As I said, this is your dream. Where do you want to go?"

"To your home."

I find myself standing just outside the crystal pool that is in the ancient city. The city's no longer old but new and fresh and bustling with life. People working and playing are living out their days.

"This was before the great illness," Shyanna explains.

Plants are everywhere. Some sit on the floor in huge pots while others hang from large baskets and their vines drape to the floor. Birds fly above and sing their songs. Off in the distance, I can hear men and women talking. It's a wonderful sound and fills my heart with longing. Merchants sell their wares from shops along the streets and children play.

"Everyone seems happy and healthy," I say.

The people are definitely human, then again, they look different. Taller maybe with thicker hair. Some have strong facial features while others have a softer, smoother look. Their skin is a mixture of brown shades. Not unhealthy ... but vibrant.

"Come." Shyanna takes my hand.

We walk a short distance when we stop at a flight of steps. I follow her and we enter a small home. The room is comfortably furnished with a table and benches that are cushioned with knitted blankets and large over-stuffed pillows. I can make out a sleeping area, a kitchen and bathroom.

"Please, sit and relax," she suggests, pointing to the sitting area. "I will make us tea."

"How come you speak English?" I ask.

"We are speaking the common language," she answers. "You call it English, we call it Saxonion. It is the oldest language of all, and we must keep it alive."

"Why?"

Shyanna carries two cups and hands one to me. She blows on hers and takes a small sip.

"We hope to one day reunite with the others, and when we do, we need to communicate. When our ancestors left our home world, laws were passed forbidding the ancient language to be forgotten."

Shyanna has a look of expectation in her eyes. I'm not sure if it's hope or longing.

"What happened to your home world?" I take a sip of my tea. It's bitter but tasty.

Shyanna sighs and I can tell she's choosing her words carefully. "It was many generations ago. We were explorers of the heavens. Not all our planets housed human life and those that were barren were intriguing to us. On those planets we found a place to relax or study. The ones that could not sustain life, we mined for resources. Our scientists were studying a distant water world when they encountered the Draconians. They are a reptilian race."

"Reptilian?" I repeat. "You mean lizards?"

"In a way, yes," she replies. "The Draconians are a warrior race. They live to fight and conquer. The scientists tried to make contact but were attacked. They hurried home and the Draconians followed.

The Draconians hunted us for food or slavery. Many of us were captured. We had no choice but to defend ourselves."

"It must have been terrible," I say, taking another sip.

"It was a very dark time. Our grand cities were all but destroyed and when they fired their powerful weapons, they affected our planet's core. Our planet stopped spinning and our world became uninhabitable. We used our factories to build ships to save as many as possible. Over a thousand ships were launched before the final destructive strike. Our world exploded and our ships felt the shock outside our solar system. The death of so many souls damaged our inner being. Pain and despair became a way of life. Even to this day, some of our children relive those lost souls from inside their dreams. We do not understand how or why, but some of our children are tortured for years. It is as if our souls are demanding revenge."

"Where are these Draconians now?" I ask.

"We do not know. They have not shown themselves since the destruction of our home world. We believe that someday they will return."

The idea of fighting a war with large lizards reminds me of a horror movie I watched as a kid. "Where's Spiderman when you need him?" I whisper.

"Excuse me?" Shyanna asks.

"Nothing." I laugh to myself, realizing, yet again, how truly different my new world is from my old. I set my tea on the table and rub my hands together. "If we can go anywhere, I wish to see the original Elders."

"I would not advise that," she says. Her face darkens and she looks afraid.

"Why not?"

"They do not know of you," she answers. "It would be wise if it stays that way, at least for a little while ... while you train."

"Train?" I ask. "For what exactly? This is just a dream, remember?"

"This is your dream, yes, but you are also in my mind. We are sharing our thoughts. You must train in order to take your place."

"My place in my dream?" I can tell that she knows more than she's telling. I'm feeling upset.

She laughs and shakes her head. "Not in your dream, Journey. I am afraid that it is time for you to return. Visit me when you can."

"Visit? Where?" I'm confused.

"You know where to find me," she says.

"Journey?" Takoda's voice echoes as Shyanna fades from my view. But as she fades, she changes from young and beautiful to the old woman from the caves. I open my eyes and my hands reach for my pounding head. Takoda whispers, "Shh, take it easy. Here, sip some of this."

Cool water slides past my lips and runs down my dry throat.

"What happened?" My vision is beginning to clear, but my head is still pounding. I'm back in my sleeping bag with a wet rag on my forehead. "More water, please." It takes several gulps before I can relax. "How long?"

"Three days."

"Three days!" I shout, trying to sit up. "Are you kidding?"

"I am not kidding. And do not sit up. You need rest. I was worried. Do you think you could eat something?"

"Maybe some fruit?"

Takoda eats and I nibble. I do feel better afterwards. Explaining about my experience with my great grandmother makes everything seem unreal and silly.

"Do you think it was real?" I ask.

"I have heard about people going through the same experience. The worker that gave you those berries, she was a part of it. She knew what those berries would do."

"Maybe when I'm better we can go back and ask?"

"We may not be able to. We are at the end of our time and will leave soon." He rubs my arm and kisses my forehead. "You really had me worried, Journey."

"I'm fine. I'm not ready to leave yet. I want to see those workers again. And I still have questions for the 3-D guy, and I wish to visit the old woman, and …"

"Shh," Takoda whispers. He bends down and we kiss. His lips are warm and sweet. He sits back and smiles. "We may have time for one more day trip. We leave for home the day after tomorrow."

"The old woman …" I whisper. Takoda steals another kiss, and her old worn eyes float through my mind.

16
AGES

THE MORNING comes all too soon. I could have slept all day. As usual, Takoda's up and preparing breakfast.

"Good morning, beautiful."

I wipe my eyes. "Morning. Any coffee?"

Takoda hands me a steaming cup as I drop my legs from the side of the bed. I take a sip.

"I wonder if this was meant to be used as a bed?" I pat the sleeping bags.

"Not sure what else it would have been for," he answers. "Come, eat."

After breakfast we try to find the people who live down below. The more we walk and search, the more we must accept that we don't know how to find them.

"We'll need to ask the Nomaddas to show us the way," I suggest.

We change our direction and head back to the 3-D man. When we find him, there are no Nomaddas.

"Isn't this just great!" I drop my backpack near the 3-D guy. "We don't know where anyone lives."

"There are several paths left to explore. We should just pick one," Takoda suggests.

The dark hall directly behind the 3-D man leads us to a set of steep wooden stairs. We stand there and stare at them.

"Do you think this is sturdy enough for us?" I ask.

Takoda shrugs. "I am sure the Nomaddas maintain it."

Our legs are sore but we climb anyway. At the top, we find a large platform that overlooks the city.

"Check this out!" Standing near the stone railing, we can see the ancient ruins that are carved from the cavern walls. The sky is visible from up here. The city is not in a cave but carved between two rock cliffs. It's these cliffs that steal the sun's rays from the streets. Down even farther, a thin red lake flows from the tip of the cavern and as far as our eyes can see.

"Is that the lava that heats the city?" I point to the thin red line.

"That is correct," a voice answers from behind us.

We start and turn to see the old woman who had greeted us from the underground city.

"The lava returns fallen rocks back to the soul of our planet," she says.

"We wanted to come to you, Great Grandmother Shyanna, but we didn't know how to find you." I cautiously approach with a smile.

She backs away.

I hesitate. "We were looking for the Nomaddas to help us find you but realized we didn't know how to find them either."

"You climbed these stairs in search of what exactly?" Her grin shows amusement and not anger.

"You," I reply. "I had to find you."

"Why?" A look of understanding almost shows in her grin. "Since you are here my daughter, please follow me." She takes a path that leads us to another set of stairs.

"More stairs," I groan.

Takoda shrugs.

"She called me daughter," I whisper.

"You are her daughter, just a few generations down," he explains. "We should call her Mother."

"Oh?"

We enter a chamber that is painted in what looks like refined gold. The walls, the ceiling and the floor sparkle. The chamber vibrates slightly and I can feel it resonating.

"Gold?" Takoda asks.

"Yes, this is the recovery chamber," my great grandmother replies. "Gold has natural healing properties. Can you feel it? And Journey … *you* may call me Grandmother. It is the name you are familiar with."

She heard us?

We follow her to a smaller and darker chamber. The old woman pulls on a large chain hanging from the ceiling. A strong light hits and makes us shield our eyes. We slowly adjust and see a long mural of men and women standing in small groups. The old woman points to a young child of about three. Her hair's a bright red and her smile lights her face. She's adorable and reminds me a little of Makayah.

"This," she says, not taking her eyes off the child, "is me."

I point to a man and woman standing behind the child. "These are your parents?"

The old woman nods.

Takoda takes pictures with his phone.

It's then that a thought hits me. "These are the original Elders!"

My great grandmother nods again.

"Where's the lady who guided the original ships?" I ask.

She points to a woman standing proudly above the others. She's holding a staff decorated with red and gold gems. Her long black hair curls around her arms. Her black uniform is similar to my school uniform. She's wearing the same hat as the one I wear every day. Two couples stand at her side.

"This is the mother of the original two?" I ask. "Oh, what were their names?" I snap my fingers trying to remember. "Oh yes, Rhea and Hera."

"Yes," she says, nodding.

"Thank you for showing us this …" I stop talking because painted on the wall directly in front of Takoda is a portrait of Abeytu and standing next to him is a portrait of me. "That can't be me!"

"She does look like you," Takoda says, taking my hand.

"Your mother." The old woman places her hand on my shoulder.

My stomach tightens and my head whirls. "That's not my mother — she didn't look at all like this."

"That *is* your mother, my child," she says.

Takoda studies the portrait. "She looks like you. In the eyes mostly and around the mouth, and the nose, and the cheeks."

"Okay, okay, so I look like her but that doesn't prove anything. My mother was blonde and shorter than me."

"… and her hair, her forehead, her body type, her …" Takoda kisses my fingers "… hands …"

"Okay, if that's my mom, then how does my father fit into this equation? How can I be the great granddaughter of that young girl over there, Shyanna, if my mother is over here standing next to Abeytu? Takoda, check the walls to see if my dad's here … or if there's anyone who looks like him."

I run along the mural checking all the portraits. There are seven sets of families displayed on the wall. The original captain and her two children with their mates are in the middle. Then there are other families. All six children with their wives and husbands. The first child of each is scattered about the room. From what the 3-D guy said, each of these kids had six of their own. If only one grandchild is present, then this room was painted in the early part of their reign. No names are listed, so there's no way to tell who's who — and there's no portrait of my father anywhere.

"I captured all the paintings," Takoda says with pride. "How can these be so clear and colorful? They must be thousands of generations old. Why have they not faded over time?"

"They keep it dark in here," I reply. "My question is how can that old woman still be alive … and where did she go anyway?"

My great grandmother is nowhere to be found. I still have so many questions for her. I run into the golden chamber but she's not there. I return and study the portrait of my so-called mother a little more closely. She's young. Maybe in her teens, and she does look just like me, or I look like her. Her parents are standing behind her — Shyanna has her hand on my mother's shoulder.

"Wait!" I yell out. "This can't be my mom! The people in these paintings are all mixed up. Shyanna is in two places."

"What does that have to do with anything?" Takoda asks.

"Look, that is the lady I saw in my dreams … Shyanna. She said she was the mother of my grandmother, Lylillea. Lylillea had my mom. But Lylillea is over there, not over here. And Lylillea looks just like my sister. Why would she lie to me?"

"Actually, that makes everything come together," Takoda explains. "In this picture she is a child with her parents. In that portrait, she is a wife and mother standing with her family — your grandmother." Before we leave, he takes one last look at the Captain. "I wonder what her name was."

"Great, great, great grandmother," I say, counting on my fingers.

17
TOMORROW

I'M SAD to leave our beautiful ancient city. I have learned so much but still need to know more. The answers are here somewhere, I just know it. I make a silent promise to return someday. It's a long hike to the jeep. This time, I have no fear of the creatures eating me for dinner. We camp in the clearing where we spent the first night together. However, I would have rather stayed on the cliff so I could watch the stars.

"It'll be strange to be home and at school again." I lay content in the warm embrace of Takoda's arms.

"Yes, it will." He yawns. "What will you do with all this information now that you have it?"

"The problem is I have more questions than answers." I look into his beautiful eyes and my heart melts. "I can't ignore what we've learned and I know I must tread lightly. What we learned can be deadly if the wrong people find out, and I can't stop wondering about my mother."

"Perhaps that is a question for your father," he says, bending over to kiss me on the forehead. "Now that I have you, I never want to lose you. We will tread this dangerous path together."

"I love you, Takoda."

I'm feeling secure in our love as sleep takes hold. I just close my eyes when a large explosion rocks the ground and lights up the skies. Booms echo throughout the darkness as a second explosion shakes the ground beneath us. Takoda's up and hauling me to the jeep before I'm fully awake.

"What's going on?" I yell as Takoda's maxing out the speed.

"Unknown," he yells.

Another explosion hits nearby, making the jeep lurch to one side. My head hits the window and I scream. I'm shaking as I grab the seatbelt trying to lock myself in. Before I can, another explosion hits directly in front of us. The jeep flips and lands back on its tires. I'm bleeding but I'm more worried about the stupid seatbelt. The click causes me to sigh with relief as another explosion lights up the sky and rocks the jeep from side to side.

"Who's firing at us? Are we at war?" I grab hold of anything to steady myself.

"Unknown!"

I freeze as a large fireball heads straight for us. I scream. Takoda swerves onto another dirt road. The fireball hits behind us and the area erupts in flames. It takes all his concentration to keep us from running head-on into a tree. We drive a little farther before skidding to an abrupt stop.

"Get out now!" Takoda yells, jumping from the jeep.

He grabs our packs and whatever else he can reach in less than a few seconds. We run as fast as we can away from the jeep. Just as we lose sight of the road, another fireball roars over our heads and lands right where we left the jeep. The impact sends us soaring several feet into the forest. I lay crying and shaking on the ground when a pair of strong hands pick me up, and we start running again.

We dash through the thick jungle until the morning light crests the nearest ridge. Only when the explosions are a distant rumble do we finally slow down. My ears are ringing and my head is pounding. Blood's still dripping down my face, and my legs and arms are scratched and bruised. We eventually come to a small stream with fresh running water. We stop to rest and take note of our situation.

"How hurt are you?" Takoda asks, dipping a rag into the cool water. He softly wipes my face and dabs the cut on my head.

"Ouch."

"That will need a stitch or two," he says, pulling out some bandages.

"What just happened?" I'm shaking and can't stop.

Takoda shakes his head. "I honestly have no idea."

"It was as though they were aiming right for us!"

"I hate to agree, but I think you are correct. Whoever it is, they were tracking that jeep. That is why we ditched it."

"How do we get home?"

"Not sure yet," he answers.

"Why us?"

"You really need to ask that question?" he asks.

"No, I guess not."

We bathe in the small stream. It's painful because the water's so cold. Takoda finds an area covered by large trees and sets up our badly torn and bent tent. It's pretty banged up but should work. We lost one sleeping bag and will have to share. At this point, nothing matters except that we're both still alive. We're afraid of our phones and Takoda smashes them between two rocks. He then buries them.

"We cannot risk being tracked," he explains when he sees me staring at him.

We're now totally on our own. It's several days before we pack up and head out — on foot. Our bodies needed time to heal. Not wanting to run into anyone, especially anyone with a fireball, we head deeper into the forest. We thought about returning to the ancient city but felt it too risky.

We're living off the land and I'm thankful for Takoda at my side. I don't know the first thing about finding food in the wilderness, especially on another planet. He teaches me to hunt with a small wire and a stick, and how to fish with a sharpened branch. We never light a fire at night, only at midday to cook our food. I learn what plants are poisonous and which ones are safe to eat. Takoda makes us bows and arrows from limbs of small trees, and we soon have enough equipment to be comfortable.

Our feet hurt and we're constantly fighting off blisters. I finally give up on the shoes and decide to go barefoot. Takoda scrapes the bark off a strange looking tree and makes us sandals that we tie to our feet with a strong vine. They look stupid, but they work. Although we sleep each night in each other's arms, the days are spent working on our survival. We must ensure that we have enough food and fresh water.

We keep track of the days with a strand of rope. Each morning a new knot is added, and it isn't until we have six strands with five knots each that we find a small community nestled in the forest. We cautiously enter the village. My heart pounds as I search for any suspicious characters. Then again, everyone looks suspicious.

Six homes sit side-by-side with a small field behind each. Our arrival draws attention and we're soon surrounded by curious people. An older man with a long, white beard and white hair that is pulled into a ponytail approaches. He's cautious and searches us with questioning eyes. I'm not sure how dangerous we look but we're definitely filthy. Our clothes are torn and ragged.

"Do you speak the ancient language?" the man asks in English.

"Good day to you my friend," Takoda replies and nods to the right.

"May we offer you sustenance and a place to wash?"

"Please," Takoda says.

Takoda holds out his hands for the man to examine. It's a gesture of submission when meeting someone for the first time, a cultural thing I was told. When they serve food, the white-haired man sits with us.

"How did you get here?" the man asks. I doubt if he trusts us.

"We are on Trials," Takoda answers. "We chose the *Ruins of the Wicked Lady.*"

"That's a very dangerous place. Did you see the Nomaddas?" he asks. His expression is serious.

Takoda glances at me and I answer, "No, it was actually very boring. The city was empty except for rodents and insects."

"I see," he replies. I'm not sure if he believes me.

"Did you hear the explosions?" I ask.

The old man stares directly at me. "Yes, we were wondering what that was."

"A fireball hit our jeep and destroyed it," Takoda says. "We must now walk to the trains." He picks up a piece of bread and dunks it into his stew.

"You're a long way from the station," an older woman from across the room interjects.

"Your stew is delicious," I say. "Thank you very much." I smile, trying to steer her off the subject. "This is very kind of you."

"Are you from the city or are you Council?" she asks.

"Harriett!" The man scolds the woman.

"It's fine," I say. I feel it important to not cause trouble. "We're neither. My Uncle is a Statesman and my father works for the government."

"Government?" the old man asks, staring at me.

"She means the Council. Her father is Consultus for the Natioprobo. My name is Takoda and this is Journey."

"A scum digger." He growls, shaking his head and laughs.

"A what?" I ask, looking over at Takoda.

"You would call him a lawyer," Takoda explains. "Your father works for the courts." It's obvious Takoda doesn't want to start a debate with the man.

"You know about lawyers?" The old man snickers. "Enough of these stupid questions. Where are you from, exactly?"

"Well … exactly … I'm from North Carolina." Not thinking anyone would know what that means, I felt safe saying it. But the man and woman gasp at the same time. "You know where North Carolina is?"

"Yes," the woman replies. "I'm from Ohio and Jed's from Texas."

"How in the world did you get here?"

"They tell us we're somehow related to the Elders," he says. "Seems they want our DNA."

"Why?" I ask.

"Have no idea," he answers.

"How long have you been here?" Takoda interjects.

"We're not sure," the woman replies, refilling Takoda's bowl with stew.

"Well," I say, standing up and offering the man my hand. "We are very pleased to meet you both." As we shake hands, he seems to relax.

"It's nice to finally meet another from Earth. We are a small community, about twenty of us. All from around the United States. It's a relief to know others are out there — somewhere."

"Is there any way we can get to the trains from here?" Takoda asks.

"We can help with that," the woman replies. "Isn't that right, Jed?"

"We'll get you there," the man adds, rubbing the back of his neck. "Going to check on horses. Be back in a few, make yourselves ta' home."

"Thank you," Takoda replies, finishing his second bowl of stew.

Sitting on the porch under the night's sky with Jed and his wife, Harriett, others come to greet us and introduce themselves. All are from Earth and none know how long they've been here. In the morning after a wonderful breakfast, Jed drives us to the station. It's almost a four-hour trip. We feel guilty for him having to go so far. We say our goodbyes and agree that someday, we'll come back to visit.

We stand alone on the platform with our senses on high alert. Nothing happens. We ride the train in silence and not until Takoda's neon green jeep rolls to a stop in front of my cabin am I finally happy and pleased to be home. I'll miss Takoda not sleeping next to me, but it'll be wonderful to be in the vicinity of my father. I kiss Takoda goodbye, grab my backpack and run to my father who's waiting on the steps. He swings me around as he hugs me. He asks if I had a good time. Before I can answer, Makayah darts out of the house and jumps into my arms.

"What did you learn about yourself?" he asks.

"Too much to explain tonight," I answer, following Makayah into the cabin. My father grabs my backpack.

"That is fine. You need to wash and get a good night's sleep. Are you hungry?"

"No, we ate on the train but thanks." I sit next to my father and rest my head on his shoulder as we watch TV. I have a million questions for him but tonight is not a good time. My mind needs to sort through everything I've just experienced. Tomorrow I'm going to find out who tried to kill us, and who in the world is my *real* mother. How do I explain it all to my dad?

18
THE LIE

I'M LYING in bed trying to decide on whether to get up or be lazy when my dad's phone rings. I know who it is before my father hollers out my name.

"Coming!"

"Phone is for you," he says with a wink.

I roll my eyes as I place the phone to my ear, "Hello?"

"Thinking of you," Takoda says.

"Good morning to you too."

"I will pick you up soon," he says. "For now, check your backpack."

"Why?" I ask. "What for?"

"Check in your pack, you may have a surprise," he adds just before he hangs up. "Just found mine."

I grab my bag and run back to sit on my unmade bed. I place the bag on the floor. The front and side pockets reveal nothing. Perhaps Takoda's toying with me but then I remember the small pouch on the back that I never use. I unzip it and glance inside. The opening is small and my fingers barely fit. I can feel something thin. When I pull it out, my heart skips a beat. I'm holding the reddish-gold disc from the 3-D man between my fingers. Now I'll just have to figure out how in the world I'll play the thing.

"Good morning, Takoda," my father says from the living room.

"Good morning to you, sir." Takoda's sweet voice echoes down the hall. "I will spend the day with Journey. We plan to have lunch at the ruins if that is approved by you."

"Of course, Takoda." I hear my father's footsteps coming toward my room. As his head peeks around my door, I slip the disc under my pillow. "Takoda is here."

"I'll be right out," I reply. I'm not even dressed yet.

"Everything okay?" he asks, with a slight frown.

"Just a little sleepy, that's all." I grab my jeans from off my chair. "Can you entertain him for a few?"

"Certainly," he replies, closing my door.

I pull my old school's sweatshirt over my head. I glance at the mirror.

"What am I going to do now?"

Something has to be done about my people but what? What can I do? I'm only sixteen. I'm just me. I drop the shiny disc back into the small pocket on my pack. I know that no matter what I decide to do, I will never be the same person again.

Takoda smiles as I enter the kitchen. I smile back. My father tilts his head as he gives me a strange glance, then he smiles too.

"How is your report coming?" he asks, sipping on his coffee.

"We will work on that today," Takoda answers. He takes my pack from my shoulder.

"Thank you." I kiss my father on the cheek to say goodbye. "I won't be late."

"I guess you will tell me later everything that happened. Particularly, why you are so banged up?"

"Of course," I reply, staring at him. I'm still not sure how or what to tell him. It's important I speak with Takoda first. "Later, Dad." I turn to leave.

"Journey." I turn back and look at him. "You do know you can talk to me about anything. And I do mean anything."

"Of course." I glance at Takoda.

I can't seem to get out of there fast enough. As we drive down the long country road shadowed by overhanging branches, I stare out the window.

"Something is bothering you. Want to tell me about it?" he asks.

"There's nothing to tell."

"You are bothered."

"I just can't get the way the Nomaddas have to live out of my mind. It's disgusting and filthy. And why are they down there to begin with? Why aren't they here with us? Then there's my family. To know that my family killed millions."

Takoda pulls the jeep to the side of the road. "Come here." He takes me in his strong embrace. "You are someone special. I knew it the moment I met you. You will figure this out, and you will do the right thing."

"How can I do anything? I'm not in charge of anything, not even me."

As I rest in Takoda's arms, a huge yellow truck barrels down the road. I know who it is. I duck down.

"If he stops, I'm not here," I whisper.

Abeytu slows but doesn't stop. I no longer feel safe in that man's presence. I do not trust him. Takoda pulls back onto the road and when he no longer sees the ugly yellow truck in his mirror, he says, "It is safe for you to sit up. You will have to tell me what that was all about. I hope you are not ashamed to be seen with me."

"Please," I reply. "I don't know, I just don't trust anyone right now. Except you. I feel better not having everyone know where I'm going and what I'm doing."

"We are not doing anything." Takoda laughs.

"I know," I reply. "I can't explain it. I just didn't want him to see me, that's all."

Takoda shakes his head and continues to drive.

"We have to write a report?" I ask, trying to change the subject.

"Yes, and I brought my tablet so we can work on it."

At the ruins, we find our special spot, and I help spread out a blanket. The area is deep inside the crumbling building under the canopy of the large trees. I feel at home here, and this place makes me feel good. Takoda packed us a great lunch filled with fruit, cheese and bread. He's always so thoughtful, and I love him for that. I stare at the basket and wonder if I'll ever be hungry again.

"We should write down what we know," Takoda's words pull me from my trance.

"You mean for our report?" I ask, unhappy that he disturbed me.

"I have already completed that," he says. "No, I am talking about creating your family tree. From what we learned, we believe your mother is not your biological mother. The question is whether George is your biological father. You and your sister resemble him, so I would conclude that as a yes. To be sure ... here, use this ... please." He hands me a small rectangular box.

"What's this?" I turn the box over in my hand. The writing's not English.

"There is a swab inside. Before you eat, wipe the inside of your cheek. I acquired samples from your dad and sister."

"How?"

"Your sister was easy. I told her it was for my biology class. As for your Dad, I stole his razor from his bathroom. Unless someone else is shaving in his shower, the hair should be from him. My father is a chemist and has access to equipment that will analyze your DNA. Do not worry, he will be discreet. No one will know but us and him."

"How can you be so sure?" I'm not convinced this is such a good idea.

"Believe me, my father trusts these people less than we do. Go on ... swab."

I hesitantly swab the inside of my cheek and place the tip back into the plastic bag and then inside the box. When I hand it to him, Takoda tucks it into his pack. He leans over and kisses me. I melt into his touch and can think of nothing else.

"You are a part of me, Journey," he says, staring into my eyes. "I will never want another."

"Please, you'll want to marry and have kids someday. And we know it can't be with me. The laws forbid it."

"We will figure out something," he says, "for us to be together, I promise. You will bear my children. Your grandmother found a way."

I shake my head and grin. At sixteen, having children is the farthest thing from my mind. Then again, I hate to think of Takoda with anyone else.

"Let us work," he says, turning on his tablet. "We start with you and your sister." Takoda pulls up a graphic program and lists me and my sister at the top of the page. "What do we know?" He glances at me.

"I can't verify that the old woman is my great grandmother. I mean, how old does that make her? Is it possible she's still alive?"

"Remember, Journey, your ancestors were scientists. They were trying to extend their lives and, from what we learned from our 3-D friend, they succeeded."

"It's all I can think about," I add. Takoda strokes my hair and grins.

"Again, what do we know?"

"Oh, I almost forgot!" I jump up and grab my pack that's leaning against a tree. From the bag, I pull out my binder my father gave me when I first arrived.

"What is this?"

"My father gave it to me," I answer, sitting down next to him. "If my mom wasn't my mom, then who was she?"

The first few pages are of my sister and me at different ages. As I flip through the pages, Takoda studies the photos carefully.

"May I?" he asks, reaching for the binder.

"Sure." I dig through the food basket and pull out a bottle of lemonade. "What do you think?"

"Not sure yet," he says, removing a picture of my mother who's holding me as a baby. Takoda slips the picture on the screen and within seconds the picture displays on his tablet. "Something looks wrong."

"Like what?" I ask, chewing on a piece of fruit.

After placing the picture back into the binder, Takoda enlarges the photo until only pixels fill the screen.

"Look," he says, with a frown.

"I see squares."

He sighs. "Look closely, Journey. See how the colors change all along here?"

"Not really, but I believe you." I can't see what he's talking about. "Explain?"

"These photos are fake," he adds, studying the picture more closely. "Do you remember any of these being taken?"

"I can only remember those of me and Makayah." As I think about it, I realize I have no memory of any of the pictures with my mother.

"What are your earliest memories of her?" he asks, scanning some of the other photos. "Do you remember her being pregnant with Makayah?"

"Not really," I reply, glancing around the ruins. I didn't want to admit to what Takoda was hinting at.

"How old is she?" He scans a picture of my father into his computer.

"Ten," I answer. A tear rolls down my cheek.

"You are sixteen, so that would make you six when Makayah was born. You should remember something about the pregnancy."

"But I don't." My tears fall.

"Journey, do you want to stop?" He rubs my shoulder.

"No, I need to know the truth." It takes all my courage to look at Takoda. Somehow, he always makes me feel better about myself.

"I feel your pain, Journey."

"Okay, this is a little too weird." The statement's more of an accusation. "What's going on between us? It's as if you can feel what I'm feeling."

"The only fake photos are the ones with your mother," he says. He's obviously trying to change the subject.

"Don't ignore me," I demand. "Explain, please, about us."

Takoda stares at me and my stomach tightens.

"I'm afraid," I say, close to tears.

"No, I am afraid," Takoda adds, lowering his eyes. "I am sorry, Journey."

"Sorry for what?"

"Sorry for … for us," he replies.

"Okay, talk." This conversation is going nowhere fast, and I'm never any good at guessing games. "Spill it."

19
REVELATION

I REALIZE that Takoda's breaking up with me. We've gotten too close, too fast. I can hardly breathe and panic pulls me into its tight embrace. I have to run. I have to get out of here as fast as I can. If he speaks the words, I will die. I'm running, running for my world, my life. Running to escape the truth that's haunting me, chasing me.

"No!"

I have no idea where I'm going but it doesn't matter. The ground gives way and I'm falling. Falling through a dark black rabbit hole. As the last bit of air escapes my lungs, cool hard ground slaps my world into darkens. I hear a crack as the back of my head slams against the hard floor.

"Journey," Takoda whispers. "Journey, my love. Why did you run? Journey, please open your eyes, baby, please."

Slowly, my eyes open. Taking in a deep breath doesn't help, my body cries out in pain.

"Where are you hurt?" Fear emanates from his begging voice.

"Takoda, I'm sorry."

"Sorry for what?"

"For loving you so much!" I cry.

"Oh, my baby, my beautiful baby." Takoda places his cheek next to mine and cries with me before checking my body for breaks or cuts.

"I think I'm okay. I don't think anything is broken, but I smacked my head pretty hard."

"That was really stupid, Journey. Why were you running like that? What scared you?"

"I didn't want to hear you say the words."

"What words? What are you talking about?"

"You're breaking up with me, and I don't want to hear you say it."

"Breaking up with you? Never." It takes a couple of seconds for the words to register in my thick brain. "You were feeling *my* pain. The fear was mine." Takoda sits back and rests his arms on his knees as he studies me.

The realization of what he's saying hits me harder than the floor slapping me on my back. I look at him with a fear now growing inside me.

"I am the one that is sorry," he says, with tears swelling in his eyes.

"Come again?" I gasp.

Takoda looks away as he speaks. "When we bonded, when I went through the change, I never had the chance to explain everything. It all happened so fast."

"Did I do something wrong?"

Takoda leaps to my side and embraces me. He rests his chin on my head as he continues his explanation.

"You did nothing wrong, Journey. Nothing."

"Then what is it?"

"The Kupatanna," he whispers. "The Kupatanna made us one. We can never part. If we do, we could die."

"One?" I do not understand.

"One," he repeats. "If I cry, you will cry. If I am hungry, you will be hungry. If you laugh, I will laugh. Deep feelings, deep emotions we now share."

The force of the realization dawns on me and I laugh. I'm laughing so hard that with every wave of joy my body screams in protest as pain hacks at my bones. Takoda starts to laugh too.

"I'm fine, Takoda," I finally say once I'm able to catch my breath. "My hip hurts, my head hurts, but I think I'm okay. Can you help me up?"

"Certainly."

"We are quite the pair, you and me. What do we do now?"

"Crawl back to our site?" Takoda asks.

Brushing off the dirt, I stare at Takoda. I love him so much. He hugs me.

"Sometimes I am not sure if you love me, or if you are mimicking my feelings for you."

"Takoda, you listen to me and you listen good," I state as firmly as I can. I stare so intensely into his eyes that they widen in shock. "I loved you the moment you turned around and looked at me when we were in town that day. Every time you take my hand, it's all I can do not to melt. You became a part of me before that Kupatanna thing ever happened. To me that means nothing, you are what's important. Do you understand?"

Takoda nods and his tears smudge the dirt on his cheeks. I laugh and try to wipe it away with my sleeve. He takes my hands into his.

"Union with me, Journey," he begs. "I love you and want to be with you forever. Union with me."

"I'm a little too young for that. Besides, I have to be home for dinner or George will come looking for us."

"I am serious, Journey," he replies.

"I am too." I smile.

"I do not know what the future holds but I do know that I want to be with you forever. If this is all we can have, then I am satisfied.

I can settle for just about anything, as long as you are a part of it. Do you understand?" He nods and rubs my cheek.

"I believe I do."

It takes us a while to get back to our blanket, but it's a relief when we see the food and drinks. We were lucky, the ruin I fell through was just one of the many ancient buildings that's sprawled through the complex. A door was just a few feet away from where I landed. We really had no issues escaping from my self-made prison. After we eat, we rest holding hands. The birds fly from tree to tree, and I never want the afternoon to end. On the way home, we're silent. Our bodies are tired and our emotions drained. It's dark when we enter my driveway.

"Try to write down what you do remember about your family," Takoda suggests, getting out to walk me to my door.

"I'm fine," I argue, raising my hand to object. "Don't walk any farther. Go home and take care of that ankle."

"Tomorrow then?" he asks.

"Tomorrow," I agree with a smile.

Takoda makes a fist. He touches his cheek with his knuckles and opens his hand out to me.

"This is how we address our other," he explains. "The one with whom we are to union."

I do the same gesture. It seems that we are one now. We share emotions and it's almost as though he can read my mind. He's so beautiful with his long hair and amber eyes. I'm in deep and I know it.

Dad and Makayah are playing cards when I enter the cabin.

"What happened to you?" Makayah asks from the table. I must be a mess. I pull a twig from my hair.

"What the Most Holy, Journey, what happened?" My father asks, running to my side.

"I fell down a hole," I reply, feeling a little stupid. "It's my fault, I wasn't paying attention to where I was going." It isn't a complete lie. "I need a shower."

"Abeytu came by this morning. He said he passed Takoda's jeep on the road but did not see you." George looks a little puzzled.

"That's weird, I was there," I reply, nonchalantly.

"Why were you parked there anyway?" he asks.

"I thought I'd forgotten something. I was looking through my pack before we got any farther."

"That makes sense," he replies, satisfied. "You would forget your head if it was not attached."

"Very funny," I holler from my room. The hot shower is wonderful. I examine my new cuts and bruises. I wonder if my body will ever go back to being normal. That night I lay in bed thinking about Takoda and our connection. Can I push it farther? If I concentrate hard enough, could I actually hear what he's thinking? And for that matter, can he hear what I'm thinking? The thought, although comforting, is also slightly disturbing.

My dreams begin, Takoda and I stand together in our small apartment in the ancient city next to the waterfall he built especially for me. I'm happy and feel loved. The city is busy with everyday life. I leave the apartment and glance over my shoulder. Two guards are only a few paces behind. My stomach clinches and my hands shake. I don't know why, but I feel I'm in trouble. It's important I get out of here — fast. The guards are laughing. They're making jokes and the taunts are aimed at me. I hurry but the faster I walk the faster they walk. My father's store is only a few more paces ahead, and if I can make it there, I will be safe. Only a few more paces.

Before I take another step, strong arms pull me into a dark alley. A large hand covers my mouth, I can't scream. The harder I kick, the firmer the hold. My feet scrape along the side of the stone structure. My heel hits something sharp. Pain shoots through my leg. I have to get away, my life depends on me getting away. Stars splash across my eyes as my head hits something hard. My robe's yanked over my face. I feel the cold rock digging into my back. They're touching me, and I can't scream. A hand is covering my mouth and nose. I can't breathe. My hips shout out in pain as he falls on me. I know what is next and panic fills my soul. I bite his hand as hard as I can. He yelps and draws back. I'm slapped hard across the face. His other hand pushes up my chin so fast that I know it's going to break my neck.

Intense pain echoes between my legs and I scream, but no air escapes my lips. My hands slap at the man holding me. I scream. I'm not going to let anyone do this to me. I fight, fight hard and with every ounce of strength I have left …

"Journey! Wake up!" my father screams. "Journey, wake up!"

The ringing pulls me from my nightmare. I can hear Makayah answering the call. Dad continues to yell, but the stinking breath of the guard is still hovering just inches above me.

"No!" I scream. "No!"

"Sweetheart, it is only a dream. Wake up, baby," my father yells again.

A splash of cold water shocks me back to reality. I shake my head as my father releases his grip. I wipe the water from my eyes and glare at a laughing Makayah who's holding an empty glass.

"Sorry, sis," she says with a giggle. "But you needed that."

"Thanks, I think," I say.

"Takoda's on the phone for you," she says, holding it out to me.

George sighs and runs his fingers through what's left of his hair. "Are you okay now?"

"Yeah, sorry, Dad. That was a really horrible dream."

"Sounded like it," he adds, standing. "I think I will make some hot chocolate, since we are all awake anyway."

"I'll help," Makayah adds. She has a little hop in her step. How in the world can she always be so cheerful?

Takoda's voice echoes from the phone in my hand. "Are you okay? I just had the worst dream."

"Me too." I really don't want to relive it. "I was about to be raped."

"And I was a guard about to rape a young girl."

"It's weird. Why would *you* be *my* rapist?"

"We are one, Journey. We are sharing past memories. We have no choice how it happens. I know you are safe. I will let you get back to explaining things to your father."

"Thanks, good night, Takoda. I love you."

"Good night to you, my love."

Makayah dashes into my room to let me know the drinks are ready. We spend the rest of the night sitting on the porch sipping hot chocolate, and never once is my nightmare discussed.

In the morning, George and Makayah leave early. When Takoda arrives, we're alone. I'm not expecting my family home until close to dinnertime. We use our private time to do some research on my family. My new computer arrived while I was away. We stay in my bedroom, me on my bed and Takoda at my desk. He's scanning the Internet, or this planet's version of the Internet, to see what he can find. I use Takoda's tablet to examine the pictures he took of the murals from the golden room.

"I wonder which one is Hera and which one is Rhea," I say. "Any way to find out? They look the same."

"They are twins," Takoda answers. "Journey, look at this."

On my computer screen are parts of the same mural. However, under each of the portraits, text was added. I can't read it, but Takoda can.

"The one with the blonde hair is Rhea. The dark curly haired one is Hera. I bet you are from Hera."

"Does it list Hera's kids?"

"Let me see," Takoda types Hera's name into the search box. Nothing popped up. Then he typed in Rhea and chose the first option. Up pops a picture of my great grandmother just as I saw her in my dream.

"That's her!" I scream, slapping my hand over my mouth. "Sorry."

"No problem, so that is … who?"

"Shyanna. I'd recognize her anywhere. What does it say about her?"

"It says she had one child, a daughter — Lylillea. Lylillea unioned with a Swetaachata, Chawanna. They lived on Journey for most of their lives."

"And their children?" I ask.

"Lylillea and Chawanna had three children. Two girls and a boy."

"Names?" I dance around the room. I must know.

"Their youngest child is a daughter, Lylianna. She married someone named Lagardo and they have several children. In the middle, was a son, Chatello. He married Donaphia from Earth, which is where they are living today." He glances at me and raises his eyebrows. "Are you ready for this?"

"No, but spill."

"Their first child was a girl, Chawlya. Pronounce it with a *sh* sound, such as ShaLieAh."

"And?" I urge.

"Chawlya married a man from Earth, named George Gordon. They had no children."

Takoda turns to me as I remain frozen to the floor. I clear my throat but can't talk. Takoda takes me in his arms. I just stand there. After a few moments I slowly speak.

"See, she's not my mother? My mother's name was Rachael. Maybe my mother is my dad's second wife."

"Maybe." Takoda replies. "But then again …"

"Wait, wait, wait!" I yell, running to George's bedroom and digging into his closet. "Found it!"

"Found what?" Takoda asks, from the doorway.

"Our family records," I say, digging through a box. "Here it is." I pull out some papers. "I just remembered these were here. I had forgotten all about 'em. But when you mentioned Chawlya I just remembered."

"What do you have?"

"Our birth certificates," I state, tears running down my cheeks.

"What do they say, Journey?" Takoda kneels beside me.

"Chawlya Gordon is listed as mother," I cry out.

"Then my suspicions are correct," Takoda explains. "If our Elders had known there were children involved, they would have been imprisoned and the children killed. That is why you were raised on Earth. Your Earth mother's early death must have changed things. Your father was able to bring you here because Makayah is now over the age of maturity. He felt safer raising you as Earth children. He probably registered that he was married to Rachael and listed her as your biological mother."

"Do you think she's still alive?" I ask.

"Who?"

"My biological mother," I whisper.

"Yes," he replies. "She is still alive and she is one of the Elders on the council."

"Oh my … but wait. Abeytu said I was expected to attend classes. That *I* was an Elder. I heard him say so myself."

2

I sit in the darkness waiting for my family to return. My heart pounds when I hear the truck come to a stop. Makayah runs up the stairs with her hands full of bags.

"Wait 'till you see what I got!" she yells, running past. "We picked up some things for you too."

"Great," I say, keeping my eyes on my father.

Abeytu helps unload and nods as he enters the cabin.

"Have a good day, sweetheart?" my father asks. "Any new bruises?"

"Very enlightening day, Dad," I say, without emotion.

My father stops and studies me and then shrugs. Abeytu and Makayah enjoy a lengthy conversation about one of her new gadgets. Dad keeps glancing at me with concern. Abeytu eventually excuses himself saying he has an early morning meeting. After kissing Makayah and me goodbye, he leaves.

We have a somewhat quiet dinner. Makayah does all the talking, not sensing the tension between me and Dad. I wash the dishes then watch as Makayah gives us a fashion show of her new outfits. It isn't long before Dad sends her off to take a shower and get ready for bed. I sit on the porch swing and wait. Dad stands silently in the doorway staring at me.

"You want to talk about it?" he asks.

"No," I reply, gathering my courage.

"Then, what do you want to talk about?" he asks, taking a seat on the swing. "It is obvious that something is wrong."

With a deep breath, I say as softly as possible while staring straight ahead, "Chawlya."

Dad doesn't say a word. We sit for a long time without speaking to each other. Makayah comes out to say good night. I stare at the moon's reflection on the lake and wonder about life in general. Finally, my dad stands and walks to the door and waits for a second before speaking.

"Not tonight," he says.

20
MOTHER

I AWAKE and the house is quiet. I can't hear Makayah but someone's in the kitchen. Time for me to rise and face the judge and jury. Afterall, I do have a right to know the truth about me and my ancestors. After changing into my day clothes, I inch my way into the kitchen.

"Abeytu took Makayah out for the day," my father says. He stands at the counter holding his coffee and pushes another cup my way. "It is not poisoned." He grins a very odd grin.

"What a strange thing to say to your daughter."

After a couple of sips, I smile. He smiles back and takes a seat across the counter.

"They mix up names," he says, staring into his cup. "It is the Swetaachata custom."

I squint and frown.

"Takodaovi … his mother was Takeya and his father is Fretoda. Combine the two. The Ovi is from one of his grandparents. I am not sure which one."

I nod and take a sip.

"I met your mother at school. She was sent to Earth to learn. Earth and Traveler share a lot more than what most are aware of."

"Why?"

"I am told that religion is too strong on Earth. Many would not accept the idea that intelligent life lives throughout the universe."

"Oh."

He turns and stares out at the lake. "Your mother ... she is beautiful, smart ... magnetic. I fell for her the moment I saw her. We unioned right after graduation ... while still on Earth. We attended Earth college together."

I nod.

"Your mother is half Swetaachata. Never know it by just looking at her. She is the spitting image of her mother, and her mother before her. Strong genes."

"And ... her mother before her," I add. "What about me and Makayah."

"You have some of my great looks ..." George drags his fingers through is thinning hair and smiles. "Well, some of my looks, anyway."

He pulls out a picture that he had hidden under the counter and hands it to me. The woman is absolutely gorgeous. Thick, long, curly hair that swirls down past her knees. She's wearing the same uniform I wear every day to school. I can see myself in her. Now I understand what Abeytu meant when he first saw me ... I look a lot like my birth mother. He wasn't talking about Rachael. He was definitely referring to Chawlya.

"I love that woman," he says as a tear rolls down his cheek. "She is my life partner."

"Where is she now?" I ask.

"She lives and works on Journey. Chawlya is a half-breed, which is forbidden by Council law. Chawanna, her father, did not have the deep bluish skin as most Swetaachata. As he aged, it has darkened. Made it easy for them to pass as somewhat of a normal couple. His eyes were not as pronounced as Takoda's."

"Why isn't mother here with you ... us?"

Dad ignores my question and continues his story. "We met our first year of high school. The following year she was requested to return to Traveler. We played the system and eventually she returned to Earth where we finished college. Eventually, I was accepted as an exchange student, here."

"Exchange student?" I repeat. "Since when does Earth have students from other galaxies?"

"There is much you do not know. As I said, not everything is shared with the people of Earth as it is here."

"Okay, go on." I shake my head. I'm not sure how much I should believe but I listen anyway.

"Shortly after I arrived here, Chawlya was in an accident and transported to the health center. Lylillea and Chawanna were detained and arrived after the doctors had examined Chawlya, which meant that they discovered her true heritage and contacted the Council." I watch as my father explains. My heart aches for him but at the same time I need to know. "Your mother has two hearts and four kidneys like most Swetaachatas. Not something that is easily over-looked during a physical."

"I guess not."

"Lylillea and Chawanna were imprisoned, however, the Council had a more serious problem. Chawlya was proof that the union between the races did not create a mutated child. The question was … what to do with your mother and her siblings." Dad stared down at his hands. "We worked hard to have her parents released … me and Abeytu. Eventually we were successful. It took a very long time."

"How did you get them out?"

"We fought through the legal system," he replies. "The courts here are not the same as back home. It took us almost ten Earth years. During that time, we hid Chawlya, her sister, and brother on Earth at my family's farm and that is where we eventually married. She gave birth to you and Makayah at my parents' home."

"You said I was born here, on Traveler," I argue.

"Journey, it is hard to know what to say. I still have trouble sorting through everything."

"Just tell me the truth, Dad. I want to know the truth."

He nods. "I will stick to the truth but you may discover things you do not want to know."

"Let me be the judge of that. I'd rather know than not know, even if it means hearing something terrible. Understand?"

"Understand." He winks. "You are stronger than I first thought. I am proud of you." He kisses me on my forehead and after a brief hug, continues with his story. "It was reported to the Council that we had two children. The Elders forbid her to bring you or Makayah back to Traveler or even register your births. To punish Chawlya, the Council refused me passage back to Earth.

"The truth is that you were born here. We tried to hide you in this cabin but someone told the Council. When you were still just a baby, Abeytu warned us that the Elders were coming. Rachael agreed to raise you on Earth as her own. Your mother and Abeytu took you there. I had to remain here. When Makayah was born, Rachael took her to Earth too.

"Rachael felt it best if you believed that she was your birth mother. The chance that Chawlya would ever return was not good. Chawlya wanted to visit you often. You called her mother until you were about six. It was at that time when the Council forbid her to ever return to Earth.

"Our Council was ready to go to war over you two. We were almost annihilated during the Tarkadian siege. We couldn't afford another conflict. To counter the gossip, it was decreed by the Elders that Chawlya would take her place among the Council Elders."

"I don't get it." I say, rolling my eyes. "I thought they hated her for being mixed. That they didn't want her coming back … so they put her on the Council?"

"We are not sure why. Perhaps as a way to keep her close, to monitor what she is or is not doing. When she was ordered to return to Traveler, Chawlya had to return without her daughters. In fact, she was ordered to denounce her babies."

He pauses and stares at me. After a couple of sips of my coffee, I stand. My father turns and, again, stares out at the lake. My silence seems painful for him. He takes a large gulp of his drink and sits down. I sit next to him. He waits a few seconds before continuing.

"Leaving you two behind almost killed her." Dad continues to stare out at the lake. "She was never the same after that. The only thing that kept her sane were the reports she received from Rachael. She loved you two more than life itself." Dad chuckles. "She even has clippings of your hair and Makayah's braided into a draping and wears it to this day. She never removes it."

"Draping?" I ask. "My hair was made into a draping?"

"Takoda wears them," he replies with his voice cracking.

"You mean the leather and beads that dangle in his hair?"

"Yes, those are called drapings. Now you know that I am still unioned to your birth mother, Chawlya. Rachael was my sister, and I love and miss her greatly. That is why she cried all the time. She missed me and wanted me home."

"Aunt Deborah?" I ask.

"She is my eldest sister, and she knows the truth."

"Is that why you have no issues with me being with Takoda?" I'm not sure how much I want him to know about how our relationship has grown. "That any union is forbidden?"

He sighs and chuckles. "I am not blind, Journey."

"It's that obvious?"

"It is very obvious," he teases.

"Where's my birth mother now?"

Dad again ignores my question. "We know that you loved Rachael and thought of her as your mother. We do not want to take that away from you or Makayah. Chawlya knew what she was doing when she left you on Earth."

"Then why *did* she leave us? Why is she not here now?"

"To protect you and to stop a war between our planets. She is loyal to both worlds and only wants to do what is best. She now sits on the Council of Elders as a voting member. Not everyone on the

Council knows the truth about you. Abeytu was able to conceal some of the facts but it has been difficult."

"Who knows about us? Me and Makayah?" I'm now concerned about my sister's safety.

"Abeytu and I have kept your heritage a secret from just about everyone."

"You put us in school. How secret is that? Doesn't the school know who we are?"

Dad shakes his head as he talks. "They only know that you are my Earth children. We reported Rachael as your biological mother. No one individual knows the whole truth. The Council Elders have never been to Earth. They do not know of my family."

"This is so not right!" I yell. "All wrong … all wrong!"

"Journey, you need to understand, we only did what we felt was best for everyone."

"Best for who?" I ask. "You? Makayah? Me? My … mothers?"

"We thought it best if you had a chance at a normal life, or as normal as possible."

My anger's rising and it takes all my strength not to run from the room. I learned my lesson about running blindly away from a problem when I fell into that hole and hit my head. No, it's time to stand up for what's right, and to fight for what's wrong.

"I want to meet my real mother," I say.

He looks shocked and when he answers his voice cracks. "I am not sure if that is possible."

"Oh, it's possible," I snap. "And you're gonna make it happen. I wish to meet the woman who gave birth to me. Don't make me go looking for her!"

"Journey, please," my father begs. "Promise you will *not* go looking for her. I will do what I can. If anyone discovers who you are, they will not hesitate to —"

"To what? Kill me?" I finish his sentence. Dad looks away. "Seems to me that this planet is just as screwed up as Earth after all!" I scream out the words at him. The tears fall and I can't hold back the waves of sadness that's overwhelming me. "This is so wrong." I cry inside my father's embrace. "This is so wrong!"

"You cannot tell Makayah any of this. She is happy. If you say anything to her, it could upset her. She only remembers Rachael as a mother. She has no memory of Chawlya. She was only a year old when she left you and —"

"You mean my real mother left me alone for good when I was only six? What kind of a mother leaves her baby and a six-year-old child on another planet?" The thought of her abandoning us makes me want to hate her.

"She left to protect you. She loved you and had no choice ... no say in the matter."

"No! You're wrong. A mother fights for her children. She doesn't just run away and hide. No! That woman is a *coward*. You know what?" I face my father. "She is *not* my mother! Rachael is my mother."

I run to the lake. The sun's hidden behind a thick layer of fog. The lake is dull today, no reflection. I sit next to the lifeless water and cry. Frogs croak in the distance and I wish I could go home. Home to Carolina ... back to my mountains.

As I struggle to understand everything, two strong legs and arms wrap around me. I'm now cuddled by a familiar aroma. Takoda leans in close and hugs me tight. We sit in silence for several minutes before I finally have the strength to speak.

"Thank you." Is all I can say.

"Feeling better?" he asks.

"A little, now that you're here." I lean in deeper into his embrace. "I guess you could sense I was upset?"

"Just a little."

"What's a family without a little drama now and then?" I muse.

"Actually, you have not met my family yet." Takoda laughs.

21

AN ATTACK

I CAN'T face anyone right now. I'm just too upset. I walk around the lake and enjoy the view. I've been here almost a year and this is my first time actually walking completely around the lake. Maybe I should spend more time with just me. Takoda left to help his father with something at home. I'm on my own for a while. A perfect time to reflect.

Being in the same room with Dad is unbearable. All this talk about my heritage makes my heart ache for my mother — my real mother, Rachael. I miss her so much and need her advice more than ever.

I walk down the well beaten path into the dark and damp forest. The air's crisp but not cold enough to deter me. The ferns tower over my head. When I was here last, I could at least see the landscape. Now, I cannot even see past the next bend. It's a little unnerving but I'm not stopping. I survived the ancient city, fireballs and creepy animals, so I can survive this little hike behind my cabin.

The wooden stairs are just a few feet ahead. I climb to the top and find the place where I was first amazed at our valley and lake. It's all as I remember. For some reason, the colors are not as vibrant today. Kind of mimics how I feel.

I round the small cliff and below me is the vast valley with the huge trees who's branches spread out for miles. Our blue and white moon, Makayah, is just above the horizon. My namesake, Journey, is nowhere in sight. I sit back against the cliff and allow the memories to attack.

I have fallen in love with an alien. I know that much. I was drugged and spent the afternoon with my great grandmother. Someone who should be dead. I discovered that my mother is not my mother but my aunt. What a world … or should I say … worlds?

Feeling sorry for myself, I contemplate. *What else could go wrong?* The sun will set soon and since I forgot a flashlight, it's probably not a good idea to be up here after dark. I stand, brush off my jeans and turn to head back home. Something hovering near the horizon grabs my attention. It's still a long way away but it looks huge from where I'm standing.

Looks weird to see a craft just floating because back home only helicopters hovered. I strain to hear the engines. All's quiet. No insects, no animals and no wind. In fact, it's too quiet and my inner alarm sounds.

I need to get home!

A bright light explodes along the horizon. I fall to the ground too frightened to move with no noise or wind. The bright light lasts for only a few seconds before I see the shock wave speed toward me. Now is the perfect time to panic. Caring about my life, I dive down the path and into the bushes. My ankle hits the rocky surface. Pain echoes through me and I scream. Just above head, everything explodes at once.

The air's pulled from my lungs as dirt, plants, rocks and small trees are ripped from the ground and yanked into the sky. Half running … half limping, I dash for the cabin. Just before I reach the lake, I hear my father's voice. But just barely.

"I'm here!" I scream out.

My father and Abeytu run toward me.

"What's going on?" I ask, to anyone who might answer.

"Not sure," Abeytu replies.

"Takoda! I need to get to Takoda," I plead.

Abeytu stares directly into my eyes and says, "You will know if anything happens to him. Seek yourself and know he is safe."

Abeytu is correct. Deep inside, I know Takoda is fine. I can sense that Takoda, his father and his little sister are waiting for us on our porch. Takoda runs to us as soon as he sees us.

"She is fine, Takoda." Abeytu is carrying me. "She just sprained her ankle."

"Do we know what happened?" my father asks Takoda.

"Father heard from the Council. It was confirmed. A particle beam attack." Takoda frowns.

"Why did the mirrors not stop it?" Dad asks.

Before anyone can reply, I add to the conversation. "It wasn't a beam!"

"What do you mean?" Takoda asks.

My father interrupts and addresses me. "There is no way you could know what we are talking about, Journey."

"I saw it!" I yell.

"What did you see," Takoda asks with understanding and love in his voice.

"There was a huge craft … on the horizon." I point to the mountains. "It looked huge from where I was standing. There was a flash of light. It lit up the whole sky and a few seconds later the shock wave hit. I thought it was an atomic bomb but there wasn't a mushroom cloud. I did not see a beam of light."

"What the Most Holy … the transport!" my father yells. "Takoda, quickly."

Takoda must have understood for he runs to his father and after a few words his father darts into the cabin.

"Transport?" I ask.

"Abeytu, explain to her," my father says. "I must hurry."

"We have a monthly transport that is arriving about now," Abeytu explains. "You can see it from the ridge."

"Transport? Transport from where?" I ask, believing I already know.

"Earth and Ymir."

Well, I knew half the answer. "Ymir?"

"It is a planet that is in the Eridanus galaxy."

"It was not a beam attack," Takoda says as we enter the cabin.

Abeytu places me gently on the couch and examines my ankles. Takoda kneels at his side. His little sister peeks around Takoda then ducks back to hide.

"Who is *this* beautiful little angel?" I ask with a wink.

"Freya, come meet Journey," he says not taking his eyes off my feet. But his face lights with pride as he says her name.

"Hello," a soft voice sings out from behind Takoda.

"I don't bite," I say.

She's about four feet tall and her wavy reddish-brown hair almost touches the floor. As with Abeytu, her hair reminds me of corn silk. Her eyes are large and almond shaped. Her skin's the same as her older brother's, a bluish green with a slight pattern. Her rosy cheeks and full pink lips remind me of a China doll. She's the most precious little thing I've ever laid eyes on. Even Makayah can't stop staring at her.

"What a beautiful name, Freya. It fits because you remind me of a little angel. I have an angel too. Her name is Makayah." Makayah is behind the couch now smiling at the little girl.

"Hi," Makayah says it so meekly that it's hard to hear her.

"Wow, I have never heard you two so quiet before." Takoda laughs.

Freya smiles and tilts her head to one side. Her large eyes are staring intensely into mine.

"You hurt your ankle," she says.

She reaches out and touches each one. Instantly, the pain's gone. It's the same sensation as when the Nomadda touched my hip. I study the little girl and it dawns on me that everyone is somehow connected.

"Thank you," I say, sitting up.

"All better?" Takoda's father asks.

"Dad, this is Journey … Journey, this is my father, Fretoda."

"It's a pleasure to meet you, sir," I say, holding out my hand.

Fretoda takes my hand and smiles. He's the spitting image of Takoda, only a little older and very handsome. I instantly like the man. His braided hair is long just like Takoda's, and he's wearing drapings. His are a little different with more feathers and less beading. He wears many more leather strips, and they're much more colorful.

"No, my lady, it is *my* pleasure. I have heard many great things about you. Welcome to our world and to our family."

I smile at his father, "Thank you." I glance at Takoda. "We'll talk later." I whisper to Takoda as his father continues to hold my hand.

All this attention is starting to feel a little awkward. I glare at Takoda who grabs my cue and pulls his father aside. I sit back and try to hear what the other men are talking about.

"I received a call from the Council. We have a meeting tomorrow morning first thing," my father's saying to Abeytu and Takoda's father.

"Thank goodness no major damage or causalities," Abeytu says.

"The new magnetic field seems to be working for the transport," Fretoda adds.

"The attack did no damage to the transporter," Abeytu says "When it hit, the wave scattered. That is what Journey experienced from the cliffs. What was she doing up there anyway?" Abeytu turns to me.

Not wanting them to know that I'm snooping, I glance away. Takoda seems to be entertaining Makayah and Freya.

"We were attacked?" I ask, interjecting myself into my father's conversation. "Was it the Tarkadians or the Draconians?"

"How do you know about the Draconians?" Abeytu asks. It's obvious by his tone that I'm not supposed to know about this warrior race.

"What difference does it make? I know, okay?" Now that I know I'm related to him he no longer feels like a threat. "Do we know where this attack came from?"

"No," Fretoda states.

"Unfortunately, we do not," Abeytu adds.

"Could the Draconians have found us?" My internal warning is signaling me.

"We have not seen or heard from the Draconians for many generations," Abeytu adds. "We do not even know if they still exist."

I take a deep breath. "They destroyed your home world once. I understand how painful that was but they could very well still be alive. Maybe they found us."

Abeytu studies me before he replies with, "If it had been a Draconian attack, we would not be having this conversation."

Abeytu's seriousness frightens me. "Why do they hate us so much?"

"That goes back further than our recorded history," Fretoda answers. "Unfortunately, all we have are stories. No real information."

Takoda's standing next to me with his hands on my shoulders. He is warning me not to say too much.

"You have two worlds and two moons. You're friends with Earth, and that other place … Ymir. And you claim to have no written records of the race that destroyed your home world? That's hard to believe."

"It is the truth," Abeytu states a little too quickly. "We believe there is a hall of records somewhere, or there used to be. We know the ancients kept accurate accounts. Unfortunately, all was destroyed during the early Tarkadian war."

"Early war?" I ask. "You mean there was more than one?"

"This is our home now," my father adds. "Traveler and Journey are our worlds."

"You make no sense at times. What was the original home world called? The planet the Draconians destroyed?" I ask.

No one answers right away. They all just stare at me.

Abeytu finally sighs and says, "We do not speak her name. The pain is too deep."

"How can you have pain for something you've never had? None of you were even born yet." I glance over at my father. "Name please?"

After a long pause, Abeytu whispers, "Qapadhue." Abeytu frowns. "Our home world was called Qapadhue."

22

INTRODUCTIONS

EVERYTHING I'VE been through over the last several weeks has made school seem somewhat trivial. What is important now is how to change my world, the world that I'm living in … and, of course, taking care of Takoda.

The train ride this morning feels longer than before. Perhaps it's because I don't feel like going anymore. Takoda keeps asking what's wrong but I just smile and say nothing. I'm sure he feels my uncertainty and is worried.

Everyone seems happy to be back at school and eager to share their experiences. Takoda and I have discussed what we will share and what we will not. We will not share the Kupatanna thing or the meetings with the Nomaddas. The 3-D guy is also out of the equation and so is my lineage. Our final report turned out quite boring. We will discuss the ancient city and how beautiful it must have once been. Our report will cover the thermo-electric power and the plumbing. I'm lost in my thoughts when three girls approach and block our way to the main building. Takoda tenses when he sees them.

"Anneeta," he says, without feeling or emotion. His grip on my hand tightens.

The glare on her face tells the whole story. Obviously, she's not gotten over her desire to be with Takoda.

"You *two* are becoming quite the couple," she alleges as she stands in our way.

"You are blocking our path," Takoda states, glaring at her. "Please excuse us."

"Not so fast!" She scowls and holds up her hand. "I *demand* to know what is going on. Have you committed to nubere alicui? I need to know."

Takoda ignores her.

"You are making a big mistake … both of you!" Anneeta's face is darkening.

"Please excuse us," Takoda repeats but his words only add to her fury and the situation intensifies.

Several things happen at once. First, Anneeta's books hit me on the side of the head, knocking me off balance. The next thing I remember is the expression on Takoda's face. It's a combination of fear and hate. The two girls standing behind Anneeta jump on Takoda together and bring him crashing down on his back. They slap and try to bite him.

Anneeta starts for me, but after everything I've been through, my reflexes are too quick for her. I'm not sure what made me do it but I jump as high as I can and kick. My feet make direct contact with her chest, and she hurls backward as I fall to the ground. I'm up within a second.

I turn my attention to the two girls attacking Takoda. I grab a handful of hair from both and with all my strength, I yank. They're caught off guard and lose their balance, which is to my advantage. Their heads crash together and they fall to the ground — knocked out.

Anneeta is back on her feet. I grab my bag and sling it at her head. It clips the side of her face and she falls over. Before she can react, I'm on top of her, pinning her to the ground. My hands hold her arms above her head and my weight has her trapped. She's at my mercy. I bend over and lick the side of her cheek.

"I could rip your face off if I wanted to." I whisper into her ear so no one else can hear. "You come anywhere near my man or me again, and the next time I will not be so kind!"

Two strong hands pull me off Anneeta. I don't resist for I know it's Takoda. He's using his sleeve to wipe the blood from my cheek where a book cut a gash several inches long and about a half inch deep. I never felt it, I was too angry. The girls are still out. I must have knocked them together harder than I realized. My muscles have strengthened, and I refuse to be bullied.

Others run to help. One young girl hands us our packs. Strange as it may seem, no one is trying to help Anneeta or her two friends. She just stays on the ground probably too afraid to move. She never once takes her eyes off me. Men in uniform finally show. Several of the other students explain that we were attacked for no reason. Takoda gives me a kiss on the forehead and hugs me, apparently for Anneeta's benefit. He glares at her and speaks softly but firmly.

"Anneeta, I wish never to have any words with you again." He gives her an evil stare. "I spit on the ancient writings." He spits on the ground next to her. "They mean nothing. In my eyes, you are nothing."

With those last few words, Anneeta cries. She starts to say something but his voice is louder.

"We are *not* and never will *be* friends. To union with a person such as you would be a curse from the Most Holy. You are death walking and I curse you." Takoda looks at me and grins. "Now that our first day back has been established, let us go to class."

We walk together with our heads held high. I wonder how much more my body can take. We stop by the medical center so they can tend to my face. They use something like superglue to hold my cut together. They spray something into my nose and I'm told it's to prevent infection. Takoda has a few bites and bruises, and he's given the same nose spray. We're released with a note explaining that if we feel worse by evening, we're to go to our own medical centers.

"Funny," I snicker. "We were banged up worse than this during our Trials and we survived without any sprays. Why can't we make it through a day without trouble visiting us?"

Takoda laughs. "Since we were not attacked by Anneeta at the ruins, the chance of acquiring a nasty germ was a lot less."

"It's sad," I add. "She must really be hooked on you."

"She has a nasty way of showing it," he muses, as we head for our class.

The remainder of the day is less eventful, which is fine with me. Takoda meets me just before Ancient History and walks me to class. I'm never left alone after that. If Takoda's not escorting me, one of his friends is. It's almost embarrassing, but also nice to know I will not accidentally walk into an ambush.

Professor Graysonian is all smiles at the front of the class. "I cannot wait to read your reports. Tell me, how was it?" He claps his hands together. "Journey and Takoda." He eagerly heads to our table. "*Ruins of the Wicked Lady* was it not? I heard you were detained and did not return on schedule. So tell me, what terrible things happened?"

"It was not too bad, Professor," Takoda explains, speaking for us both. "The ruins are beautiful."

"Yeah, huge," I add, just knowing I'm turning red.

"Journey slipped by a pool of water and almost broke her hip," Takoda says, which makes the class laugh. Now I know I'm red.

"Really? She looks fine to me," he states. "Any Nomaddas?"

"Nope," I answer. "It was pretty quiet, actually."

"I see, well then," he says, looking disappointed. "What did you learn about yourselves?"

It's my turn now. I want to tackle this question. "Well, sir, I can only speak for myself, but I learned that our destiny is out there and is pre-planned. It's not how we approach our future, but what we know about our future that's important. We must find out where we came from in order to determine who we are going to be." Everyone's staring at me. I didn't mean to ramble it just came out. "Finding out who I am defines who I will become. To me it's important."

"Very interesting retrospect," Professor Graysonian says, standing in front of our table. *Why always our table?* "And Takoda, what did you learn?"

After a quick glance at me, Takoda replies, "I learned to never underestimate anyone. I discovered that hidden deep inside each of us is a person we never share. And it is not until the right situation presents itself that our hidden self emerges. We never know when, but when we least expect it, we will meet and have to deal with that hidden person."

Professor Graysonian stands silently for a few moments. "You must have given this some thought. I will definitely enjoy reading your reports."

The rest of class passes quickly as we hear everyone's experiences. I never knew there were so many different places to explore. It was interesting.

Our fathers meet us at the train and they don't look happy. The school officials must have informed them of our altercation with Anneeta and her friends.

"I'm fine, Dad, really," I argue as he fusses over me.

"Why would this girl attack you?" Dad asks, glaring at Takoda.

"She's jealous," I say, hoping to draw his attention to me.

"She was to be unioned with Takoda," Fretoda adds.

"I see," my father states.

"We did nothing to her," Takoda says, defending us. "They were waiting for us when we arrived. There was nothing we could do."

"You are fine so I guess no real harm done," Dad says, putting his arm around my shoulder. "Looks like the medical team patched you up pretty good. There should not be a scar."

"She threatened us, Father." It is clear that it's still bothering Takoda.

Fretoda sighs and glances at my father for support.

"I will take care of it," Dad says as he hugs me tighter. "Takoda had already broken their relationship before my daughter arrived, yes?"

"We never *had* a relationship," Takoda snaps. "The girl is crazy. Union with her would have been suicide."

"I'll agree with that," I say. "She needs a good psychologist."

"It is a major dishonor for her family if they do not union," Fretoda says. "It was agreed upon by the oracles. I want my son to be happy. I would never force him to be with someone he did not love." Fretoda winks at me.

"Thank you, Father," Takoda says. "Can we leave now?"

"Certainly," Fretoda replies.

It shows he loves his son and he's proud of him. Fretoda gives me a kiss goodbye. I know that his father approves of us. His acceptance makes me feel a little better. But I'm still worried about Anneeta.

"Dad?" I ask, on the way home. "How much trouble could Anneeta cause for us?"

"If she can persuade the authorities your relationship with Takoda is more than just friendship, you could be charged. Abeytu and I will make sure that does not happen."

"Oh great!" I say, wondering what the jail outfits look like here. *Hope they aren't striped.*

Abeytu's ugly yellow truck is in our driveway when we return. I guess someone had to stay with Makayah. Another car, a black shiny one with a colorful emblem on the door, is parked next to the truck. A driver is sitting patiently inside.

"Who's here?" I ask.

"Oh my." Dad's expression is strained.

"Could she have put in a complaint that fast?"

Dad shakes his head. After everything that's happened, I don't feel like diving head-first into more trouble. Abeytu meets us and speaks privately to my father. I can't hear what he's saying but he points to the lake.

A woman is standing by the water's edge. She looks as if she's admiring the moon's reflection. I recognize her immediately. Not knowing what I'm going to say or do, I walk slowly toward her. I need time to gather my thoughts. No one follows me. I guess I'm alone on this one. After all, I did demand to meet her.

She turns and faces me. I'm shocked for she is so familiar. The way she stands, the way she holds her hands. I remember her. Memories flood into my soul and my tears fall. She walks toward me but I hold out my hand. I need her to stay right where she is and not move.

"I remember dolls," I say as I get within earshot. "Little dolls in boxes."

"They had different colored hair," she replies. "No two were alike." Tears pool in her eyes, and she grabs her stomach.

"I remember late night movies in front of a TV with lots of blankets. I remember cookies and milk. I spilled the milk once. I thought you would be mad. You just grabbed a towel and cleaned it up. Never once did you say a word about it. We often pulled blankets from the beds and cuddled on the floor."

"Baby ..."

Again I hold out my hand. "I remember listening to your belly. You said it was my little sister. I sang to her." I hesitate for a moment trying to remember the song. But then she sings it for me.

"There was a crooked man and he walked a crooked mile..."

I remember her smell and touch. "He found a crooked sixpence."

"Upon a crooked stile." Chawlya takes a couple of steps. "He bought a crooked cat, which caught a crooked mouse."

"And they all lived together in a little crooked house." I finish the silly song. "I remember."

Everything is coming together and the bad memories also hit. I'm standing next to Aunt Rachael and holding her hand while I watch my mom drive away. The pain is deep. I felt so alone, so lost back then.

"You said you'd come back!" I yell. "You said you would come back but you never did. You never did!"

"Baby." She cries as she reaches for me.

I want to run away but I can't move. I remember the deep love I once had for her. How could she do this to me? Why did she do this?

"I have one question," I say.

"Okay," she replies, taking a few more steps toward me.

"Why?"

"Journey, I'm so sorry."

"Sorry? You're not sorry or you would have come back for us! You left us there. Thousands, millions of miles away … what kind of a mother does that? Huh? What kind of a mother does that!"

"Please, let me explain."

"I've been here how long, and I'm the one that had to ask for you?" I'm screaming now and I can't control it. "Did you even ask about me? How I was doing? What I look like? Did you even care?"

"Oh I care." She cries. "I care more than you will ever know."

She hands me a tablet. I scroll through the pictures. They're all of me, hundreds of pictures, and each one is different.

"I have another set of Makayah. Without these, I never could have gone on," she says. "Without those pictures I would have died. I have videos so I can hear your voice. You have grown better than I could ever imagine. I am so proud of you and Makayah. You are both beautiful. Look, I can show you…"

I can't stand any more. The tablet falls from my hand and I turn. I'm ready to run. Takoda's standing there holding my little sister's hand. She looks confused.

"Journey?" Makayah asks. "What's going on? Who's that?"

"That, Makayah, is our mother!" I say.

"Our mother died. Remember?" she says. Tears fill her eyes.

"Our adoptive mother died, baby," I explain. "This is the woman who gave us life. Our birth mother. This is the woman who married our father. But this is *not* the woman who raised us, who gave us love and guidance, who kissed away our tears. This person is a stranger, Makayah."

"Girls, please," Chawlya begs.

I glance at Takoda. He is looking at Chawlya.

"May I have a few moments with Makayah and Journey?" Takoda asks Chawlya. "Please don't leave, just give me a moment."

She nods and my father escorts her to the cabin. He hugs her and the love he displays startles me.

"Come sit," Takoda says. "Please."

We sit on the log that our father had pulled from the forest. I'm crying and shaking, and Makayah has tears in her eyes. She's confused and so am I.

"Let me just say a few words, then if you still want to hate her, I will understand." Takoda watches us.

We nod and he continues.

"It is different here. Our world is guided by the Elders. They are our government. They are the law. They have the power that if they decide you are to die … you die. They determine where you live and what you will become. When a person breaks the law, they take a chance of losing everything.

"Chawlya did nothing wrong but be born a child of a forbidden union. Chawlya's mother is from here and her father is from Journey. He is Swetaachata just like me. His coloring is not as vibrant because he was born here on Traveler. He started Kupatanna early and Lylillea, your grandmother, was there to help him through it. The same as you did for me, Journey. They bonded. They were marked, as we are marked. Their destiny was written for them, just as ours has been written for us."

My stomach hurts but my love for Takoda keeps me calm. I listen even though I don't want to.

"Chawlya," he continues, "knew she should never have children and if she did, she would be punished and the children put to death. She loved your father very much and did not have the strength to terminate the pregnancy … terminate you, Journey. After you were born, she did not want you to be alone, so they tried for another. The differences inside us make it difficult, and a generation had passed before Makayah was born." Takoda places his fingers over my mouth to silence me.

"I researched and discovered that the law is finite. She had no choice but to take her place on the Council. Just as someday, you will take yours. If she refused, they would have come for her. Imagine a craft as large as the one you saw the other day suddenly showing up over North Carolina or Colorado? What would have happened?"

I'm sure my eyes are swollen from crying but I nod because I do understand. "The military would try to bring it down."

"Yes and we would have been at war, and we are far more advanced than Earth. No one would have had a chance. You would have been put to death the moment you returned."

"Won't we still be killed?" I ask.

"Once you reach the age of understanding and can think for yourselves, your souls are considered complete. A complete soul is considered sacred. Once a mixed child reaches the age of about ten Earth years, the Council cannot harm them. It is a law put in place by the original captain. Her name was Gaia and she was known for her caring and understanding. Even when people broke the laws, she realized there were reasons, and sometimes those reasons are more important than the law themselves.

"Journey, you must understand. If Chawlya did not return when she did, Earth could have been destroyed. Would you allow another planet to be destroyed because of what you want?"

I shake my head.

"Then how could you expect your mother to do the same? And if she brought you back with her, you would have been put to death. What would you do to save our babies?"

I suddenly understand why she did what she did. "I would have done the same thing. I guess I should talk to her."

"I am here."

I feel her hand touch my shoulder. When I look up, I'm staring into my mother's swollen eyes. I grab her and hug her harder than I've ever hugged anyone. I bury my face deeply into her thick hair.

"Mommy," I cry. "Mommy, I have missed you so much."

"I know." She's crying too. "I've missed you too."

Makayah just sits there and stares at us. She really doesn't understand any of this. My father steps ups and hugs Makayah.

"Everything will be okay, Makayah," he says, gently. "I will explain everything later. I would like you to meet your mother, your real mother. The woman I love, the woman I married."

"Hello," Makayah says in a meek voice.

Her hello is just enough to break the tension. We all laugh. My mother can't seem to take her hands off me. She keeps touching my face, my hands, my back. I'm hers and she isn't going to let me go again.

23
DECISIONS

BETWEEN CLASSES and getting to know my mother, my life is pretty hectic. We spent so many hours talking that my final month of classes is a complete blur. Everything is great, until that horrible day when my mother suggests we move to Journey. She wants us together as a family. I sit and listening to George and Chawlya making plans — plans for where we will live, where we will attend school, and where we will vacation. Makayah is excited. Abeytu stands silently and listens.

I can't take any more of this happy family reunion and head to the lake. Abeytu is not far behind me. He places his hand on my shoulder. We admire the reflection and the birds singing as they fly overhead. Neither of us speak for some time, we just enjoy the moment together.

"I don't know what to do," I say.

"You will have to tell them," Abeytu says, tossing a rock into the lake.

"Tell them what?" I ask, glancing at him.

"That you and Takoda shared Kupatanna while on Trial." He says it so matter-of-factly I take a step back.

"How did you find out?"

"It does not take a rocket scientist to see that you have bonded," he replies with a grin. "He shows up whenever *you* are upset or hurt. You carry no phone. How would he know? Unless …"

"Unless we've bonded," I say. "I need to keep that phone with me."

"You must tell them. You cannot leave Takoda behind."

"I know, but…"

"It is personal and you were not expecting it to happen?" he suggests. "Am I correct?"

"You're right," I answer.

"Your parents are not stupid, Journey. Your mother's parents, your grandparents, went through the same situation. Believe me when I say they will understand."

"But…"

"There is no reason your mother cannot come here to be with you," he adds. "Besides, I do not want you to leave. There is a little selfish motive here too."

"I know you're my uncle," I add.

"You learned a lot on your Trials," he replies, giving me a hug. "I hope you do not mind sharing my bloodline."

"I don't mind as long as when I'm ready you'll give me answers."

"Not a problem." He laughs. "I will answer any question you have. For now, you have news to give to your parents."

"Great." I aim for the cabin.

Being only sixteen, it feels weird to tell my parents I'm sort of engaged. Or at least that's how I feel. Things are definitely not turning out the way I'd expected. In fact, things are getting more complicated every second.

The secluded little village Takoda and I had stumbled upon during our Trial seems like a nice place to be right about now. But when I run, I'm the one that gets hurt. I don't believe that my body can take much more. When Takoda and I are alone, everything feels so natural, so perfect. Add other people to the mix and everything gets all jumbled.

"Excuse me, you two," Abeytu says as he enters the cabin. "Journey has something to say. Something you must hear before finalizing your plans."

"Oh?" George stares at me.

Abeytu laughs a little. "You may want to sit down."

"Oh no!" Chawlya states with a sorry expression.

"I'm not pregnant!" I yell out. "If that's what you're thinking."

"You bonded with Takoda …" George blurts it out so fast that it shocks me.

I nod.

"That *does* change things somewhat," my mother says, sitting on the couch.

"Come and sit, Journey," My uncle suggests.

I sit on a kitchen stool. It seems important to keep my distance.

Makayah runs in and screeches to a stop. "Okay, now what?" she asks. "I don't like these looks you get. It means there's something going on that no one has told me about … and it's *always* bad news."

"How about if you and I ride into town, little one," Abeytu asks Makayah.

"Yep, something's definitely going on," Makayah states firmly, crossing her arms. "Okay, I'll go. But you've got to tell me everything. Deal?"

"Deal," he agrees as they leave together.

Now I really feel stupid and embarrassed. I wonder if girls my age feel this way when they have to tell their parents that they're pregnant. It's almost the same thing, right? Only this problem can get us arrested. This is oh-so-not-good.

"It is not the end of the world," my mother states. "We just have to change our plans a little, that is all."

My dad stands behind my mother looking dumbstruck. He doesn't look so good.

"I'm so sorry," I say, meaning every word. "If I ever —"

"Journey, do not apologize," my mother adds, jumping from the couch and startling my father. "My mother had no control over her bond with my father. Even though her life was tough, she would never change any of it."

"Not even the prison time?" I ask.

"Maybe that part. She never regretted loving my father or having me."

The phone rings and startles us.

"That will be Takoda," I announce.

"He knows you are upset," my mother says with a little laugh.

She hugs and kisses me on the cheek as I talk to Takoda. I tell him everything and he says he's coming over. We wait for him. When he arrives, he has his father and little sister with him.

"We need to discuss what to do next," my mother says, trying to control the situation. "I understand what happens to their souls after Kupatanna. We cannot separate them. They could become ill and some have been known to die. It is serious. They receive their strength and health from being together. For some reason when Kupatanna is not between two Swetaachatas, the chemistry is much stronger and much more dangerous. We still do not understand everything about it."

"They are too young to union," Fretoda states.

"No marriage … no union … or whatever you call it." I stammer, surprising even myself. "I'm too young for this."

"No one is suggesting a union," my mother replies, smiling.

My father has a look of pure horror. If I didn't know better, I'd say he's a light shade of green. I'm so glad we don't have a shotgun in the house.

"Everyone just needs to calm down," my mother says. "All we have to do is make sure they stay together. Simple enough?"

"How much together?" my father asks with a very weak voice.

"For the sake of the Most Holy, George," my mother states with a smirk. "Sit down before you fall. They do not need to live together, although that would not hurt. Just being in the same vicinity should be enough. How do you two feel at night when you are apart?"

"Well …" Takoda starts to say.

"We're not exactly alone," I add.

"What?" my father shouts, standing again.

"Wait." I hold up my hands. "We are in our own rooms, in our own homes, okay?"

"That is a relief." Dad sits back down and wipes his forehead with the back of his hand.

"What I meant is that —" I start but my mother finishes my sentence for me.

"You can communicate mentally." She sits next to my father looking as though she's now in shock.

"You can what?" Fretoda asks, staring at us as though we just grew an extra head or something.

"It is rare, but we have seen it happen," Chawlya says with enthusiasm. "I have never met anyone who could do it, although, I have read about it. Can you actually communicate with each other?"

I nod. "A little."

"We share dreams," Takoda adds.

"Dreams?" she asks. "Now I am impressed. Celestial merging, I thought it a myth. Who discovered you could do this?"

"I did," I offer, glancing at their eyes for approval. "I wanted to see how far I could push our connection."

Dad sighs and rubs his eyes. He tries to speak but nothing coherent comes out. Finally, with a lot of effort, he says, "I need a beer." And aims for the refrigerator.

"I could use one too," Fretoda says, frowning.

"This is more information than I needed to know." My mother whispers before aiming for the kitchen.

"This subject is as sensitive to a Swetaachata as sex is to humans," Takoda whispers.

"Ah man!" I holler and run out to the lake to be alone again.

Takoda is right behind me. We had to get out of there. It was getting way too personal for our liking.

"That went well," Takoda muses, walking with me.

"Stop, please," a soft voice echoes from behind.

We wait to allow Freya to catch up with us. For the next hour, we walk around the lake and talk. Takoda holds my hand and my heart fills with love. Only when I'm with him do I feel safe. When we return, they're discussing politics, which is a relief. I'm tired of being the center of attention.

"Hey," I say.

"Oh," my father exclaims. "We have plans. We are staying here until your classes end. Then you will go to college, together, of course. Once you graduate, we will plan your union."

"I thought a union was forbidden ... illegal. I really have no desire to spend part of my life behind bars."

"We are going to change the laws," my mother says as if it's nothing.

"This is going to be interesting," Takoda says.

24

THE ATTACK

CLASSES END and it's wonderful knowing that I no longer have to worrying about tests or homework assignments. It's also wonderful knowing that Anneeta will not be in my life for several *masikas* ... or weeks. Although she doesn't threaten us anymore, her stares from the back of the room still burn. How she's able to do that is beyond me. Summer's approaching and since this world is only slightly tilted on its axis, there's no strong seasonal change. It does get a little warmer but nothing drastic. My birthday's just a few days away. I've passed my required physical and was told that I'm in perfect health. My mother already announced to the Council about me and my sister. Since we are over the age of maturity, they cannot harm us.

I receive gifts from everyone except Takoda. A new jeep from my father and it's gray — not canary-yellow or neon green — and I'm delighted. Abeytu gives me a robe and a pair of sandals. He winks when he hands them to me. I have to laugh.

"I know how much you love my attire," he chuckles.

My mother gives me a matching mirror and brush set. Both are inlaid with colorful gems and the carvings are exquisite.

"They were *my* mother's," she says, as she hands them to me.

I don't know what to say. It feels good to have something of my family, but at the same time, I don't feel right in accepting such a personal gift.

Takoda made reservations for us at a nice restaurant. Money and buying things are different here and I still don't understand how it all works. It's based on a point system, and they use something similar to a credit card. I even receive points for attending classes. Not a lot but enough to pay for transportation and a lunch now and then. I can't complain.

We arrive at the restaurant just after sunset and are seated right away. Our table overlooks the huge valley that I'm always admiring from our cliff. I'm excited to finally be in the valley and not above it. Trees as huge as, if not larger than, a house extends out as far as a city block. Their leaves are of average size but their trunks and limbs are enormous. I gasp as thousands of lightning bugs sparkle in the darkness.

"Oh!" I exclaim when I see them. "I love lightning bugs."

"Those are not bugs, Journey."

"What are they?"

Takoda laughs and takes a sip of water. "Nasty little creatures that will rip your skin right off, given the chance. Be thankful these windows do not open."

"Really?"

"Really," he repeats. "They resemble an Earth wasp, but their body is much larger. They breathe as we do, not through their skin as an Earth insect. They are categorized as itophilus. Nasty little critters and only found here in this valley. They look small, yes?"

I nod.

"They are larger than my hand." Takoda holds out his hand. "That is why this area is not as populated. They live in the ground and spread quickly. Even if you build over them, they eventually make their way through the foundation."

"Are we safe in here?" I glance around for any sign of the little things.

"Yes. They inspect the buildings often to ensure they have not drilled through."

"Drilled?"

We're interrupted by the waiter. "My name is Lentel and I will be serving you tonight."

He reminds me of Abeytu with his long, white hair. He's wearing a black robe with black sandals just like all the other employees. "May I take your orders?"

"Yes," Takoda says. "We will have the greens and soft rock, well-done, please."

"Excellent choice, sir," the young man states nodding to the right. I'm getting so used to everyone nodding that I hardly pay any attention to it anymore.

"Greens I understand, but what's soft rock?" I ask.

"It is similar to chicken."

"Have you ever had chicken?"

"I have eaten steak and it was not bad. We now have cattle here. Many of Earth's food has transitioned, including chicken. Swetaachata never ate meat until the Council introduced it. Now people cannot seem to get enough of it. I have trouble with the heavy fat. The way they fix it here, it is okay. It is called rock."

"Well, this will be fun." I look out at the nasty little creatures. "I still like watching 'em."

"How is your relationship with your mother?" Takoda asks, taking my hand.

With his touch, my heart leaps. His eyes cut right through me. I squeeze his hand and smile. "I really enjoy my time with you, Takoda." I study his face and amazing features.

"I enjoy you, Journey. Now quit changing the subject. How are you and your mother?"

"Distant," I reply, glancing at the flying, little creatures to avoid his prying eyes. "It's hard. I miss Rachael so much. When I look at Chawlya there's a sense of belonging … of memories … but …"

"But?"

I take a deep breath and let it out slowly. How do I explain to someone if I don't understand it myself? "Something is missing."

"Maybe time?"

"Yes, like time. All the days that have passed and she was not there has affected our relationship. Maybe it is the time that I'm missing. She's still a stranger."

The waiter returns and I take a bite. The food is very good — a thick soup loaded with chunks of vegetables and herbs. The few chicken chunks I find I push aside. The greens are a combination of a leafy vegetable and fruit. After dinner, Takoda drives us to our ruins and I see that a blanket is waiting for us by our old tent. I laugh because the tent is barely a tent anymore.

"I've missed not having you by my side," he says, when we stand in front of the small campsite. "I need to be with you alone, and it does not feel right unless we are in a tent or the wild."

My heart melts and I hug him. He smells wonderful and his strong embrace makes me feel safe and secure.

"Journey?"

"Yes, Takoda."

"I love you."

"I love you, too."

We lay together under the stars enjoying each other's company. We talk about anything and everything. Takoda is wonderful and always the perfect gentleman. Just before we fall asleep, he hands me a small box.

"What's this?"

"Your birthday present. I understand you celebrate birthdays with a gift. This is my gift to you."

I pull out a draping and study it. "Oh my." I am not sure what to say. Between my fingers dangle a long, thin strap of leather entwined with beads and tiny colorful feathers.

"This was my first draping. I want you to have it. Every birth generation of our life, we receive a new strand. After a while, there are too many to wear at the same time. We pick and choose each day. On Journey, it is different. They add to their drapings and as they age, there is more leather than hair."

I laugh. I can just envision an old man with nothing but a leather wig of feathers and beads that's falling down his back.

"If this is your first one … oh Takoda, I can't …"

Takoda places his fingers over my mouth to quiet me. He takes the draping from my hand and attaches it to my hair. It's a little heavy but not uncomfortable. My heart skips as I take in its meaning.

"My mother made this for me while she carried me inside her. She died giving birth to my sister. This is what I have left of her and I want, no, I need you to have it. I need you to understand how important you are to me. How much I love you."

He kisses me. I melt into his strong arms and gentle touch. His warm lips invigorate me. I fall asleep inside his embrace. It's wonderful.

The bright lights wake me before the noise. Men wearing uniforms are everywhere. Growling dog-like creatures barely on leashes tear into our already damaged tent. We're yanked from the sleeping bags. They beat Takoda with a whip and I squeal as they struggle to hold me back.

"No, stop!" I yell until my throat is raw. "Leave him alone!"

Takoda's dragged away and his blood leaves a thin and dotted trail. The pain on my back echoes throughout my body. Takoda never makes a sound although it has to be excruciating for him. I yell and I cry. I kick. I bite anyone I can reach. They restrain me before aiming for a vehicle.

A high-pitched screech escapes my lips as my head hits the frame. Stars clog my vision. My body aches and my back is on fire. Fear consumes me but I push it back for this is what Takoda's feeling. I must be strong.

My heart's breaking for Takoda. I feel helpless as my anger rises. I yell out and kick the inside of the vehicle. I crack a window and by the time we arrive, the grid, separating me from the driver, is dented. They have to drag me inside because I'm not going willingly.

I'm thrown into a cell and I scream when my elbow smacks against the cement floor sending waves of pain up my arm. I bounce up and grab a guard before he can slam the door. The sound I make reminds me of the first scream Takoda and I heard at the Ancient City — high-pitched and evil. When the second guard tries to pull me off the first, his eyes widen with terror. I grab hold and bite down with such force that he roars and his voice echoes through the room.

Jerking my head back, I spit the torn flesh on the other guard who's still stunned. I'm going in for another bite when several guards pull me off the severely injured man. Blood's running down my chin and I'm screeching and growling. Another guard pulls off his belt and starts beating me with the buckled end. The first blow hits me across the back of the head and stars fill my eyes as the room spins. Something hard hits me on my left hip, the same hip I cracked by the pool at the Ancient City, and I feel the bone split. My screams of pain ricochet down the hall.

Other prisoners yell and scream in my defense. I'm being held up by two guards, so with my good leg I kick and catch someone who then flails across the room. They hit a wall and I hear a loud crack just before they fall to the floor. The two guards who are holding me laugh as another guard beats me. I deliberately drop to the floor and the two guards holding me lose their balance. They crash together headfirst. I push them away and jump to my feet. My left hip is killing me, and it takes all my concentration to not fall. A new guard enters and points a gun at my head.

"Move, Princess, and you are dead!"

It only takes a second for me to respond. I jump and slam my feet toward the guard. He fires and the bullet enters and hits my right hip. The bullet shatters the bone as it exits but my feet still find his chest. We make contact and he falls backwards against the hard steel door. His head hits the edge and he stops moving. I fall to the floor and my blood is everywhere. The pain should be unbearable, but I'm just numb. I lay there panting and gasping. With fear gripping deeply into my soul, I reach out with my mind for Takoda. He's there, telling me to calm down.

"Someone will pay for this!" It's a woman's voice. She laughs an evil hysterical laugh. "Looks like several already did. Medics! Over here, now!"

Gentle hands pick me up and place me on a stretcher. Just before I pass out, the woman's face comes into focus.

It's my mother.

25
THE DREAM

I WAKE in a dimly lit room, covered with a light blanket. A beeping echoes through my aching head. Everything's blurry and my mouth's dry.

"Water," I mumble.

"Honey?" It's my father's voice.

"Water," I beg.

Cool water drips onto my tongue. It isn't enough, I need more. I reach out for the liquid to quench my thirst but only find my father's arm.

"Calm down, sweetheart," my father coos. "I cannot give you too much, it will make you sick."

As he continues to drop water into my mouth, an angry voice comes from somewhere.

"I want those responsible for this to be brought to me immediately. Nothing … I repeat, nothing will be done to them. You bring them to *me*. I will deal with them."

"They are being detained, Madame Magistrate," a man's voice replies.

"See to it that my orders are carried out." I hear a curtain being drawn. "How is she doing?" It's my mother's voice.

My father replies, "Not sure."

"Through the eyes of the Most Holy, George, she will be fine. You always overreact."

My vision is starting to clear and I can see more than just shadows. My mother's face is hovering just a few feet above me. She leans over and kisses my forehead.

"How are you feeling?" she asks.

"I've been better," I mumble. "Where's Takoda?"

"We do not know. We are looking for him."

"What?"

"There is a faction of rebels fighting the Council for control. They wanted you, not Takoda," she explains, sitting softly on the bed. "My men were able to rescue you. You would know if he was killed."

Takoda's in pain because of me? "I thought they were taking us because we were together."

"No, sweetie," she says. There's no feeling in her words and I'm bothered by that. "They are after you, and they are still after you. They want you so they can take us down. But you are here and we will not let anything happen to you."

"How badly am I hurt?" I ask, afraid of the answer.

"They operated on your hips earlier and gave you medicine to help your bones heal. You will be here several masikas. The nurses will have you up in the morn. You should be fine in about a gawo."

"Gawo? I don't have a month! I need to be up now. I need to find Takoda!"

"If she wants up, we will get her up," a doctor says from the foot of my bed, startling everyone.

My father protests. "She was almost killed! She needs to rest."

"George," my mother scolds, "I am sure the doctor knows what he is doing."

The doctor was as good as his word. By that afternoon, I am up and hobbling down the hall. Whatever they gave me is definitely healing my bones faster than they would have healed on Earth. My left hip hurts more than my right but they're working, and that's all that matters.

I'm going after Takoda, and I need my strength back. For the next several days, I walk up and down the halls. If I'm not walking, I'm in the exercise room. Every machine they have, I use. The therapist begs me to slow down. I ignore her. I now have scars along both sides of my body where they repaired my hips. They give me a salve to rub into them to make them fade. I kind of like my battle trophies. I want them to remind me never to let my guard down again.

It's night and my parents finally leave. Maybe I can plan now. A young Swetaachata nurse enters and smiles.

"How are you feeling? Do you need anything for pain?"

I shake my head.

"Something wrong?" Her gaze looks sincere.

My body is healing but I'm still exhausted. She pulls up a chair and sits beside me.

"I overheard about your friend," she says, lowering her eyes. "Did you two experience Kupatanna?"

My inner alarm sounds. Knowing to trust my inner-self, I remain quiet.

"I may be able to help," she says. The young nurse seems honest.

My mind reels with questions — can I trust her and should I trust her?

She leans over and whispers, "You can communicate with him if you are bonded. I can help."

"Why would you want to help?"

"I know he is Swetaachata," she explains. "I heard your mother talking on the phone. Is she on the Council?"

I nod.

"I do not believe she is good," she says.

"Excuse me?"

"Her conversation was not that of a worried mother," she explains. "It was more of a concerned Council member. I do not believe she is worried about your friend."

"Why should I trust you?" I whisper. For some reason, I feel it important to keep our conversation private, and with the guards just outside my door it will be hard to do.

"Your friend is Swetaachata," she says again. "We protect our own."

"Tell me how to communicate with him, Moytuya." I saw her nametag when she first entered my room.

"If you bonded with him, if you experienced Kupatanna, your souls are one. So are your minds. He can hear your thoughts and you can hear his. That is how your mother knows he is still alive."

"How do I reach him?"

She glances out the door and smiles at a guard. Pulling the door shut, she nods to the left. As she reaches for my hands, she says, "I will guide you. Take my hands and close your eyes."

I grab hold and close my eyes.

"Think of him," she says. "Picture him inside your mind."

I concentrate on Takoda's face and his voice. My heart pounds as I experience his smell and the taste of his lips. Through my mind, I can feel his skin as my fingers tracing his green and blue swirls. At first nothing happens.

All's quiet, then I hear Moytuya talking to me from inside my mind. "Listen to your heart, Journey."

With a deep breath, I relax and concentrate. Little by little, Takoda's essence intensifies. It's as if he's lying right next to me.

"Takoda!" I yell, from inside my mind. "Takoda, answer me!"

At first, I hear just heavy breathing and I'm not sure if I'm listening to my breathing or to Moytuya. The breathing is sporadic and heavy. My soul panics when I realize it's Takoda, and he isn't breathing right.

"He's in trouble," I say out loud.

"Through your mind, Journey."

"Takoda," I say, silently. "I'm here. Can you answer me?"

"Journey?" Takoda whispers.

"Do you know where you are?"

"A trailer … woods … not sure where."

"Are you hurt?"

"Yes … drugs."

"Sleep, my love," I reply. "Sleep, I'm coming for you." Opening my eyes, I stare at Moytuya. "Thank you."

"You are welcome," she replies.

"Tell me what you heard my mother say," I whisper.

Moytuya glances at the door. I can tell she is afraid. "She said that the boy was expendable but they could not allow the rebels to capture you. That your powers are too strong." Moytuya glances down at her hands and frowns. "She said you were more trouble than you are worth."

Tears form in my eyes. "I knew something wasn't right. If she loved us, she would have come to see us as soon as we arrived. It's been an Earth year. No, I knew something was wrong. Thank you, Moytuya."

She nods to the left.

"No need to apologize," I whisper. "It is not your fault. You are just the messenger."

Moytuya leaves me to my thoughts. It hurts to learn the truth about my mother but at the same time it is also a relief. Now I know not to completely trust her or her Council.

I'm out of the hospital and back home within the week. Aside from a slight limp, I'm almost back to normal. At least my bones don't ache and that's important. The following day after dinner, I approach Chawlya about Takoda. Knowing that I can't trust her makes it difficult to face her. But I must, so I can find Takoda.

"What do you know about the people who took him?"

"Quite a bit, actually. We just do not know where they have him."

"I think I know how to find 'em," I say, remembering my vision at the ruins.

"And how would that be?" my father asks.

"In my dreams," I explain. "While on Trial, I was drugged by someone and met my great grandmother, Shyanna. If I go back, maybe I can find whatever they gave me. I can find Takoda through my mind."

"I do not know about that," my father says, frowning.

"Well I do and I need to do something," I state.

"We have no idea what they have done to him," my mother says.

"He cannot be very far," Abeytu says from the door.

"I'm going back to the Ancient City!" I state not allowing anyone to persuade me differently.

"No need to go anywhere," Abeytu says. "I have what you seek."

"Absolutely not," Dad yells, standing next to me. "You are not drugging my daughter with that weird shit."

"Honestly, George," my mother replies, looking stern. "If I did not know any better, I would argue that you are not the man I married. You seem afraid of your own shadow."

"I know what these drugs can do," Dad cries out. "Too strong for a sixteen-year-old."

"Seventeen," I state.

"Seventeen ..." Dad blinks at me. "I have seen it. I have experienced it and so have you, Chawlya!"

"If I were afraid of everyone or everything that threatened me, I would be nothing but scared all the time," Chawlya argues back. "No one harms my family and lives to talk about it!"

"What happened to those guards?" I interject hoping to stop their arguing. Studying my mother, I'm wondering whether she took acting classes.

"You knocked out three all by yourself," she explains with pride. She winks.

It's starting to make me nervous knowing I share DNA with this woman. She's a little on the freaky side.

"I can set everything up if you still want to find Takoda in your dreams," Abeytu suggests from the door.

"What are you thinking?" I ask, not sure who to trust anymore.

Abeytu points to the lake. I glance out and see several Wanderers praying by the water. "They are here for a reason, Journey. I believe *you* are that reason. This *is* sacred land and it would be such a waste not to use its hidden powers."

I glance at my mother and she nods, but my father looks like he's going to faint.

"George," my mom says, patting him on the back and giving him a quick hug. "Journey will be fine. She is taking her own path and there is nothing we can do. It started with her Trials and it will not end there." She kisses him and he smiles a crooked little grin.

"Okay," I say. "What do we do first?"

It takes forever for the sun to finally set behind the tall mountains. As Dad starts a fire near the lake, Abeytu collects pillows and blankets from the house. Fretoda arrives with Freya. Makayah runs to greet them. Several hours after sunset, the fire is blazing. The sweet aroma seems to be calming everyone, especially me. Abeytu waits until we're seated and settled. He tosses a couple of new logs onto the fire. I watch as the flames shoot much higher than I expect.

"The logs were prepared for this," he whispers to just me. "I need you to pay attention to what I am about to say. I will hand you a small bowl. Drink what is in it. You will feel lightheaded. The Wanderers will chant to keep your spirit tethered to us, to this realm.

If you find yourself lost, simply start talking. We will bring you home."

I nod.

"If at any time you see or hear anything that frightens you, come back and …"

"Talk to you?"

"Exactly, if you are in serious trouble …"

"How can I get into serious trouble? I'm in a dream?"

"Was not your great grandmother real to you? Was any of that a dream?"

"It didn't feel like one," I reply, understanding.

"The drug is very strong. Drink all of it as quickly as you can. Your mouth will numb and that is normal. Drink it all before your throat goes too numb or you may choke. Once you crossover, call out to Takoda. Freya will help you."

She smiles when I glance at her. She seems young and frail. I'm not sure how she's going to help. Makayah waves and blows me a kiss. I blow one back.

Abeytu asks, "Do you have any questions, Journey?"

"What do I do when I find him?"

"Start describing where he is the best you can. Your spoken voice will come through to us."

"Let's do this," I say.

I'm determined to find Takoda no matter what I'm required to do. I watch as two bowls of red liquid are placed before Abeytu. He hands one to Freya and the other to me.

"Wait, she's taking the drug too?" I'm not sure if this is such a great idea. "She's only a kid!"

"She may be young," my mother explains, "but she is a Gemanaga. Her mind and body is made for this. She will be fine. You just worry about you."

"Gemanaga?" I ask. "What's a Gemanaga?"

"Do not worry, Journey." Freya ignores my questions. "I have traveled many times."

"That gives me the warm fuzzies," I muse.

"Are you ready?" Abeytu asks and I nod. "As I bring the bowl to your mouth, drink as quickly as you can and do not stop."

Abeytu lifts both bowls simultaneously and guides them to our lips. He stares straight ahead, chanting. The Wanderers also chant, soft and deep. I gulp the tart nectar. My tongue goes numb immediately but I continue swallowing until all the liquid is gone. A Wanderer sits behind me and places his hands on my shoulders. Another does the same for Freya.

Suddenly, I'm floating above the fire. I reach out to touch the flames that are only a few inches away but I can no longer feel the heat. A tree limb brushes against my arm and I reach for it. I grab the leaves and drop them into the fire. Instantly they explode into the flames. My mom and dad are staring into the bright light. *What are they looking for?*

I can still see me and Freya sitting in the circle. Our eyes are closed and we're not moving. Is this what it's like to die? Can this be real?

"Our bodies are where we left them," Freya says, floating next to me. "Our souls have left but do not worry, Abeytu will not allow anything to happen to us. We are well protected until our return."

"How long can we remain like this?" I ask.

"Time does not matter here, Journey." Freya takes my hand. "Come, let us find my brother."

We fly, allowing our spirits to be drawn to where our inner souls take us. Our journey is guided by our inner selves.

"I feel sick," I whisper.

"Close your eyes," she suggests as we soar through the sky.

Closing my eyes does seem to help make the trip a little more bearable. When I open them, I'm standing in our destroyed campsite. The tent is beyond repair for the fabric is sliced in several places and the poles are broken. Our blanket is crumpled and covered with leaves and dirt. Tears fill my eyes as I remember that night.

"Takoda!" I yell.

All remains quiet. Something in the grass catches my eye. It's the draping Takoda gave to me.

"Did Takoda give that to you?" Freya asks, picking it up.

I nod.

She giggles. "A man gives a draping to the woman he plans to union with. It is our custom. Takoda loves you, Journey." She attaches the draping to my hair. "There … you are now complete. You are one of us." She kisses and hugs me.

I dry my eyes on the sleeve of my old sweatshirt.

"Takoda!" Freya yells. "Takoda, where are you? Journey, help me search for him."

"How?" I ask.

"Look for clues. What do you remember?"

"Lots of blood and he was dragged through here."

"Dragged?"

"Over here," I say, guiding her.

Freya pushes the leaves aside and smells the ground. "He was here!" She examines the soil. "They went this way."

"How do you know?"

Freya pulls me down. "Here, touch the soil."

I place my hand over Takoda's blood and a sensation pulsates through me. I'm not sure what it is, but I know that Takoda is lying down. His blood is not red but a deep purple. It almost kills me to see his precious life force spilled and left to rot. I reach out and as soon as my hand touches Takoda's blood, my soul awakes within his and I can now clearly see the tracks. I can now find him. Vibrations reverberate up my fingers. I clearly taste, sense, smell and hear Takoda.

"Takoda?" I whisper.

"Journey?"

He is weak and I know I must hurry. Freya and I stare at each other and nod. We have found him, but where exactly, we do not know.

"We follow the trail," Freya says.

The sense is strong and doesn't take long for us to determine which way to go. We hover for a brief moment before floating toward Takoda.

"Wait!" I yell, yanking us to a stop. "We need to remember the way so we can bring others later. We must fly slowly."

Freya nods.

We come to the main road and I glance around nervously. "I know this place," I say.

We continue past the train station, and I make mental notes and remember what Abeytu had said, 'Talk through my mouth.'

"Can you hear me, Abeytu?" I ask.

"Yes," Abeytu replies.

"We know where he is," I explain. "I don't know how I know."

"That is good. What do you see?" Abeytu asks, coaching me through this nightmare.

"We're following his sense. It left a trail."

"That is good," Abeytu answers. "Can you describe where you are?"

"We're on the highway heading away from the train station," I answer. "I've never been this far before. Large white buildings … we're passing white buildings."

"The civic center," he says. "I know where you are, sweetheart, do not panic. I am following you."

"You're following me?"

Turning around to see Abeytu, I almost run into a tree. But Freya grabs my arm and pulls me to her.

"Pay attention, Journey!"

"I am not physically with you." Abeytu laughs a little. "I know where you are. I have been there before."

"Oh, okay. We're crossing a very long bridge. This thing is huge! Is this an ocean? No, just a big lake."

"Keep talking," Abeytu says.

It is good hearing his voice. I feel grounded, secure. "We're slowing down, there's a sign," I say, nervously. "I can't read it. It's in another language."

"What does the sign look like?" he asks.

"It has white letters or symbols."

"I know the sign," he says.

I sigh with relief as we soar. "We're on a dirt road," I continue, "it's leading toward a mountain. We're passing farms. Lots of trees."

"You are doing good, Journey," he says.

"We're turning again."

I try to find a landmark but can't and panic. I glance around for anything that will remind me where to turn. But nothing. Then I see it — a broken log pushed up against a tree.

"Write down to make a right turn at a log. It's more of a path than a road. We're slowing, there's a light up ahead … and trailers! Takoda said he was in a trailer."

"Watch yourselves, others can hear and some can actually see you," he warns.

"Great," I whisper, glancing over at Freya.

We slow and hide behind the trees. I need to get a good view of where we are.

"There are several trailers," I whisper. "Men wearing camouflage are holding rifles … looks like Army rifles. Lots of big trucks. They have dogs … big black dogs. Wait, one's heading this way."

The dog walks straight for us, growling.

"What is it, boy?" a guard asks, following the dog.

The dog steps up to me and sniffs. His deep bark startles me and makes me fall onto my butt. A twig cracks and the guard grabs his gun.

"Who is there?" The man's pointing his gun directly into my face. I freeze.

"They cannot see us," Freya whispers. "But the dogs can sense us. They know we are here. The guards do not. We need to be careful."

Freya takes my hand and we float upward. I'm not ready to leave and try to pull away from her. "I need to see if he's here," I plead.

"We will," she says. She pats my back, I guess she's trying to calm me but it's not working. "We need to get away from those dogs."

I nod and follow.

We hide high in the trees for some time before we feel safe enough to head for the trailers.

"The doors are blocked by the dogs," I surmise, frowning.

"We are spirits, Journey, we do not need a door or window."

"Yes, of course." *If I cannot use a door, how will I get in?*

"Concentrate or you may become stuck inside the structure. Get through it and out as quickly as you can. Watch me."

Freya sticks her head into a trailer and pulls it back out. Now if that wasn't the weirdest thing ever.

"Got it," I say.

"You look in those over there. I will take these."

I'm not sure about this *sticking my head through a wall* thing. The first trailer is huge and filthy. Holding my breath, I fling my head at the trailer knowing I'm going to bang the crap out of myself but my head falls right through. I feel nothing. There are men playing cards and drinking inside. The next trailer is empty, as is the third. The last is secluded and has one guard sleeping near the steps. I float to the back and step inside — body and all. Takoda's asleep on a bed. He's bloody and dirty but alive.

"Takoda," I whisper. My hand goes right through him.

"Dag-gone it," I say more loudly than I mean to.

"What is wrong?" Abeytu asks.

I had forgotten about everyone else in my excitement at finding Takoda. "I found him, but I can't wake him. I can't touch him! What do I do?"

"Use your mind, Journey. Talk to him through your mind," he suggests.

I concentrate and feel Takoda's mind touch mine.

"Journey? Is that you?"

"Takoda, my sweet!" I yell out. "Takoda, we have found you. Others are coming."

"Hurry," he says, groggily. "They are moving me in the morning."

"Do you know where?"

"No. Thank you for finding me."

"I'd never not find you."

Freya pulls on my arm. "We must go."

I try to kiss his cheek but almost fall through him. We're hovering over the trailers now. Freya grabs my hand and we speed home. I see our campfire with everyone staring into the flames. The Wanderers are still chanting. I cannot hear them but their mouths are moving. Pain explodes along every nerve as I re-enter my body. I gasp and try to push myself back out. When air fills my lungs, my body tightens and I have the urge to throw myself onto the ground. The Wanderer behind me uses his knees to hold me steady. He grabs onto my shoulders. I cough. Abeytu wipes my face with a wet cloth. Each breath is filled with agony and makes me cough and gag.

"Oh my, God!" I gasp. "This freaken hurts!"

"Coming back is never an enjoyable experience," Abeytu says, rubbing me vigorously. The more he rubs the more normal I feel.

"I found him," I cry and cough. "But we've got to go now!"

"They are moving him in the morning," Freya says, from her father's lap.

"We've got to go now!" I scream.

"Your mother is working the issue," Abeytu whispers in my ear.

His warm hug is soothing but we have no time to waste.

Several black helicopters land next to the lake. Uniformed men jump out and greet my mother and father with salutes. Abeytu helps me up and we climb aboard. I'm dizzy and the ride is mostly a blur. My stomach wants to expel whatever's in it, but I can't be sick now.

This ride is taking forever. Freya and I were there in only seconds.

We finally land on the major highway. There are too many trees to land any closer. Almost a dozen jeeps wait for us at the landing site.

How did they get here so fast? "I hope these are the good guys," I say to Abeytu.

"These are the good guys," he confirms, with a reassuring smile.

We climb into a jeep and ride down the dirt road until I scream for them to stop. My head's hanging out the window like a dog's. I'm searching in vain for that stupid broken log. I spot it just as we're about to pass it.

"Stop! The log ... the log!" I scream.

"We are here," Abeytu tells the driver.

The men jump from the vehicles. They look creepy with their night-vision goggles. Each seems to know his position as soon as we enter the forest. Men climbing trees or crawling under the brush, reminds me of a World War II movie. The commander shouts directions through his radio. The men receive their orders and follow close behind. Dogs barking in the distance tell us we're nearing our target, and my internal warning system blares.

"Takoda's in trouble," I whisper to Abeytu.

"There is nothing you can do now," he states, holding me firmly by the arm. "Stay with me."

Shots ricochet off a tree near my head and jolt me to action. My senses awake and it's as if I'm watching everything happen at once. Men shoot wildly from the trailers. The dogs are set free and attack the uniformed men on the ground. Yelps echo through the forest as dogs are shot or stabbed. Several explosions ring through my ears as grenades are thrown wildly into the wilderness. I must get to Takoda — and fast — or they will kill him. Abeytu refuses to let go of my arm. Shots ping over our heads and we drop to the ground. My mother, father and Takoda's family stayed with the helicopters, while Abeytu and I followed the men into the forest searching frantically for Takoda.

"Journey," a whisper flies into my ear.

"What?" I ask, Abeytu.

"I did not say anything. Stay down!" he orders.

"Journey, help me." Another cry echoes through my mind.

"Takoda?" I whisper.

"What?" Abeytu asks.

"Nothing," I lie.

I'm afraid to confide in Abeytu. We lay on our stomachs waiting for the shooting to stop. But it never does. The explosions sound closer, which means the men are advancing. Whether our guys can take them down or not is not my concern. My goal is Takoda. Abeytu looks the other way for just a second after an explosion, and I take my chance. I roll under some ferns and start crawling. If my memory serves me right, a small footpath winds behind the trailer and should be here somewhere. I have to find that path.

"Journey!" Abeytu's yelling for me but I ignore him.

I crawl as fast as I can toward the footpath I know has to be here. A crack of a twig announces someone's coming. I scoot under a plant with large leaves and hold my breath. Ah man, it's one of the men from the trailers. Phew, he passes without stopping. I start crawling again and my hands stick to the damp soil. A sigh of relief escapes when I touch the solid dirt path. My hands are bleeding and my knees scream with every rock they hit. Still, I continue to crawl.

A thorn embeds itself into my palm and I want to cry. I use my teeth to pull out the little spike. I use my sleeve to clean the wound before continuing to crawl. Tears sting my eyes. I keep crawling. Bullets ping over my head and pieces of trees and rocks pelt me as an explosion hits nearby. I can't see a thing but I know the trailers are about a hundred feet ahead, and Takoda's in one of them.

"Takoda," I whisper inside my mind. "Help me find you."

A flicker of light excites me. I squint and can just make out the outline of a wheel. Memories of Takoda teaching me how to live in the wild run through my mind. I frantically search the forest floor for a stick or rock, anything I can use as a weapon. My fingers search through the darkness around me. Something slices one of my fingernails and I gasp as pain shoots up my arm. My finger's throbbing and I cringe as I suck on another wound. I just want this terrible night to be over. As I suck on my finger, I use my other hand, a little more carefully this time, to search through the fallen leaves. My heart jumps as I feel a rock that just fits in my palm.

Good, this will work.

After a few more cautious moments of searching, I find a stick I can use as a knife. It's as thick as my finger and about a foot long. The pointed end will hurt. I pray silently that I'll have a chance to get Takoda out alive. It's difficult crawling and holding a rock and stick, but I have no choice. The stick I carry in my mouth, but the rock I keep in my hand.

The trailers are right there only a few more feet. Someone doused the fire but I can still see the red embers in the smoldering ash. They help me to know my location. Pushing myself to my feet, I remain in a crouched position. Takoda's wisdom from our travels echoes through my mind, reminding me of what I should and should not do.

A grenade explodes several feet behind me and throws me to the ground. Dirt's pushed into my eyes, nose and mouth. After I spit a few times and wipe my eyes, the ringing subsides enough for me at least to hear some sounds. Suddenly, I'm very sleepy and have to shake my head to stay awake. Damn, they've drugged Takoda again. I'm feeling what he's experiencing. That's why he isn't answering me. He's sleeping.

A branch scrapes my leg. As I rub my new scratch, I smile at the blue willow that towers above me. Blue willow is a stimulant. I remember Takoda telling me. Using the stick, I dig into the bark. Chewing on the tart fiber, I shove a few pieces into my pocket. A few deep breaths to clear my mind, and it's time to head for the trailer at the very back. As I crawl closer, a deep growl threatens me from the darkness. It's one of those damn dogs. If he barks, it's all over.

"Where are you?" I whisper.

It's so dark I can't see a thing but I can almost smell the dog's breath. I can't tell where he is. Another little step and the growl deepens. I make a chirping sound and the dog quiets. Searching the dark, I move just a little and it growls again. Slowly, I turn my head and then I see it. It's about six feet away. I chirp again and the dog cocks its head. That's my sign. I throw the rock and it's a hit. The large animal yelps once before falling over. I'm on it before it has a chance to recover.

I inch my way toward the trailer. Mumbled voices — I can hear men talking but can't make out what they're saying. Takoda is probably not alone and there's only one way in and one way out.

Think, Journey … think!

I crawl back to the dog and remove his collar. Cautiously I unscrew the stem cap from the tires. Using the little prong on the buckle, I release the air. It's not making enough noise. Shaking my head, I pound on the trailer with the rock. Two men jump into the darkness to see what's going on. They cannot see me as I stand in the shadows of a large tree. My eyes have somewhat adjusted to the darkness, and I can see enough to do what I need to do.

The first man walks around the side of the trailer. I throw my rock. It clips him just above the left ear and he stumbles. I see the other man's feet from under the trailer. He's walking in the opposite direction. It's a far chance but I have to take it.

I jump from the shadows and hit the first man with such force that he falls backwards. I shove the stick through the man's throat before darting back into shadows, grabbing my rock and stick on the way. I'm watching where the rock lands so I don't lose it. The man struggles madly, I must have broken his windpipe. He can't breathe. He's kicking the trailer and flailing his arms.

The second man runs to his friend's aid, and when he bends down to examine the wound, I throw my little rock. It hits the man squarely in the back of the head. I hear the crack from where I'm standing. He falls on top of the first who's still struggling to breath. I jump onto the semi-conscious man and stab my stick into the back of his neck. He jerks once then quiets. The first man has stopped struggling too.

With my bloody stick and my favorite rock, I peer around the trailer — no dogs, no men. Trying to stay in the shadows as much as possible, I dart for the trailer door. It was left swinging open. An explosion rocks the trailer and almost knocks me over. Seeing this as an opportunity, I stumble up the steps. The place is empty.

"Takoda!" I whisper. "Where are you?" *This has to be the right one.*

I pray he's in the back. As quietly as possible, I inch into the darker part of the trailer. Lights from the outside illuminates only the entryway. The windows are blackened. Although the guards had hung lights in the trees, it doesn't help much in here.

I'm not sure if I'm walking into the arms of a man with a knife or will find Takoda sleeping. Each step is agonizing but also feels right. With my stick and rock at the ready, I slowly move to the back. The bed takes up the whole end and there's no walking room around it. I crawl onto the bed. I can't see a thing. With just a rock in my hand and a stick in my mouth, I feel across the top of the mattress, blankets and pillows. No Takoda. I crawl a little and feel a little … crawl a little and feel a little … crawl a little and … ouch!

I run into a wall. *Dang.* I hear a moan and freeze. If it isn't Takoda, I'm in trouble. I take another breath and hold it for a second before letting it out slowly. I feel a little better. Holding the rock ready to strike, I crawl in the other direction and find a … leg.

"Takoda?" I whisper, making my way to the head.

I can feel a hip … a waist … and then a shoulder. He must be lying on his stomach. My hand finds the head. Whoever it is, is warm and alive. I lean over and can smell his essence. It's my better half.

"Thank you, God," I whisper. "Takoda, you have to wake up."

Bullets fly through the window splattering glass into the entryway. I can see a small bathroom with a bowl on the floor. I take a quick glance outside. All's quiet again. In the distance I only hear the muffled sounds of gunfire. After filling the bowl with water, I find Takoda again in the dark and say a little prayer. Not able to see a thing, I aim the water the best I can and take my chances. He moans when the water hits him.

"Takoda?" I whisper. "It's me. Wake up! I've got to get you out of here."

I'm feeling helpless again, just like back at the crystal pool. Takoda moves and moans as I pull him into my arms.

"Takoda … please wake up, my love, please!"

A hand brushes the side of my cheek and I jump. "Journey?"

I sigh. "Takoda, can you move? Are you hurt?"

"I do not know if I can walk. I am dizzy and sleepy."

"Take from me, Takoda," I plead. "Take what you need from me!"

"No, I do not want you feeling this."

"That's what's going on. You're trying to shield me." My anger's rising. "That's why I couldn't sense you. I'm not leaving!"

"Leave me," Takoda whispers. "Save yourself."

"Look, fool," I whisper back. "I risked my stupid, miserable life to save your sorry self. I killed two men outside. I'm tired and hungry. Don't piss me off! Now take what you need and let's get out of here."

"Journey, do you know what you are asking?" he whispers, grabbing my hair.

"Yes, now do it before someone comes."

It could have been a truck that rammed me. My body's wracked with pain and I fall onto Takoda as waves of throbbing pain strikes over and over again. I gasp as my lungs tighten and release with each contraction. Being shot in the hip was nothing compared to this. Every nerve in my body is exploding.

I want to scream but I hold it in. I can't let anyone know I'm here with Takoda. Then as quickly as it came, it's over with. The terrible pain is gone. It was Takoda's pain venting through me as he pulled strength from my body.

"Takoda?" I whisper. I'm still panting. "Are you all right?"

"Better," he whispers, "I believe I can walk now."

"You've got to stay close to me."

We struggle getting to the door and I'm relieved when we finally reach the edge of the forest. I need to protect him, get him far away from the guns and the men who stole him. I'll tend to his wounds once we're safe.

Takoda leans on my shoulder. We walk until we find a shallow stream. For some strange reason I'm reminded of the fireballs. We make our way through the damp forest until we find a small clearing surrounded by high bushes. We hide throughout the night. It's chilly but I still sleep soundly curled inside Takoda's arms.

It's the best sleep I've had in many nights.

It's morning and I'm feeling wonderful although my wounds are stinging and my finger is throbbing. I yawn and roll over to greet Takoda. I can't believe I'm staring into those beautiful amber eyes.

"Do not talk loudly," he whispers. "The air is thin and our voices will carry."

I nod and whisper, "How're you feeling?"

"Much better now that I am looking at you." He smiles.

"What?"

"You amaze me, Journey. Is there anything you cannot do?"

"Failure was not an option," I whisper.

"What do we do now?"

"We wait," I reply.

"What are we waiting for?" he asks.

"Journey! Takoda!" A loud male voice echoes across the early morning mist.

"For that," I answer feeling proud. "Abeytu put a tracker in my shoe. As long as I keep my shoes, I can be found."

"Journey!" Abeytu yells again. "Please, sweetheart, answer me. It is safe to come out. I know you are here somewhere. The signal is going crazy."

Takoda and I stare at each other. We hold hands and kiss.

"It's time," I say, cringing as I stand. Every bone and muscle protest. "Abeytu! We're over here."

"Thank the Most Holy," Abeytu shouts. "I have your jeep with me."

"Do you have food?" I yell back.

After a long chuckle, Abeytu replies, "I have food."

26
JOURNEY

WE EAT as Abeytu drives. I sit next to Takoda and rest my head on his shoulder. There's no way I'm staying one more inch away than I have to. If I could, I would climb onto his lap but there's not enough room.

"You will tell me everything when we return?" Abeytu asks.

"Of course." We answer at the same time and laugh.

"Uncle?" I ask.

"Yes, niece."

"You must answer me honestly." He turns and glances at me briefly before looking back at the road. "Yes."

"Can I trust you? Do you plan to kill us?"

Abeytu sighs and shakes his head. "It *is* a shame when you cannot trust your own blood. It was like this before the war. No one trusting … looking over their shoulder. My little one, you are safe when you are with me. You can trust me, Journey, I love you."

"I appreciate that."

"Unfortunately, you will be making that decision for everyone who enters your life from here forward. Obviously, there are people who want to hurt you."

"Obviously," I repeat, looking down at my swollen finger and bleeding hand. "What happened to the guards?"

"A few escaped into the forest," he says. "The others are being questioned. Journey, you disobeyed me. I told you to stay with me. You could have been killed."

"Sorry, Unc, but I *had* to find Takoda before they hurt him again."

"Did you tell him about the fireballs?" Takoda asks me.

Abeytu glances into the rearview mirror with a funny expression. "What fireballs?"

"Eyes on the road, Unc," Takoda adds with a grin. "You did not."

"I haven't said much of anything to anyone."

Takoda nods. I'm sure he understands why.

"I guess we will have a long discussion at dinner tonight," Takoda says.

"I guess we will," Abeytu replies.

We finally enter my driveway and everyone runs out to greet us. My mom has a doctor waiting to care for our wounds. I cry when Takoda removes his shirt. I hate those who did this.

We're patched up, cleaned up and fed. After a short rest, Takoda and I meet the Wanderers at the lake. I had already explained to Takoda how Freya and I had found him with their help.

"Thank you," Takoda says with his arms reaching out and his hands cupped together.

"No need," a Wanderer replies. He nods to the right and holds out his hands to Takoda. "We are very grateful that you are safe. Safe travels, my lord."

We watch as they walk around the lake and disappear into the afternoon sunlight.

A tight grip on my shoulder announces my mother. "Tomorrow," she states, "You two will come with me tomorrow."

"What's up?" I ask.

"There are a few people I need you to meet," she says, with a wink. "We need to discuss what we are going to do with you. I cannot work and worry whether you will survive the day."

"How *do* you get to work?"

"What?" That was obviously not the question she thought I'd ask.

"You work on Journey, our sister planet. How do you get there? Do you dematerialize here and rematerialize there? Do you ride in a star cruiser? How do you get to Journey?"

"We have ships," she explains.

"I see." I'm not sure if this makes me happy or sad. "Space travel, huh? I rode in one once although I don't remember it."

"How would you like to meet your relatives?" she asks.

"Are you trying to get rid of me?"

"No, just trying to think of a safe place for you," she answers.

"How about a job with the Council?" Takoda suggests.

She looks a little puzzled at first but then says with a huge grin, "What a good idea."

"What would we do?" I ask not looking forward to being a bean counter.

"Hmm," she hums. "Allow me to think about that. I have a few ideas. Be ready to leave in the morning."

"I will be there, Madame Magistrate," Takoda says, nodding to his right.

"Please, Takoda," she says, nodding to the left, "no formalities around me. Only if we are in front of the Council do you need to be so proper." Chawlya gives Takoda a quick hug. "Feels almost like hugging my father. See you tomorrow."

I watch as she slowly walks back to the cabin. "Are you leaving now?" I ask.

"No, your dad said I can stay for the next few days … until we are fully healed. I will sleep on your couch."

"Too cool!"

The morning is warm and a little humid. Not at all like the other mornings. George explains that Journey is approaching our side of the planet again and therefore the air is warming. That's great news for me — I love the heat.

A government car arrives right on time. The days here are thirty-two hours long versus twenty-four as on Earth. Swetaachatas require at least fifteen hours of sleep every night. I only need about eight, but the extra hours gives me more time for private stuff.

The workday, I'm told, is between ten to twelve *nyna* ... or hours. I think I like Earth time better. Eight hours is more than reasonable for a full day of work. The driver greets us, formally. Takoda and I are wearing our school uniforms. My mother explained that when we're away from our community, we're required to dress formally, which means our uniforms.

At least, it takes the guesswork out of what to wear.

That morning, I see my mother in her uniform and it reminds me of what Gaia, the Captain, was wearing in the mural. It's actually kind of cool, seeing everyone so formal. Makes things seem more important. The driver stops in front of the huge air station, which is miles outside of the town. The building looks like it's over a hundred floors tall. In reality, the building's only a few floors with a large gap between the top and bottom.

The crafts don't actually land on the ground, they hover and dock on the upper floor. There's one air station on this continent and one in the north.

My mother explains that this is the spaceport. People come from all over to catch their connecting flights. Unlike home, where a city springs up around a central hub, the spaceport is in the middle of a huge empty field — no businesses or homes or hotels.

"Our flights are efficient," she explains. "Weather is never an issue and our crafts do not break down, there is no need for people to stay here for long."

"Interesting," I reply.

"You have much to learn. It is very different from what you are used to on Earth. We are more efficient, more world friendly."

"More controlling," I add.

She gives me the *look*.

We board the small craft, which could carry about fifty passengers. It reminds me of a small plane. The pilots announce we're to buckle up and ready for launch.

"Now that's something I never heard before," I muse.

The ship floats from the docking station. Very odd sensation. I watch as the ground falls away beneath us.

"Good morning, Madame Magistrate," the pilot's voice interjects over the intercom. "We are cleared for departure. Artificial gravity will be engaged once we are free of the atmosphere."

"Very well, Willis," Chawlya says into the air. "We are ready here."

"Thank you and please enjoy your flight," he replies, as we leave the planet.

One minute Traveler is there and the next it's gone. Only darkness is outside my window now. But the darkness lasts only a brief moment before there are stars everywhere. It's then my stomach encroaches upon my throat and my feet float higher than my head. My hair is simply ... everywhere.

"Mom!" I yell.

"Hold on, Journey, any minute now, he will turn on the ..."

Slap! I'm back in my seat and my feet smack against the floor. But my hair is still all over the place.

"... artificial gravity," she finishes, laughing. "I should have warned you. On these smaller ships they do not turn it on until they are away from the planet."

"I see." I'm trying to get my hair back in place.

"There should be a brush in the ladies' room. It is mine," she suggests. I take her up on it. When I return, she says, "I almost forgot." She hands me my draping. "Where did you find this?"

"By the campfire, the night you searched for Takoda. You must have dropped it," she replies, pulling out her tablet.

"Takoda?" I whisper, handing him my draping.

He attaches it to my hair and kisses my forehead.

"I lost this at our camp site. Freya found it that night and attached it to my hair."

"I am glad," he says, not understanding.

"No, you don't get it," I reply, pulling on his arm. "We were traveling as a ghost when we found it. That means I brought it back with me from the spirit world!"

Takoda stares at me, puzzled.

"It means we can bring stuff back with us. And, if that's the case, we should be able to travel both ways with stuff in our hands, or maybe even people!"

I sit back to ponder the possibilities.

Takoda stares at me. Then he says, "That is something worth researching."

"I've got to figure out how this spirit-world stuff works," I add sitting back and thinking hard.

The rest of the short flight is uneventful. With my hair tied back and my draping firmly attached, we leave our ship. I can't wait to explore a whole new world. My namesake, Journey. The station has huge viewing windows that allow visitors to enjoy the sights. I walk to the edge and stare out at the horizon. It's very different here. The colors are more vibrant but fewer than on Traveler.

"Journey? Coming?" my mother asks.

"Yes." Before I leave the viewing area, I make a whispered wish. I make an appeal to the mother of this planet. "Can I please not break any body parts here?"

All remains quiet. I cross my fingers just in case.

Takoda is waiting patiently and laughs as I finish. He nods with understanding of my request. Holding hands, we walk together to the elevators. A car with a driver is waiting for us on the street and the car has no *wheels*. It's floating only a few feet above the ground. Now this is just way too cool.

"Mom?" I ask, as we approach the vehicle.

"Magnets," she replies without looking at me.

"Magnets?"

"Cars here are as the trains. Have you ever put two magnets together?" Takoda asks and I nod. "Then you know that the sides stick together. However, when one is reversed, they push away from each other." Takoda uses his hands to demonstrate what he's explaining. "Our vehicles have magnets and so do the roads. Our cars push away from the ground as they hover."

Understanding the basic concept, I have to ask, "Then what makes them go?"

"The magnets are turned on and off, rapidly. Too fast for your eyes to see or your body to feel. When it happens, the cars move forward or backward."

"Then you cannot drive these things off the road?"

"You can only drive where there are magnets."

"In a way it's the same on Traveler and Earth. We keep our cars on the road," I surmise. "We could drive into a field but some cars would get stuck."

"My jeep can go anywhere," Takoda boasts.

"That's because yours has four-wheel drive," I add.

We ride in silence as I enjoy the landscape. The sky is not blue but more of a green with light streaks of yellow. In school, I learned that two major elements give the planet a bluish-green color from space, and it's what makes the people here more on the blue side.

The buildings are different here too — almost prehistoric with large rocks placed strategically together to support the heavier upper floors. Carved into the stone are intricate sculptures of men, women, children and various animals. Windows are mostly stained glass.

Each building looks self-sufficient with its own mini-electric grid. Meticulously landscaped gardens are everywhere. Only blues, greens and yellows form naturally here and create a weird sensation for the senses. The colors red and brown are absent.

The aroma of the planet seems sweeter than Traveler and reminds me of being inside a candy store or bakery. People greet us with a friendly nod or warm smile. Unfortunately, I can't understand a word they're saying and no one seems to be in a hurry. It's very relaxing and a nice change from what I'm used to.

"I like it here," I say.

"Our planets are very different," he replies. "Just depends on what you want from life."

"I want to live here someday," I muse, hugging him.

"That could probably be arranged," my mother adds, turning and smiling at us.

"Eavesdropper," I joke and she laughs.

The Council center is an extraordinarily large but beautiful building. It reminds me of the Roman Colosseum back home. Six levels with curved windows that are large enough to be doors. We enter through the main lobby and a portrait of Hera and Rhea greets us. The gold frame has the same carvings as the entryway of the Ancient City. I stand and study the painting. The girls stand side-by-side, neither smiling nor frowning. The artist captured their haunting eyes. It's as if they're watching my every move.

"Impressive?" My mother asks from over my shoulder.

"Spooky is more like it," I reply. "Why is this here? These two ruled Traveler, not Journey. And I thought our worlds are now ruled by the Council."

"They are," Takoda says from my side.

"I don't like this," I whisper. "It's as if they're still alive and judging me."

The women are portrayed in full uniform with their berets sitting only slightly tilted on their heads. Each holds a golden staff and chalice. What really grabs my attention is what's behind them. The two women are standing in the golden chamber of the Ancient City. I can just make out the murals of the ancient families behind them. Two owls rest at their feet. Clouds hover above their heads and something shiny grabs my attention. I step closer to get a better look.

"Journey, we do not have time for this." Mom grabs my arm and guides me away.

"Just a moment," I whisper, yanking my arm away.

A flash pulls me from my thoughts. It's Takoda taking a picture of the large painting. He winks and I nod. I'll be glad to study it when I have more time.

As we walk to the security office, I keep glancing at the portrait. The eerie painting haunts me, and I'm not sure why. There's something about it that bothers me. My mother hands a guard her badge and we're allowed entry. It only takes a few minutes for Takoda and I to receive our passes.

The elevator to the second floor enters into a normal office, except everyone is blue with long gray hair, just like Takoda. Although their hair is red on Traveler, on Journey, Swetaachata hair is a dull shade of gray.

A young female employee compliments me about my draping, and I thank her. We meet with a supervisor and discuss our past work experience, which doesn't take long because we don't have any. The Swetaachata woman shakes her head and grins.

"How about I just ask what you enjoy doing?"

"We love to travel and explore ruins," Takoda explains.

Not looking up, she scribbles a few notes on her tablet.

"And we love to meet people," I add, wondering if we are qualified for anything.

After several grueling minutes of not having anything important to share about our work experience, she assigns us to the social welfare department.

"Oh goodie!" I say.

Takoda frowns as we're escorted to our new office.

27
THE COUNCIL OF ELDERS

"SOME OFFICE," I say, standing next to a very small table. "I bet this used to be a broom closet."

"Do you have a fetish for broom closets?" he asks, scanning through some documents on his tablet. "We are supposed to read about these cases and make arrangements to visit their homes."

I walk around the table that fits only two stools, one on each side, and sit.

"Well, I just walked our whole office. Wow, that sure took a while."

"It is not a big room," he agrees, "but it works."

"I guess we're lucky they gave us stools to sit on."

Takoda laughs as he reads the record. "What about this one?" he asks, turning his tablet so I can see his screen. "It is an elderly couple. The wife tossed her husband out of the home."

"Why would she do that?" I ask, my heart breaking for anyone being treated that way.

"I do not know. It will be our job to find out. Let us visit this couple and hear the whole story." Takoda tucks his pad into his pack and we leave.

No reason to lock the room. There's nothing in it but a table and two stools. The train schedule is every fifteen minutes or so.

Not a lot of time to look around but enough for me to enjoy the fresh air.

The thick clouds dim the sunlight. Everything is cast in shades of green or blue. The small station, a kiosk and bench, is empty. My mind wanders to a large tree that is behind us.

As Takoda buys tickets from his phone, I take the time to enjoy the scenery. As far up as I can see, the branches spread out in all directions. The tree is enormous. Large leaves curl and drape creating a bluish kaleidoscope of yellows and greens that's almost mesmerizing. A sweet aroma tickles my nose, I breathe it in and sigh slowly.

"That tree has been here for as long as I can remember," Takoda says.

"What is it?"

"A tree," he says, laughing.

"Very funny. I meant what kind?"

"No idea," he replies. "There are many different types on Journey. Some larger, some smaller." He pulls off a leaf and hands it to me. "Here, put it in your bag. After a while, the bag will smell as the plant does now."

The train comes to a full stop and I carefully place the large leaf into my backpack. I smile as the sweet aroma follows me onto the train.

The countryside is amazing with all the different foliage. Unlike anything I could possibly imagine. It's as if God mixed a jungle with a forest and allowed everything to grow freely. We step off the train about twenty minutes outside the city. I have to calculate in Earth time because it is all I have. Saxonian time is just too confusing for me.

A young girl greets us when we enter a complex that houses six families. She looks about my sister's age. Her long grey hair is entwined with drapings of various lengths. Her large amber eyes shine with excitement. She must be excited to see strangers.

"My nam ... Akaya," she says, with a heavy Swetaachata accent and points at my chest. "Ou patee."

She's difficult to understand but I believe she's trying to tell me I'm pretty.

"Thank you," I say, nodding to the right.

Takoda asks her a few questions in their native tongue. She nods and points to a small apartment near the back of the compound. I follow Takoda as several sets of amber eyes follow us. No one is smiling. Instead they all stare with dark and solemn expressions, which is not normal for a Swetaachata.

"These people look sad," I whisper. "They don't seem as happy as the others from the city."

Takoda glances around but makes no comment.

We knock on the door that the young girl had pointed to. An elderly, white-haired woman answers. Her skin is blue but most of the swirls of green have faded. She motions for us to sit on her couch, which is just a block of wood with pillows. We sit. She drops to the floor in front of us and crosses her legs. The old woman bows her head and says a few words in their native language. Takoda nods to the right. She is frail looking but quite limber for an older woman. She's wearing a white robe and her feet are bare and worn.

Takoda sighs. "It is as I thought."

"What?" I'm feeling sorry for the old woman.

The barren home is empty except for the block of wood we're sitting on. I see no kitchen or bathroom, no bed or chair. The home makes me uncomfortable because Takoda and I are feeling the same emotions, which doubles the effect.

"These people were brought here against their will," he explains.

"Brought here?" I repeat. "From where?"

Takoda shakes his head. "No idea."

"Then ask her!" I order. "Translate for me, please." I turn to the woman and say slowly, "Where were your homes?"

Not understanding a word I'm saying, the woman looks at me with a quizzical expression.

"Takoda, translate, please."

Takoda talks to the woman, and their conversation lasts only a few moments. His eyes lower as he sighs. "Their home was on the other side of Journey. On the continent of Shabeelah. She said the trip took many dzanas. The Council confiscated their land with a promise of a better life. They have no way to support themselves here. These people only know how to live off the land. They have no idea what to do here."

"This is a better life?" I ask, jumping up and pacing the room. My anger's rising and my mind is running through all the reasons why. I do not like what I'm concluding.

"I guess this is the Council's idea of a good life," he replies.

"What about the old guy who was thrown out?"

"He was not thrown out, he left," Takoda explains. "She said he refused to stay and demanded to be returned to his homeland. He was ignored and therefore left. She begged him not to go but could not stop him. The authorities picked him up and are detaining him."

"Detaining him? Where was their homeland and what does the Council need it for?" I ask.

Takoda pulls out his tablet and searches until he comes to the case about the old couple. He reads through the text and growls.

"What?" I know what that sound means — something's wrong.

Takoda stands and walks to the door. "We must go."

I stand and follow him outside. I'm confused. Isn't he even going to say goodbye?

Takoda leaves but I stay and nod my head to the left and say, "Um, goodbye and it was nice to meet you."

When I catch up with him, I grab his arm. "What is wrong with you? That was rude!"

"We have no business here," he says and continues to walk toward the train station. It's as though he can't get out of here fast enough. Not until we're on the train and alone does he explain. "Journey, those people … that woman …" He can't seem to finish his sentence.

Tears form in his eyes and his hands shake. I've never seen him so angry. I concentrate and can see his visions through my mind. I can feel his reverence and spirituality as Takoda's mind tries to sort out the situation.

"These people are special?" I ask, knowing the answer before he says a word.

Takoda nods.

My stomach tightens as Takoda's feelings surge through me. My hand finds his and I squeeze it to let him know that I'm there. "We'll fix it, whatever *it* is."

❦

When we return, the city is busy. We find a bench that's away from the crowds and under a tree. It amazes me how large the trees are around here. Nowhere on Earth are there any as big as these, not even the redwoods in California.

The sun's rays are barely penetrating through the thick cloud layers. However, the large leaves, covered in dew, still sparkle as if sprinkled with diamonds. It is too beautiful to put into words.

Takoda stares into my eyes and holds my hand. My mind races through the issues as I try to understand. The look on Takoda's face is a mixture of concern, anger and pity.

"Journey," he says. "My people are a proud race. We are not formally educated in schools the same as you. We are taught by the old. We learn their wisdom and how to be understanding."

Knowing his need to explain, I just sit and listen.

"We live as one with our world and our environment. The Most Holy feeds us, clothes us, and gives us warmth. We have no seasons, only dzanas and usikus or what you call days and nights. Our world is us and we are our world. That old woman," he says, with tears. "She is one of the ancients. I could read her thoughts. Her people are of the first people. Her lineage goes back many, many generations."

"You mean as old as my family?" I ask.

"Your lineage is short compared to hers because your family artificially extended theirs. Instead of living a hundred years, they now live thousands. That woman's family evolved over time and is probably more than a million generations from her first mother.

"According to the records I pulled earlier, her DNA is from the original ancient line and I do not believe we were supposed to know about that."

"Wait." I need a moment to grasp what he's telling me. "If she is from the original settlers, then her DNA must match that of the Captain Lady … um … Gaia … and if she's related to Gaia, then she's related to … me … to us!"

"No, only to you."

"Then she is related to the Council members somehow," I surmise. "Every member is related to me. So why isn't *she* on the Council? And why did they bring her to that dump? And how *is* she related to me?"

"I do not know," Takoda admits.

"Maybe they brought her here to humble her, make her feel bad about herself or maybe they just wanted her land but that doesn't make sense either. This planet is so large there is no reason to fight over land. Unless … there is something special about that land."

"Special?" he asks. "Special in what way?"

"Abeytu and my dad both said that our cabin is on sacred ground. What makes ground sacred?" My mind tries to piece together the puzzle. "Think about it, Takoda. Earth people kill for land that has gold or diamonds."

"I see your point," he agrees. "We do not have precious metals or stones. The other planets in our system provide us with whatever we need. We have no reason to fight for it. There is no benefit from having gold or jewels here."

"Okay maybe not minerals," I reply. "But there's more going on than we know. This planet has … I don't know … special powers? There has to be something. Let me ask you this, why do the

Wanderers pray to the other world? Just because it's hovering over their heads. Of course not. If you're born here and see something cross through the sky all the time, it becomes normal. Not something to be worshipped."

"What are you trying to say?" Takoda asks.

"Seeing Journey over my cabin was amazing but it was the first time. After many years, I may not feel that way. People here don't worship the sun do they or the moons? We need to talk to Abeytu. We need to get him alone and really rack his brain. There's something he is not telling us."

"Journey, we already have people trying to kill us. I am not sure about this but we need to be careful."

"We need to find out why they're after us, Takoda. We need to find out who is after us. Maybe if we dig into what's going on around here, maybe we can figure out the whys. There is a reason my mother wants us here and not on Traveler. She's hiding something too."

"Here you are," my mother says, making us jump. "How was your first day?"

"Interesting," I answer. "Ready to go home?"

"Day is over," she says, with a smile. "We can leave."

"Mom," I say, as she turns to guide us to the car.

"Yes."

"Why is the Council immigrating people around this world?" I probably won't get a straight answer but it's worth a try.

She doesn't reply. Instead, she glances around. She stutters as she answers. "Journey, you have to understand that most of the Swetaachata are undereducated and live in very poor conditions. We are trying to help them."

"I saw the one-room help from the Council. Just one room shacks. Where did you pull these people from? A cave? That family didn't look happy, and I would not consider their new home anything but trash."

"Journey," she scolds. "You are asking questions about situations that are none of your business. You are only going to cause trouble."

"Trouble for who, Mother?" I demand. "For me? Or you?"

"We will discuss this when we return home," she says, nervously.

"By the way," I add. "I met my great grandmother the other day. Ever met the lady?" It feels good to throw little bits of information at her and catch her off guard. Maybe I'm hoping she'll tell some of her secrets.

"Of course," she replies. "Do not be silly, Journey."

"You should talk to her sometime," I say, walking away and holding onto Takoda's hand.

The ride to Traveler is quiet and strained. Chawlya, my mom, keeps glancing at us. Takoda and I do not discuss what we saw today. Instead, we play on his tablet.

George has dinner on the table when we return and he hugs us. After we eat, I walk with Takoda by the lake.

"I don't like working for that social department," I say, when I know no one can overhear us.

"It may prove useful," he replies. He picks up several rocks and throws them into the lake.

As I watch the ripples, I frown. "What we do affects others. I believe that now. Look how Anneeta affects me. If we can affect in a bad way, then we can also affect in a good way."

He tosses another rock. "I believe that."

"We will not be going back," I state. "I believe we can do more good from the outside than the inside. We are being watched and monitored there. I guarantee it." I pull out my phone.

"Who are you calling?"

"Abeytu," I reply. "We need to tell everyone at the same time that we will not be working for my mother after all. I want everyone on the same playing field. No more surprises. No more talking behind our backs. And … no more secrets."

Makayah is working on her school project while we have our family meeting. She's still listening and perhaps that's a good thing. My classes are over for the term but Makayah's school stays in session all year, or whatever they call it around here — about three months on then two weeks off.

We sit on the porch. My mom and dad are on the swing and Abeytu leans against the door. Takoda sits on the top step and I stand next to Abeytu.

"Since we're all here," I say, "I think now is a good time to tell you something." I glance at everyone. They remain quiet waiting for me to continue. "Takoda and I will *not* be working for the Council this year."

"And why not?" my mother asks, standing up.

"For one thing … I don't appreciate sitting in a broom closet." I smirk.

"They put you in a broom closet?" Abeytu chuckles. "I can see that happening."

"It is not a broom closet," my mother says. "It is just a very small room."

"Anyway," I continue, ignoring them. "Takoda and I prefer to travel this summer."

"Oh?" my father says, speaking up.

"I have credits saved," Takoda interjects. "That will cover the costs."

"I see," my mother says not looking very happy.

"Maybe next term I'll be ready for work. For now, I wish to visit my relatives," I add.

"The Council is family," Chawlya defends.

"I mean my immediate family," I say, defending our decision. "My grandmother for one and Takoda's grandmother for another."

"I think that is a wonderful idea," Abeytu says, giving me a hug. "I did not like this *working for the Council* decision. You need to explore your surroundings while you are still young enough to appreciate them."

"Are we not forgetting something here?" my father asks, interrupting Abeytu. "What about the people that are after them ... what about Takoda's abduction?"

"I have thought about that," Takoda adds. "My father said there is a class we can take over the break that teaches defense and other useful skills. We plan on signing up tomorrow."

"I see," Dad says not sounding convinced. "I just do not know if this is a good idea."

"Your father is right," Chawlya states holding onto George's arm.

"Oh, so now he's right?" I ask. "The other day he worried too much, but since he doesn't like our plans, you are suddenly agreeing with him? I think I'm old enough to decide for myself. I will not be returning to the Council, and Takoda and I will be taking that class and traveling this summer."

"I guess that settles it," Abeytu says.

My mother looks furious and my father looks like he's going to be sick again.

"Is there something you are not telling us?" I ask.

"Now what could anyone be hiding?" Abeytu stares at my parents and shakes his head.

"Nothing," my mother replies and my father glances out at the lake.

"Right," I sigh. "You tell us everything, don't you? If it's all settled, then I'm going to bed."

"And, I am going to the couch," Takoda adds, with a grin.

28

GRANDMOTHER

TAKODA'S GRANDMOTHER lives on Journey. Being a Council daughter, we cheat and hitch a ride on my mother's private spacecraft. Mother Vviaa lives with the family tribe in a remote village. Therefore, once we've landed, I find myself strapped to my backpack riding a train into a vast wilderness.

Excitement invigorates me just knowing I'm about to meet Takoda's tribe. Even though the ride through the mountains were at an incomprehensible speed, our trip still lasted several hours. I'm exhausted stepping off the train. I stare into the darkening sky and frown. The air is still warm and a slight mist clings to my hair. Without a formal station, we stand in the darkness holding hands, alone.

"Not much out here is there?" I laugh. My nerves are crawling and if I don't say something, panic will soon consume me.

"It will be okay," he replies. "It is only a short distance down the road."

It is not a road but a dirt path and it's not used much. The foliage continuously fights to take over and I believe it's winning. Takoda uses a machete to hack his way through the thicker brush. I'm reminded of a jungle with flowering vines and plants with leaves larger than my body. Cries of animals screech out from the shadows and wakens my inner alarm. By the time we reach his family, I'm sweaty, tired and ready to explode.

Lights filter through as the last few leaves are cut. We stand at the jungle's edge and stare into the small but busy village. The huts are amazing. I've never seen anything like them. One large hut sits in the middle. Other huts surround the main one with connecting hallways. Stairs lead to the upper huts that are built on stilts. Above them are even more homes that are wedged between the trees. A whole city had been carved into, or should I say, from the jungle.

"This way," Takoda says, taking my hand.

A large fire is off to one side. It looks like something is roasting over the open flames. Several women are tending to the evening meal. White wraps hug their slender frames, which makes their skin darken and radiate. Drapings cling to their hair. I can hear them tingling from across the yard.

Takoda yells out to the women in his native tongue. They turn and wave. A couple scream and run to us. Hugs and kisses are freely exchanged as I stand and watch. I'm not sure what to do or say. Takoda reaches for me and pulls me in. He says only a few words before I'm whisked away by several beautiful Swetaachata women. My hair is pulled in all directions, my face is touched and stroked, and my hands are studied.

Before long, Takoda's at my side hugging me. He's laughing and talking to the women. When they slowly back away, I take in a deep breath.

"You okay?" he asks.

I nod.

"These are my cousins," he says. "This is Veevaa, Eevva ..." the introductions are endless.

There is no way I'll remember everyone's names. I can see a family resemblance but since I can't understand a word, I'm at a disadvantage.

"Takoda?" It's a woman's voice. "Takoda, is that you?"

"Vookda!" Takoda yells grabbing on tightly to the beautiful woman. "I have missed you."

"I have missed you," she replies. "You brought a friend?"

"Yes," he says, wiping his eyes. "This is Journey, my Kupatanna partner."

My heart leaps through my throat and flies into the heavens. As my eyes cross, the world twirls and my legs melt. Before the ground slaps my face, Takoda steadies me.

"Journey," Takoda asks. "Are you okay?"

"I need to sit down," I reply, knowing that my face is glowing red. How could he say that as if it was nothing?

"Please …" Vookda says, pulling on my arm. "Bring her to my bed."

As I'm dragged through the village, my emotions run wild. I stare into the eyes that are fixated on me. I can't believe Takoda told her we had bonded! We enter the private hut and Vookda hands me a glass of water.

"Journey, sit. Be comfortable," she says, pushing the hair from my eyes. "Oh my … you are sweaty."

Vookda runs into another room and returns with a wet cloth. She wipes my face and the back of my neck. As I sip on the water, the room finally stops spinning.

"Feeling better?" she asks.

I nod.

"And your father?" Vookda asks. "He is good and Freya too?"

"Yes, they are fine," Takoda replies.

She is not asking about us bonding. Why not? After Vookda chases her family from her hut, she studies me and I study her. The woman is tall and slender. Her color is similar to Takoda's but her swirls are larger and less wavy. Her eyes are amber and huge. Gray hair falls down her back, reaching to her knees.

"You are pretty," she says.

"No," I reply. "You are!"

"Journey," Takoda says. "This is my mother's twin, Vookda. I believe you would call her my aunt."

"Yes," I reply. "You are correct. Nice to meet you, Vookda." I nod to the right and hold out my hand. She kisses it and nods to the right.

"She has a good heart," she says. "Not like Anneeta. It is good Anneeta is not in your life."

"Yes, that is good," Takoda adds, squeezing my arm.

"You come to stay awhile?"

"A dzana or two," Takoda answers.

"I wish Journey to meet Mother Vviaa. How is she?"

"She is not young," Vookda replies. "She is with us only for now. We are on borrowed time. Final meal is almost ready, let us eat and I will take you to her."

Dinner is something else. The roast was not an animal but a large plant stalk that was covered in herbs and spices. My mouth explodes with every bite. A bowl of cut fruit is offered and I can't resist. A glass of water tops it off and I'm soon stuffed.

As we walk through the main hut, an enchanting melody captivates my soul. Not recognizing the instruments, I follow the sound. Several people sitting in a circle are enjoying the evening. Others come up to me and stroke my hair or kiss my cheek. I'm more interested in the music. I can't get enough of that beautiful sound.

"Journey?" Takoda asks.

"I love this music," I reply. "What is it?"

"Bowls," Vookda answers.

Between the legs of each musician is a colored bowl. After wetting their fingers, a beautiful melody escapes as they run their hands around the glass rim. It's amazing and I don't want to move.

"We can teach you to play," Vookda says.

"Really?" I ask. "It's beautiful!"

"Yes, it is," Vookda adds. "Our children learn young."

"Come, Journey," Takoda says, pulling on my arm. "We can come back. I wish for you to meet my grandmother."

We walk through several huts. Each have several rooms and are comfortably decorated. Takoda holds my hand. We approach an elderly Swetaachata woman who is sitting comfortably in a chair. She is covered with blankets. Her hair is almost gone but many drapings have taken its place decorating her face with beauty. Her skin is fair. The blue has long since faded with time. The wrinkles that adorn her eyes give her a look of wisdom. I'm instantly taken by her.

Her eyes open and they twinkle as soon as she see Takoda. A huge smile grows and almost lights the room. "Takoda," she whispers. "My boy, my beautiful boy."

Takoda kneels next to his grandmother and places his head in her lap. She rubs his head.

"I love you, Mother Vviaa," he says. Tears fill his eyes.

My heart aches for I know she will not be on this world much longer.

"Do not cry, my beautiful boy," she whispers. "When I leave to be with the Most Holy, I take with me the knowing of love."

Takoda lifts his head and kisses her. "Mother Vviaa, I wish for you to greet my nubere alicui."

"Ah," Mother Vviaa says, reaching out her hand to me. "Kupatanna, you have bonded."

I take her hand and instantly everything changes. No longer am I standing in Mother Vviaa's home. Instead, I'm on a mountain ridge. Next to me is a beautiful Swetaachata woman wearing a scant cloth that barely covers her. Drapings cling to her long hair. Below is the valley and above are the clouds.

"Where am I?"

"You are with me," she says. "We must talk privately."

"What happened?"

"I am Gemanaga, Journey, and I have suspicions as are you."

"What's a Gemanaga?"

"Someone with the ancient blood running through their veins," she explains.

I stare at her.

"You are special if Takoda pledged himself to you," she says. "He does not give his love freely."

I nod.

"I believe you are very special, Journey," she says. "When we touched, the Most Holy gave me a message for you."

"A message?"

"Do not trust your mother," she replies. "She is not what you think she is."

"I've already figured that one out."

"The Council is not what you think they are either," she adds.

"I have not met the Council yet."

"Wait as long as you can," she adds. "You need to be introduced to your powers first. I believe you will find yourself but not today, and not tomorrow. Maybe in yesterday is where you will meet."

We're now back in her home, and Takoda is still kneeling next to her.

"That was interesting," I say.

"What is interesting?" Takoda asks.

"It is interesting that you are here, my boy," Mother Vviaa says. She places a finger over her mouth and waves it back and forth. Then she smiles. "Come sit by me, Journey. Let me know you better. Tell me about your home world."

We sit together and share stories. I tell her about the large cities of Earth and how many people live there. She seems interested in how we live, work and play.

"Tell me about you, Mother Vviaa," I say.

"There is not much to tell," she replies. "I was born here in this hut. Takoda also woke up here. Freya, however, was given on Traveler. I unioned young. Too young. I never bonded but we loved each other. My fears kept me alone for most of my life."

Takoda is now visiting privately with Vookda and I grab at the chance. "What is a Gemanaga?"

"The ancient blood is strong and powerful," she replies. "The Council removed all life that showed the signs. There are only a few of us left."

"But what is it?"

"Gemanaga … the ancient bloodline. The blood of the Most Holy."

"I believe you are tired, Mother," Vookda says, interrupting our conversation.

My heart drops. I want to know more but I also do not want her to tire. Takoda and I retire to Vookda's hut. As sleep greets me, my mind juggles through the conversation with Mother Vviaa. How did we get to the top of that mountain, and why didn't anyone notice we were gone? How did she look so young? So many questions without answers.

@

Mother Vviaa died that night as we slept. Her body was burnt the next evening. Distant family came to pay their respects. Takoda's father, Fretoda, and his sister, Freya, arrive just before the service. Tribal clothing with family colors brighten the service, all yellow and green. Takoda cries on my shoulder as the fire blazes. My heart breaks as I watch the family mourn. The night before we leave, Vookda says her goodbyes.

"This is for you," she says, handing me a small cloth.

"Me?"

"Yes, from Mother Vviaa," she replies. I open the cloth and in my hand is a beautiful draping.

"Why?" I ask.

"She believes in you, Journey," Vookda replies. "She said to wear this, and when you have a daughter, you should pass it on."

The draping is long and golden threads decorate the thin strap. Tiny feathers and beads cling to the strand. On the end dangles a tree with a snake. The snake is gray and glitters in the light.

"She said your heart is good and this draping will announce your greatness. Wear it with pride."

"I will," I reply, knowing I would again meet the old woman in my dreams.

29
GAIA

WE LEAVE before any of the others are awake. My heart aches for the ancient mother I just met. She was sweet and loving. Before we left Traveler, Abeytu had given me directions to my grandmother's home on the small water moon, Makayah.

We arrive at the station and find our flight, a small ship similar to my mother's. This flight, however, is a few hours longer than our previous flights since Makayah is now on the other side of Traveler. Makayah's only station is on the largest of the islands.

We now must ride a ferryboat to my grandmother's home. It's weird being on the moon, all I see in any direction is water. Traveler is so large that I can see it hovering just off the horizon. It is sunny today, no clouds. Large whale-like creatures jump from the sea splattering us. I laugh but Takoda frowns as he wipes his face. It's not a short ride to my grandmother's island. We eat lunch on the ferry and work on our tablets. Being out in public it's important that we look like friends and nothing more. We do not kiss or hug each other but we do hold hands.

"Okay, we are registered for the kickboxing class. It starts next masika," he says, shoving his tablet into his pack. "It is not the official title, however, it is what you are calling it."

Takoda looks at me with a saddened expression. I can sense he's thinking about the people I killed to save him. He smiles and I smile back but we do not discuss it with words.

We arrive on the island shortly after lunch and find a taxi. No cars … only carts pulled by a horse-like animal. I lean against Takoda as we ride.

The house is built out of mud and brick and reminds me of an adobe village. Each room is a separate building and attached by a connecting hallway. I love it the moment I see it. One hallway is between two large trees with smaller rooms on both sides. The yard is green with soft moss. Not one flower decorates the yard.

"Ready?" Takoda asks, as we stand out front.

"Sure."

We walk to the front door together. Before we knock, the door opens and a young woman looking just like me welcomes us.

"Oh my!" she says with a smile.

"Hello, I'm —"

"I know who you are. You are Journey. I would recognize you anywhere. Come in, please."

I'm not sure what I'm expecting but the home reminds me of a home on Earth. Thick drapes frame the windows and huge pillows adorn the couch and chairs. A flat screen television hangs on the wall.

"Make yourselves comfortable," she says as she walks down the short hallway.

Takoda sits on the couch while I walk around the room admiring the pictures. There are photos of Mom, Makayah and me inside decorative frames that are placed strategically around the house. After a few moments, my grandmother returns with a tray.

"Please, Journey, have a seat," she says, motioning with her hand. "Since we receive only one transport a day, I assume you will be spending the night?"

"We can stay on the mainland," I state, quickly. "We don't want to impose."

"Do not be silly," she argues. "This is your home too."

"You look so young," I say, then wish I hadn't, taking a sip of my tea.

"When you have mad scientists for relatives there are some side effects," she grins.

"You don't even look as old as my mother," I exclaim. "How old are you?"

"Old enough to know to never reveal my age," she answers, with a wink.

I take in a deep breath and munch on the crackers. As I study her, I realize that I'm looking at myself, only a little older. "You're beautiful."

"Thank you," she replies. "And so are you." We laugh. "Are you going to introduce me?"

"Oh, where are my manners," I say. "Grandmother, this is Takoda … Takoda, this is my Grandmother Lylillea."

"We have company?" a deep voice echoes from the hallway.

"You have company?" I ask, feeling guilty for dropping in unexpectedly.

"Yes, your grandfather," she says, with a chuckle. "He lives here, so I would not be concerned. Chawanna, your granddaughter is here to visit with you. Do you need any help?"

"Of course not," he snaps.

Chawanna enters the room and I almost fall over. He's an elderly man with gray hair and a very frail body. He uses a walker and it takes him a while to get to his recliner.

"Ah, teatime. Good, I am hungry. Oh, I recognize her," he says pointing to me. "But who are you?"

"This is Takoda," my grandmother says winking at him. "He and Journey will be unioned someday."

"Another rebel, I see," he says, very matter-of-factly. "I was one of those once." He laughs. "When I had the energy."

"Yes, you were, my love," Lylillea says, patting his hand in a loving manner. The way she looks at him, I can tell that they shared Kupatanna.

"I guess Mom or Dad told you about us?"

"Abeytu," she explains, pouring her husband some tea.

"This is awkward, isn't it?" I say, smiling.

"Only for you, Journey," she replies. "We have watched you grow. Rachael sent us pictures and movies. Her letters told us all about you. It was as if we were there sharing every moment. The only thing I missed was the hugs and kisses from my granddaughters."

Taking the hint, I go to her. We hug and it's as if I've finally come home. I hug my grandfather and kiss him, though I wasn't sure how much he would remember later. It's obvious his memory is fading. I feel sorry for my grandmother, for I know he'll die someday soon from old age, and she'll live on as a healthy twenty-year-old. It's strange watching them. Her age shows in her mannerisms but her face and body are of a young woman. It's as if what our ancestors did was more of a curse and not a blessing.

We talk all afternoon and I help prepare dinner. After we eat, Takoda plays a card game with my grandfather, and I walk with my grandmother. To be alone with her for the first time is a treasure I'll never forget.

"It's great being here with you," I say as we walk. Her house is not far from the water's edge and I wonder about storm damage.

"We have no storms," she says, as if reading my mind. "Journey and Traveler's gravity is too strong and has an opposing effect on the water. Both pull on our world so there is no wind and no tide."

"Rain?" I ask.

"No rain," she answers. "The water table is high so the plants draw from below the ground. The oceans are fresh."

"Did you just read my mind?" I ask.

"You do not know about Kupatanna and its effects, do you?"

"I know only what I experienced."

"Come sit by me, Journey, my daughter's daughter."

We sit on the beach, just close enough to the water for our feet to get wet. We watch together as the sun sets behind Traveler and rises from behind Journey.

"We have only daylight," she says as she moves the sand around with her toes. Grandmother then says something that grips me from deep within. "I will die when he dies."

I'm not sure how to respond. At that moment, I understand what Kupatanna means for my future. When two people merge, their lives and souls merge too. Now I know why it doesn't bother her that my grandfather is old and dying. When he dies, she too will die and be with him forever.

"We became friends when we met in town one day," she says, gazing out at the water. "I fell instantly for Chawanna. He was so handsome. We shared Trials that year and that is when it happened. He became ill with a high fever. I had never been so afraid in my life. I thought he would die, right there, in front of me and I would be alone.

"I knew nothing of Kupatanna, absolutely nothing. It happened by accident when we were inside *The City of the Wicked Lady*."

I gasp.

"He started shivering," Grandmother continued, "so I grabbed him to warm him, and when I did, we bonded. Suddenly I found myself on his home world, and his whole life is flashing before my eyes. When he finally came to, he admitted his love for me and explained. He said it happened early and he had no idea as to why.

"We unioned right after classes ended. We knew it was forbidden but we did not care. We were young and not afraid of anyone. When I gave birth to your mother, I knew I had to hide her. They would kill my precious baby. We took her to Chawanna's family. They live deep in the mountains on Journey. We returned to Traveler when she was of age.

She injured herself in class one day, and the doctors knew she was from a mixed union. They imprisoned us for our illegal union and the creation of our abominations. Our *babies* abomination? Can you believe that? Abeytu and your father worked hard on our case. It took a very long time. We were in prison for over twelve Earth years. We did not raise our children and Chawlya has always resented us for that."

Tears form in my grandmother's eyes. I feel sorry for her. I reach out and rub her arm. She smiles and rests her head on my shoulder.

"Your life will not be easy, Journey. Many will come after you because of your love for Takoda. Your love will also be your curse. Then in other ways, your love will be a blessing. Takoda will always be true and honest to you and your children. He will love you more than any man can ever love a woman, and you will love him in ways you cannot comprehend."

"I think I understand," I whisper.

"I still do not understand why our union was forbidden." Tears roll down her cheeks. "We all come from the same family. I was taught that our people traveled to Journey and stayed. Then something happened to our worlds, and we lost our knowledge about space travel. Over time our people changed physically. Something about the air and water. They also became telepathic and more spiritual than those who remained behind on Traveler. Many generations came and went before we reunited. The time spent apart was just too great.

"The Death Plague hit our worlds, and everyone blamed everyone else. Sadly, most of the blame landed on the Swetaachatas. Journey and its people became our enemy and we became Traveler's curse. We did everything we could to annihilate one another. It was when the Tarkadians attacked that our planets began to work together for survival."

"I've been to the graveyard." Now I know where the racism originated. Although stupid, I understand.

"Truth is never pretty, is it?" she adds.

The following morning we wake early as the aroma of food fills our room. My grandmother prepared a wonderful breakfast and my grandfather's already eating when we take our seats at the kitchen table. Everything looks so good that I'm not sure where to start. Takoda digs right in.

"Journey, do you like Swetaachata food?" she asks, filling my plate with something that resembles scrambled eggs.

"What I've had so far I like. Takoda took me to dinner for my birthday at a Swetaachata restaurant," I answer, taking a bite of food. "Yum, this is delicious."

"The plants on Journey are much sweeter than on Traveler," my grandfather adds.

"Yes, and our cultures are very different," Takoda says, sipping on a hot breakfast drink.

"I thought I would take you to the caves today," Lylillea states, while filling her plate with a fruit dish.

With my mouth full, I stutter, "C-caves?"

"How can there be caves?" Takoda asks. "This is a flat-water world. There are no mountains."

"None that you can see," she explains. "Our mountains are underwater."

"We are not taught that in class," Takoda adds, taking another bite.

"There is a lot that they do not teach," Chawanna states, slapping the table. "And it is a blasted shame!"

My grandfather remains home and I feel bad leaving him behind. I promise him my full attention when we return that evening. Lylillea packs a lunch and we head for the beach that's just outside her home. My legs and feet ache and my stomach's growling by the time we stop to rest.

"What I don't understand," I say as we eat. "Why is English the common language?"

"Our ancestors came from deep inside the Fornax system," she says. "A planet called Qapadhue. It was about the size of Traveler with the same type of atmosphere. That system had one sun, unlike here, and no twin. We have no knowledge of where the people of Qapadhue came from. We do know about the ancient war with the Draconians. Our people barely escaped to other universes. Thousands of ships left in pairs. One ship could have carried all the people, but to increase the chance of survival, they used two. If one ship couldn't continue, the other would be large enough to carry everyone."

"Smart thinking," I say.

"Yes and no," Grandmother continues. "They left many behind and when the planet was destroyed, they died."

"I know two ships arrived here," Takoda said. "They settled on Traveler first. Settlements on Journey occurred many generations later."

"That is correct," Grandmother replies. "Two ships arrived here but the ancient writings teach us that one left for another universe and solar system. A planet called Tiamat."

"Tiamat?" I repeat. "Where have I heard that name before?"

"Tiamat is what Earth was called before it broke apart," Lylillea replies.

"Broke apart?" I'm surprised I never heard about this before.

"Yes," she adds, shaking her head. "It is strange how civilizations never teach their people about their history. Earth used to be a planet just outside one of the outer gas giants and twice the size it is today. The Draconians found Tiamat many generations ago. The people were warned in advance and evacuated to Mars. People were technologically advanced back then and had built huge cities in the air and under the water. We sent ships to help. When the Draconians were finally finished, it took many generations before Earth could sustain life again. We seeded it many times."

"What do you mean by seeded?" I ask.

"If a planet is knocked out of orbit, imagine the huge rocks that remain. The asteroid belt is what is left of Tiamat's other half."

"Are you saying Earth is only half of what it used to be?" I ask, surprised that our scientists never figured this one out on their own.

"That is correct," she says, as we begin our walk again. "Tiamat was big and most of it was scattered. Before the rubble settled into the asteroid belt, rocks pelted the Earth. Each time we tried to re-seed it, an asteroid destroyed everything. It was only when we were convinced it was safe to repopulate that we allowed our people to cultivate its soil again."

"Mars is dead, what happened to it? I mean, why don't we have people living there now?"

"Mars was very different at one time," she explains. "It had oceans, an atmosphere, trees, animals and cities with people, lots of people. The Draconians discovered Mars and fired their weapon. Earth was on the other side of the sun at the time, and Draconians either did not know it was there or did not care.

"Maybe they thought the asteroid belt was all that was left of Tiamat. They only fired on Mars. We could not reach the people in time and millions died. The Draconians' weapon pushed Mars from its gas giant and eventually it established its own orbit. It is still not safe to go there. The poison in the air will probably remain for many generations to come."

"You mean radiation?" I wonder if the Draconians used nuclear weapons.

"Similar, but much worse," she explains. "It not only kills the inhabitants but it actually kills the planet."

"Planet?"

"The planets are alive," she explains. "They must be in order to sustain life. They are born, they breathe, grow and die just as we do. And they talk to us through the plants. If you listen, Journey, you can hear them speak. Listen to the wind and the sounds around you."

"All I ever hear are people and cars."

"Not in the cities." She laughs. "But out here, where there is only us. Listen, Journey."

We stop walking and all is quiet. I concentrate and close my eyes. I hear something. It almost sounds like someone breathing. I must be dreaming because it's as though I can feel the ground move beneath me. She's right, the planet is alive.

"Wow," I whisper. "Does that mean everyone on Earth is related to everyone here?"

"If you think about it," Takoda states, "everyone has to be related to everyone in some manner."

"That is true," Lylillea adds, nodding her head. "We are all related somehow, although we share no DNA sequences with either the Draconians or the Tarkadians."

"Do you know how it differs?" Takoda asks.

"Humans have twenty-three chromosomes, or forty-six total. Both our races have the same. But ..." She pauses as if in thought. "... the Tarkadians have forty-six pairs or ninety-two total. Much more than us. We know nothing about the Draconians. Some argue we are related to the Tarkadians because we both have chromosomes. With that hypothesis you could argue we are related to the plants and animals because they too have chromosomes."

"Our cells ... are they the same as the Tarkadians?" I ask.

"Not really," she answers. "Their cells look different. Also, we cannot mate with them."

"I've heard that before." I glance at Takoda who smiles. "I mean, I am a mix of two races that were not supposed to be able to produce an offspring. Do you think they're trying to make a hybrid with these things?"

Lylillea studies me before she answers. "Unfortunately, I do. Give one of our ancestors a test tube and there is no telling what you will get. The Tarkadians have two arms and two legs, a head and torso but that is as common as it gets. The Tarkadians have a completely different facial structure than us. Their skin is more like a fish and they have what I call scales. The scientists call it something different."

"Are the Draconians reptilian?" Takoda asks.

"We do not know," she replies.

Takoda laughs as he adds, "I was told that the Tarkadians eat people."

"I have seen no proof of that," she answers.

"So many were taken during the ancient war," Takoda says. "We are taught in school that the people taken were used for food."

"We never found proof that anyone was ever taken." Lylillea sighs. "There is much that is not told about the war. The Tarkadians killed people. That part is true. However, we have no evidence that they actually ate anyone. We found writings inside their crashed ships. Eventually we were able to decipher it."

"What did it say?" I ask.

"It was very mysterious for they wrote about us attacking them."

"There must be records somewhere," I state.

Lylillea shakes her head. "We do not even know how the Tarkadians communicate." We turn down a small path that leads away from the beach. "We never heard their communications during the war. Even when we shot down a ship or two and dissected them, our scientists never could figure out how the things worked."

The path narrows. We can no longer walk side-by-side. With Grandmother in the lead and Takoda following, we continue our discussion.

"If we are all from different parts of the universe or from different universes, what would make anyone believe that any of our inventions would be the same? It is only common sense that our technology would be different and maybe even based on different principles of physics," Takoda says.

"We may not look the same," I say. "But we all think, breathe and live. Take our two worlds, Earth and Traveler, we are almost the same."

"Yes," Grandmother adds, stopping to look at me. "We share a common ancestor and our science centers around the same basic principles. Even though all three of our planets lost their technology after the great Draconian war, the basic principles were still there for us to rediscover." What she says is starting to make sense, and at the same time, what she explains bothers me.

"How do you know so much about all this?" I ask.

"I worked in central intelligence for many years before we were exiled. I was one of the scientists who dissected an ancient Draconian ship."

"Draconian?" I ask. "I thought you knew nothing about them."

"We do not." She laughs. "We could not reverse engineer it. Come. It is just a little farther."

"How did you ever get your hands on a Draconian ship?" I ask.

"I am not sure where it came from," Grandmother replied. "I worked on one Draconian and two Tarkadian ships. The technology between the two were very different. Those two races simply cannot be related."

"The Draconians came from inside the Fornax galaxy and the Tarkadians are found only in the next solar system, correct?" I ask.

"You have been studying," she says, nodding. "We never visited the Tarkadian world, for we cannot communicate with them. We also do not know of their heritage or culture."

We walk a little farther before she stops and studies the ground.

"It is here somewhere." She pushes the fallen leaves with her foot. The forest is thick with large and small boulders scattered throughout the trees. "Here it is!"

Lylillea disappears into the ground. Someone had carved steps into the stone. The stairs are steep and look treacherous. Water drips from the walls.

"I found this place while walking," Lylillea explains. "Each time, I explored a little more."

We finally reach the bottom and water covers my ankles. I can hear dripping all around me. We follow my grandmother down a tunnel that's no wider than I am. Being in such tight quarters makes the trek seem a lot longer than it really is. Eventually we enter a large cave. It's so big that our light does not reach the other side. A rock pedestal, about waist-high, stands alone in the middle of the room.

"A shrine?" Takoda asks, examining the carvings that are on the sides.

"Not sure what this is." Lylillea stands with her arms crossed and watches as Takoda examines the inscriptions. "Can you read it?"

"I do not believe so," he answers as he rubs his hands over the carvings. "It is written in an old dialect."

"It is that old?" she asks.

"I wish you would answer my question, Grandmother," I say. "How old are you in Earth years?"

"Let me think for moment … I believe that the last time I was on your planet was before the great flood." She says it so nonchalantly that it stuns me.

"Before the *great flood*. You mean Moses?" I almost scream out.

"I do not know who Moses is." She winks.

"Oh my," I say, standing near Takoda. "Then how did you go on Trial with my grandfather. He is much younger than you."

"On Trial you may go with whoever you wish," she replies. "Chawanna wanted me to go with him. I spent many years on Earth and other worlds before I even met Chawanna. Living a long life does have its advantages. When I met your grandfather, I enjoyed his company so much that … well, let us just say that one thing led to another and … here we are!"

"Journey, shine your light down here, please," Takoda asks, interrupting my thoughts.

"Sure, where?"

"Here." He reaches for my hand.

"Like this?"

He pushes on a rock that slides easily into the pedestal. Immediately the room lights and we cover our eyes. The room is not a cave after all.

"What is this place?" I ask.

"It is not a place," Lylillea answers. "It is a craft!"

"You mean a spaceship?"

"That is exactly what she means," Takoda answers for her.

"Is it one of ours or theirs?"

"It has to be one of ours," Lylillea replies. "Its writings are in the ancient language."

"Maybe," Takoda adds, as he examines one of the walls. "Here."

He pushes on something and consoles appear out of thin air.

"Will you quit pushing on things?" I run over to Takoda. "What did you do?"

"I am not sure," he answers.

Lylillea studies one of the consoles and pushes another button. A huge hanging screen appears. "A virtual computer!"

"Virtual, as in?" I ask.

"Virtual as in not really being there," she replies.

"Takoda, stand by that console over there and Journey, you stand over here."

"I don't really know what I'm doing," I shout out.

Grandmother runs her hands over the flat keyboard of flashing lights and things spring to life.

"Do you know what you're doing?" I ask.

"No," she says, laughing.

Takoda plays with his board and a three-dimensional display of a universe comes to life right in the middle of the room. He hits a few more buttons and the air starts to flow.

"Okay now," I yell. "Would you two quit pushing buttons before we end up on another planet or something?"

Takoda runs over to my console as the wall to my left disappears. The huge and terrifying sea is only inches away. It is being held back by just air or a force field or magic. My internal alarm sounds and I'm ready to run.

"Would you two stop!" I scream, wondering when the water will splash into the room.

"We must be under the ocean!" Lylillea walks toward the screen.

"Don't touch it!" I yell. "You'll drown us."

Lylillea reaches for my hand. "Journey, this water is not going anywhere. It is just a screen showing us what is on the other side. No water will get in here. We are sealed in."

"Obviously," I say, "someone left this craft here for a reason, and maybe that reason is because it's broken! So quit pushing the dag-gone buttons."

My internal alarm is at its breaking point, and I'm about to explode. Takoda reacts to how I'm feeling and comes to my side. He puts his arms around me and kisses my forehead.

"It will be fine, Journey. This craft is too old to go anywhere. It is only strong enough to protect us from the water."

A woman's voice echoes through the room and an alarm sounds. I almost jump into Takoda's arms.

"What's that?" I scream out. "What's happening?"

Lylillea runs to our side. We stand together like a bunch of idiots, shaking. Then as fast as everything started up, all falls silent, and the room blackens.

Takoda laughs. "There was probably not enough energy to sustain the ship. That voice is a warning that the ship was about to shut down."

"Thank goodness," I gasp, as everything quiets. I turn to Takoda and as hard as I can, I slap him on the arm. "Don't you *ever* do that again! You could have gotten us killed, or worse, stuck out in space somewhere."

Takoda takes me in his arms and pats me on the back. "It will be okay, Journey. It will be okay."

"That was fun," Lylillea says, turning on her flashlight.

"Where do you think this craft is from?" Takoda asks.

"It could be one of our ships from the Tarkadian war," she suggests. "I do not recognize the configuration and it is much more advanced than ..." Lylillea freezes and her eyes widen. "I know what this is."

"What?" I ask from inside Takoda's arms.

"Oh no," she says. "We must leave, now!"

"Why, where are we?" I ask.

"Hurry and follow me!" she yells.

We run through the water-filled hallway and climb back up the stairs. My legs burn and my heart pounds. We reach the top and continue running until we are safely on the beach.

"Mind telling me what we're running from?" I lean over and pant.

Her eyes are still wide and she looks like she had just seen a ghost. "That craft is one of the original ships that brought the people to this galaxy!" She gasps again and her tears fall.

"Gaia's ship? So what if we found it. Wouldn't that be a good thing?" I ask.

"It could not be Gaia's ship," Takoda whispers. "That would make it many generations old. Older than the *City of the Wicked Lady*."

"Why are we whispering?" I ask. "Will someone please tell me what's going on?"

"Journey," Takoda says, softly. "Gaia's ship was never recovered. There is no record of what happened to it. Our scientists searched the planets and moons for generations for that ship."

"Legend says it houses the body of Gaia herself," Grandmother whispers.

"Along with all the hidden records of her trip and where our home world is — was," Takoda adds.

"You mean ... my great, great ..." I sigh as I'm too tired to place my ancestors in the correct order. "My many-great grandmother is supposed to be inside that thing?" I don't understand what is happening and why they're so concerned about it. "I didn't see a body down there. Are you trying to tell me that no one knows what galaxy Gaia's home world was located in? What solar system?"

"The location has always been a secret," Lylillea explains. "The Elders were afraid people would want to go back."

"So what? What's the harm of trying to go home?"

Finding an ancient artifact as important as the original ship of the Captain's should be a wonderful discovery. However, they're treating our find as a curse.

"If we were to go back, we would risk running into the Draconians," Takoda replies.

"You don't know that," I argue. "And you can't live your life in constant fear."

"You do not understand, Journey," he explains, taking my hand. "The Draconians would annihilate us."

The water is only a few feet away. I take advantage of it. It's unnerving to know that just beneath me rests a huge craft that could be one of the greatest finds for these people — or be the cause of their extinction.

"How did you walk through that place and never realize what it was?" I ask.

"I honestly did not know," she replies.

"This is very weird and scary," I say, staring at her.

"We need to go," Grandmother says, taking my hand. "Promise me, Journey, you will never go inside that ship, and neither of you will speak of this to anyone. Just forget what we found."

"I can't promise you that, Grandmother," I say softly. "But I'll think about it."

30

THE PREMONITION

TAKODA'S BY my side and we're holding hands. We watch the large transport as it passes silently above our heads. The moon, Makayah, is directly over us now.

"Where do we go from here, Journey?" Takoda asks.

The baby kicks inside me and I smile as I rub my belly. Shaking my head, I whisper, "I don't know."

"You are my world, Journey," he whispers. "Wherever you go, I will follow." I lean back and enjoy his essence. "I know of one place we will be going," he laughs.

"Yeah, classes," I say, with a sigh.

I stare out at the horizon and think of my Aunt Deborah in Carolina, and all the things I've done since finding my new home. I remember my great grandmother at the Ancient City, and my grandparents' house on our moon, Makayah. The warmth from Takoda's embrace fills me with love. Even though I will face hardships, death and family drama, I'd never choose any other place than where I am right now.

"Takoda!" Freya yells from just around the bend. "You have to come back for dinner."

"Journey," Makayah hollers. "Mom and Dad said you have to come home now!"

Takoda kisses me and I melt into his embrace for I am truly home. I'm where I should be. Takoda takes my hand and we meet up with the girls. The crickets chirp and the ferns tower above my head. The afternoon sun no longer penetrates through the thick canopy. Even in the darkness, I feel safe because I'm with Takoda. The man I share my inner being with and the man I give all my love to. As we near the lake, the ground rumbles.

"What's going on?" Makayah asks. Her face looks the same as when our father first came to pick us up.

"Journey!" my father screams from the cabin.

"Quickly!" Abeytu runs toward us as we emerge from the forest. He's yelling and waving his arms but the rumbling is so loud I can't hear him.

"What is going on?" Takoda asks.

We watch his father runs hysterically from the cabin. "It is the Tarkadians! They have broken through our defenses." He is yelling and running in circles.

I scream as a ray of bright light cuts through the lake and heads straight for us. "No!"

"Journey!" Takoda's shaking me. "Journey, wake up, you are dreaming."

"No!" I scream again. "Makayah!"

"Journey, sweetheart," he says a little more sternly this time. "Wake up! You are having a nightmare."

I open my eyes expecting to see total destruction. Instead, I gaze into Takoda's eyes.

"Morning," he says, kissing my forehead.

"Where are we? The baby!" I grab myself and instead of a huge bump, I touch a flattened stomach.

"What baby?" My grandmother stands at our door staring at me. "Is everything okay in here?"

"We are fine," Takoda replies. "Journey had a bad dream."

"Are we still at my grandparents'?" I whisper.

"Yes."

"That was terrible," I state, sitting up. "I dreamt the Tarkadians attacked us. It was awful."

"It was only a dream," he says, rubbing my back. "Our mirrors will let us know if they try anything."

"Of course," I reply not fully convinced. "It was *so* real."

"Your grandmother said it is time to eat," my grandfather states from the hall.

We sit to another wonderful breakfast, but my nerves are still frayed. I can't get that terrible dream out of my mind.

"What is next?" Grandmother asks.

"We have a class starting in a few dzanas," Takoda replies. "We must return home tomorrow."

"When we start our regular classes, we have no Trials correct?" I ask.

"No Trials," he says, drinking his fruit drink. "We do have Skopocit."

"Skopocit?" I ask, glancing at him.

"It is the term for when we learn about our spiritual selves," he replies.

"I remember our Skopocit," Lylillea says, smiling at her husband. "Do you, Chawanna?"

"Oh yes, of course," he mumbles.

"And where do we go for our Skopocit?" I ask.

"We go to the northern city," Takoda answers. "Or to one of the moons or another solar system. There are many options."

"The northern city with the factories?" I ask not liking the sound of it.

"That would be the one," he replies.

"You've got to be kidding!" I exclaim. "People are murdered there. And isn't that where the criminals live?"

"Yes," he answers.

"Do not worry, dear," Grandmother says. "We survived and so will you."

31
HOME

THE FERRYBOAT ride to the space station gives me time to reflect on everything that's happened. I'm sad to leave my grandparents but happy to have had our special time together. Something deep inside me knows that I will probably never see them alive again. I'm not sure why, I just have this feeling. After many hugs and kisses, Takoda and I left with many unanswered questions.

Leaning against the railing, I watch as the whale-things play in the water. Large birds soar overhead. I stare into the water and the reflection of the sky echoes back my true feelings. I allow my mind to wander and my heart breaks. Memories of my mother, Rachael, flood my soul. I miss her so much. She'll always be a part of me. When she died, a little piece of me died too. Because of her, I have the courage to do what I know I must do. I wish she were here to tell me that I will succeed.

When I reached out to the person in the mirror this morning, she reached back. Understanding that she is me, I have to rely on myself more. We still don't know who's trying to kill us or why, but we will be better prepared the next time we run into them.

I have so many questions that I guess I'll be busy trying to answer them. At least I know the basics. I know that millions of years ago, my ancestors ran from a warrior race. They settled in this galaxy and in the Milky Way. I know that we fought a war against the Tarkadians, and that they remain a threat. I must accept who my parents are and the fact that I'm related to a group of mad scientists.

I'm an Elder and one day I will have a place on the Council. In my heart, I'm in love with Takoda. Most importantly, the number one thing that remains heavy on my mind, is my people — my people who live in suppression.

What is the truth? I don't know but I will seek it until the end of my days. Where I will find it is anyone's guess.

Takoda takes my hand and kisses it. We smile at each other. As I watch the rise and fall of the ocean, several large ships soar along the horizon. They do not look familiar. Takoda sees them too and tightens his grip on my hand. We watch as the ships speed through the air before sharply diving into the water.

"What ships do we have that go under water like that?" I ask.

"None that I know of," Takoda replies.

"Do you recognize them?"

"No," he says. "I do not."

"Tarkadians?"

"I pray to the Most Holy they are not," he says as he kisses my fingers.

Without a cloud in sight, the skies are clear and a bright blue. Holding hands, Takoda and I depart the slender, silver hover train. With my head resting against his shoulder, I immerse myself in our love. I can no longer imagine my life without him. I often remind myself that just an Earth year ago, my life was different. How can life change so much within such a short amount of time?

The rolling hills surrounding our school reflect various shades of green, yellow and red. The castle-like buildings that I adore snuggle between the snow-covered mountains. For some reason, I always expect a brave knight on a shiny black horse to gallop across the lawn. Of course, he never does for that would be an 'Earth thing.'

Takoda kisses my forehead and we start our long walk to the administration building. Beneath the blooming pink trees, I smile. I'm happy.

The gym, located on the second floor, is our destination. As we enter through the wooden doors, my heart pounds. Inside the massive lobby, vines that drape from the ceiling gather together inside the water-gardens. As always, I hold my breath. Several birds soar just over our heads and we laugh.

"I like this building the best." I say as Takoda squeezes my hand. "It's just so . . . alive."

The gym takes up the whole-second floor. The reflection from the Olympic-size pool dances across the beamed ceiling. From somewhere, the sound of balls bouncing against a wooden floor echoes down the hallway. With a renewed burst of energy, I'm suddenly eager to get started. Takoda touches my forehead with his sweet lips.

"Meet you inside," he whispers.

Today is day one of our self-defense class. Wanting to be comfortable, I wore my dark blue sweats and worn-out tennis shoes. These shoes will forever have a special place in my heart. They stood by me during our Trials last season and never once gave even a hint of surrendering. Besides, they came with me from Earth. Therefore, I can never get rid of 'em.

Stuffing everything into an empty locker, I place my thumb over the scanner. A soft click tells me it's locked. Entering the gym, I swing a water bottle and small towel. I can't help but smile when I see Takoda. He's staring at me. But something is wrong. Why doesn't he look happy?

Skipping several steps toward him, I jump to regain my balance. I must have tripped over someone nearby. As the floor rushes toward me, a strong hand grabs hold — Takoda. Turning to apologize for hurting whoever I tripped over, my heart skips when I see the familiar evil grin.

Anneeta, wearing a slinky and dark-red, skin-tight workout suit seems way too happy to see me. With her hair pulled back into a ponytail, her drapings click against her slender and sexy body. My shock must be easy to read because she's proudly displaying her evil smile of self-gratification. *How could she possibly know we'd be here?* This is no accident.

"Are you okay?" Takoda asks, handing me my water and towel that I had dropped.

"How'd she know we'd be here?" I whisper.

Glaring at her, he replies, "Class rosters are not private."

That explains it. Except … why would she want to take this particular class with us? Although, Anneeta does seem to possess the talent of making our lives miserable. Will she ever leave us alone? There has to be some way to get rid of her. But how?

"Good morning class, I'm Professor Mylee." A tall, slender-built Swetaachata counts heads with her finger as she enters. Her mannerism intrigues me. I'm fascinated by her shiny black hair. Does she dye it? Most Swetaachata's have red or brown hair, not black. "I am your instructor. Before we start, may I have a moment to gather your names?"

Not wanting to think about Anneeta, I glance around the room. The walls are mostly mirrored except on one side where a row of boxing bags swing from chains. The floor's inlaid with strips of a lightwood and the ceiling reminds me of concrete. Along a far back wall, a stack of thick black mats sits one on top of the other.

As Professor Mylee's voice echoes through the room, other students slowly raise their hands. No one says a word. In this school, when your name is called, you reply by raising your hand not by yelling out a *here* or *present*. I discovered the hand raising last term when I was the only one who yelled out, embarrassing.

Today, two students are absent. Sitting her tablet on a bench, Professor Mylee turns and states, "If you would please make several rows, arm's length apart, we'll get started."

As everyone claims a spot, Takoda and I aim for the back. We like the idea of having Anneeta in front of us. It's my turn to burn a hole in the back of her head for a change.

The class starts with a basic exercise before switching to punching and kicking. Once we're good and sweaty, she orders us to pair up. Standing next to a hanging bag, Anneeta teams with a blonde human boy. He seems surprised that she picked him. I giggle. His smile says it all, and he can't keep his eyes off her. Anneeta's sparkling red outfit is so skin-tight that she must have painted it on, instead of pulling it on.

Not wanting the class to end, I keep glancing at the clock. I have no desire to be alone in the locker room with Anneeta. You'd think after the way I knocked her and her two friends out several months ago, she'd be just a little afraid. As usual, I can sense her hatred for me from across the room.

The professor's giving one-on-one to each pair of students. By the time she reaches us, class is over. What a lucky break. Maybe I can dodge Anneeta after all.

"Do you mind staying a little longer?" she asks.

"We'd love to." I yell out. Feeling stupid for being loud, I glance away.

By the time I enter the locker room, it's empty. Just the way I like it. I change, stuff my sweats into my bag and hurry to meet Takoda.

"Not in there?" he asks, taking my bag from me.

"I lucked out." I laugh. "Where's the library?"

"On the fourth floor. Do you wish to go there now?"

"Yes, please. We still need to figure out how to play those discs, and I want to find something about the Council."

"I have been working on the disc issue. Have not had much luck."

"We may have to re-visit the 3-D guy." I push the button for the fourth floor. "Long way to go to read a disc. Just that I have a funny feeling there's something important on 'em."

Takoda nods. "I agree. Why else would someone take such a chance to sneak them into our packs?"

Cooler air greets us as we step from the elevator. "Exactly what I was thinking. And I want to know who gave 'em to us."

The elevator opened directly into the library's lobby. I'd never been in here before. The room reminds me of a gothic cathedral back on Earth. The pointed windows, filled with colorful stained glass, grab my attention. They're huge — floor to ceiling. Dark elaborately carved wood is splattered everywhere. The ceiling's beautiful with an amazing kaleidoscope of colors and geometric designs. Although I've yet to find any religious symbols on this planet, the ornate decorations still remind me of an old church. People on this world think of religion and God as a personal experience. Not a thing that's displayed in pictures or carvings. The art on this planet is for decoration only and nothing more.

"Wow." The setting amazes me.

Takoda snickers. "Do not worry. After a while, this place will not impress you as much."

"Then I hope I never get used to it."

A large round desk with a small glass lamp and a rather older-looking Earth woman sits precariously in the middle of the foyer. Must be the reference desk.

"Peace be with you," I say, as the woman glances up with a frown.

A small, forced smile lightens her face — a little. "And be with you." She pauses before adding, "May I help you?"

"Yes, please." She's obviously aggravated. Probably by the interruptions of arrogant students. My Aunt Deborah's favorite saying echoes through my mind … 'you can catch more flies with honey than you can with vinegar.' So using Aunt Deborah's philosophy, I smile and explain what we need. "I'm from Earth, so

I'm not sure how the books are arranged. We need information on the Council of Elders, and any information about Earth and its relationship to the Council would be helpful." She stares at us, so I add. "It's for a class."

The woman studies us before answering. "Our books are filed the same as on Earth. I visited libraries there once. Books are by subject and then by author and title. Sections C-14 thru C-24 are on the Council. All along that back wall." She nods toward the area. "To your left."

"Thank you." I bow to the right. Nodding comes naturally to me now and it seems impolite to speak without using it. At first, it was difficult. I now have no problem adding a little nod at the end of my sentences.

Takoda and I easily find section C-14. A book titled, *Elders in Crisis*, by Andrew J. Brookstone looks interesting. I pull it off the shelf. As I flip through the pages, Takoda shoves a book back.

"Most of our writers are from Earth," he says. "There are a couple of Swetaachata authors that are quite good." He flips through the pages of a small green book.

"I enjoyed my reading assignments in Swetaachata Literature last term. The professor did a great job explaining what the authors were trying to portray." I set aside a book that looks promising. "It was a difficult class. I had to learn about your culture before the stories made any sense. It was hard to relate to the hidden meanings sometimes."

Takoda's eyes lite. "How about this one?" He hands me a book.

The novel's written by a human, Jonathan Pentier and titled, *The Secret World of the Ancient Elders*. In the middle of the book, color photos of the original council members with their families stare back at me. The names are listed in chronological order from Gaia and her two daughters, Rhea and Hera, and end with my grandmother and grandfather's marriage. My mother's name isn't listed in the index. Must have been published before her birth.

"This looks promising." I scan through the pictures. "This is too much. Look, here's a picture of my grandmother and grandfather." The pictures are a little faded but otherwise good for being old. However, this couple looks young. "Isn't it odd how my grandmother looks the same today? Oh my, and Chawanna's very handsome. I now see what she saw in him. Yah know what, Takoda? Makayah resembles him."

"Remember, Journey, we calculate age differently than what your used to. We do not count the number of times we revolve around our sun. If we did, we would forever be young."

"Remind me, again. How long does it take for this world to go all the way around?" When my father explained it a few months ago, I was so excited about just being here that I forgot to pay attention.

"We have two suns." He winks. "Our planets circle the center one. The smaller sun is much farther out. That is why we do not see both at the same time. When they do share the same side of our solar system, we never experience darkness. It takes our worlds about twenty of your Earth's years to complete one cycle."

"That long?"

"Journey, we are much farther away from our sun than Earth is from its sun. Our sun is so large, that if we were any closer, we would burn from the intense heat and radiation. This planet is farther out than Neptune is in your system."

"I just can't grasp the size sometimes."

"Our sun is much older than Earth's, and our second sun is farther out than the planet Pluto. Any closer and we would have problems."

I laugh. "I thought our orbit was only twice as long as Earth's. I definitely wasn't paying attention when Dad explained. Wait, what kind of problems?"

"In a solar system, if the second sun is on an elliptical orbit, coming in close then slinging back out, it can push planets out of their orbits. Never a good thing."

"Ah, no. I'd say that's not a good thing. What about this book?"

I hand an old volume to Takoda. Rhea and Hera's slender bodies are on the cover. In full uniform, they look proud holding a staff in their right hands. It's written in a language I don't recognize. The picture reminds me of a portrait I once saw in the Council of Elder's building on Journey. Chills run up my spine as my mind wanders.

"This is written by a Swetaachata woman and not in our native language. I will take it home and see if there is anything of value in it. If I can even decipher it."

We pick out a few more books. Before leaving, we talk with the librarian a little. She seems happier to see us this time and even claimed to enjoy our visit. Maybe other students are rude to her.

We do not see Anneeta again, which is just fine with me. The less I see of her, the better off I am. I don't understand her deep hatred for me. Her relationship with Takoda ended way before I ever met him. I had nothing to do with their love-hate relationship. Besides, it's her fault. She's the one with the bad attitude. As Takoda said, she's not beautiful on the inside and that's what matters most. I could totally accept if she just didn't like me as a person. But her deep hatred goes far beyond anything I've ever experienced. There has to be something I can do to fix it, other than ask Takoda to go back with her, which of course will never happen.

On the train ride home, we skim through our library books. As usual, I'm the one to break the silence with a stupid question. "Takoda?"

"Yes?"

"What do you call the library here?"

"We called it a librarium." He doesn't remove his eyes from his book.

"And you call the books, what?" I ask, holding one up.

Still not looking at me, he replies, "Libraria."

Scratching my head, I giggle. "I may be wrong, but a lot of your words sound Latin."

"Latin? Yes, I believe you are correct. Latin is a major part of the ancient Saxonion language." He puts his book down. "Our ancestors are called Fornaxians. They came from somewhere outside the Fornax galaxies. We have no proof of course, but our scientists have a theory. They believe our people originated from somewhere in the Saxonian galaxy. It is just an ancient rumor but interesting. You should ask Abeytu. After all, he is a Celestial Engineer, or what you would call an Astrologist."

"He said he's my father's research assistant. I'm still not sure how much I trust him."

"His statement is not incorrect." Takoda glances up and smiles. "He does conduct research. Just that he researches the universe. I am not sure about his current project, but he does extensive research for the Council of Deep Space Observatory."

"We have a council for everything around here, don't we?" I shake my head.

"There are many. We have the Council of Elders that rule over all the other councils; then there is the Council of Salus, Council of Health. We have a Council of Centuries and a Council of Tribes and that is about as far as my council knowledge goes without my notes. Abeytu can explain more. I try not to get involved in Ordinatio or what you call Government."

"Holy ancient Roman, everything is coming up Latin!"

"Ever thought that maybe our languages and heritage come from the same ancient civilization? Maybe Saxonion is the original root language. Maybe even an earlier civilization from where that one comes from. Languages and cultures change and evolve through the generations."

"Or years?" I laugh.

We load up my jeep with our books and packs. My turn to drive. Takoda believes it's important for me to be familiar with our roads. Just in case I need to go somewhere alone, which I hardly ever do. Ever since Takoda's abduction, tracking devices inside our abdomens allows our parents to keep tab on us. Thank goodness, the procedure was quick and painless. I woke with just a little scar about a half inch above my belly button.

Since it's almost lunchtime, we stop by Takoda's cabin and pack a small bag before heading to the ruins — our favorite place to be. Every spare afternoon, we are there, exploring. Over the last several months, we've mapped out almost the entire area. Takoda thought it was once somebody's home. But, after a lot of research and exploration, we discovered that the ruins were actually a small ancient community. Although, we have no idea who built it. With our blanket spread out on the grass as usual, we lie on our backs and study the clouds.

"Oh, before I forget," he says, pulling out his tablet. "With everything that's happened, I forgot to give you your DNA results."

"I forgot all about that." I scoot over to see the report better.

"Your father is your father and Chawlya is your mother. Nothing out of the ordinary there, but ..."

"But what?" My internal warning system blares.

"Your sister."

I don't like his expression. He seems worried. "What about my sister?"

"She is from your mother, but her DNA does not completely match your father's."

"What? She looks just like him, how could she not be?"

"I did not say she was not his, her DNA is just different."

"Different? How?"

"My dad is still working on that. I did some research on your father." Takoda grabs my hand. I hate it when he does that. It means he's trying to console me just before he upsets me. "What do you know about your relatives from Earth?"

"On my dad's side? I know very little. Never really thought to ask about them. Seen some pictures, but I thought they were all dead. He never talks about 'em."

"Then this should be fun ... ready?"

"I hope so."

"George, your dad, was born on Earth … and his Earth name is Gahege … which means Chief."

"Chief?" Now, I'm confused. "Chief … you mean as a Native American? Then where did the name George come from?"

Takoda stares at me before continuing. "His mother … your grandmother … was from Chicago. Her name is Cecilia … Cecilia Aryee Plantaino. Her family was from some place called Italy."

"Italy's a country." Takoda looks confused so I explain. "We have different countries that have many different cities. Each country is ruled by a different Government … lots of differences on Earth."

"Confusing," he says, as he continues reading from his tablet. "Cecilia met George's father, your grandfather, while at college and his name is Kachada. Kachada means … White Man … ironic because he married a white woman."

"My dad changed his name from Gahege to George?" My father is so proud he can't bring himself to using his birth name? He just had to change it to George?

"He now goes by, George K. Gordon. Perhaps the K is for his father's first name … Kachada. Gahege almost sounds like George."

I pull a drink from the lunch sack and twist off the top. My head is reeling with unanswered questions. My father's part Native American and he never said a word about it. Then why would he if he's ashamed?

"Do you think they're still alive?"

"Who?"

"My father's parents."

"Have no idea." Takoda pulls a drink from the sack.

"What do you know about my great grandmother … George's mom's mom."

"Here's the full lineage. You can read it later. It is your grandfather's lineage that's interesting. It seems your father is a direct descendent of Tawa, the great Hopi Sun Sprit. He would be your father's great, great, great grandfather. In the writings, his name was Masauwa, but he was also known as … Skeleton Man." Takoda raises his brow and growls. "He was considered the Spirit of Death."

"Great, I have the Grim Reaper in my family tree. Who else, Satan?"

Takoda ignores me and continues. "Masauwa is listed as an Earth God and he was the door keeper to the Fifth World or the Keeper of Fire."

"Sounds like the Devil to me. Not a very flattering title. Only in my family … Fifth World … really? What happened to the other four?"

"What is really strange," Takoda gives me a funny grin, "is that this Masauwa wore a mask to hide his face. He was either very handsome or a bloody fearsome creature because no one ever saw him without his mask."

"I'll pray for the handsome. I need something positive right now. So, who were my ancestors on this weird masked-man's side?"

"Let me see, what else." Takoda scans through his tablet before continuing. "Kachada's parents, your dad's grandparents, were Aponivi and AHOTEb. Aponivi means Where the Wind Blows and she was beautiful, look …"

Takoda shows me a picture of a woman dressed in formal tribal attire. Her hair is a deep black, wavy and long. Her dark skin seems to radiate in the sunlight. My skin tingles just knowing I'm related to her.

"Great Grandmother Aponivi was beautiful. Makayah has her eyes! They're shaped exactly the same. Too bad I can't see the true color."

"She was unioned … I mean married to AHOTEb. AHOTEb means Restless One. He would go on long exploratory missions for masikas at a time."

"Sounds like us," I add.

"His parents were Mongwau and Qaletaqa. It says that Mongwau was a strong woman and ruled the tribe after her husband's death. Her name means Owl and Qaletaqa means Guardian of the People. He was a strong ruler and fought hard for his tribe. He died protecting them."

"Native Americans were exploited by our Government for years. Almost everyone was mean to them, and a lot of people died because of prejudices."

"Same here with our Council of Elders." Takoda shows me a black and white photo of Mongwau and Qaletaqa. "They look like proud people."

"They do," I say with a frown. "It's a shame how people treat each other. Always wanting to kill … to do harm."

"It is sad." He rubs the back of my hand.

"If you can't kill 'em, you ruin their life by taking their land or their only means of support. It seems that people have a need to feel more important than others."

"Maybe it is just something that is innate to humans," Takoda suggests. "People seem to be the same on both our worlds. We know that you share ancestors from the humans here. The 3-D man said that two ships had arrived. That one of those ships continued on to Earth. You are therefore from Qapadhue. And you share a home world deep in the Saxonion galaxy."

"We're living in the Fornax galaxy now, right?"

Takoda pulls up a star chart. "This group of stars is the Fornax cluster. See this larger star here?" He points to a round white ball near the edge. "That is our sun … our center sun. That small dot is our second sun. Your home world, Qapadhue, would be way out there somewhere. We have over fifty-eight galaxies in our Fornax system."

"Fifty-eight?" I repeat. "With fifty-eight there could be millions of stars, which could mean billions of planets."

"It does," Takoda adds. "Look at this."

"Beautiful." I stare at the white and yellow cloud that's loaded with shinning stars.

"This is how our star clusters look from Earth."

"Cool. So how does my galaxy look from here?"

After he taps on the screen, I stare at a large spiral galaxy with a bluish-white ball in the middle. "I think my galaxy is prettier than yours."

"Ours is a mass of different smaller galaxies where yours is one big one. The Milky Way *is* a very beautiful place, Journey."

"I was only joking." I cringe knowing I've just insulted him.

Takoda rubs my cheek. I take his hand and caress his fingers. He drops the tablet and takes me into his arms. We kiss with such longing that for a moment I think we're in trouble. When he releases me, I lean into his embrace staring into nothing.

"I love you, Journey."

"And I, you."

Standing under the cool shower, I take a deep breath. Our instructor gave us an extra heavy workout this morning. I call the class *kickboxing*, while others call it Self-Defense. The official name is Survival 1101-A42. A tiny Swetaachata girl nicknamed the class, *Torture 101*. Professor Mylee is sweet, but at the same time, she's someone you would not want as an enemy. Although slender and beautiful, her fighting moves are quite impressive. Throughout the class, I take meticulous mental notes. Anneeta never showed again after that first day, which only strengthens my argument that she just wants to cause trouble. The human boy, who has obviously fallen madly in love with her, asks every day if anyone knows what happened to her. Personally, I don't care as long as she isn't there.

After class, I sit with Takoda as we eat and talk with friends. The morning sun passes slowly overhead, and we enjoy our precious time together. A sparkle from the far side of the valley announces that it's almost time to catch our train for home. The friendly debate over who's really in charge of the Council of Elders continues as we stroll down the path that runs between the shade trees. Far off in the distance, deer-like creatures graze peacefully on the tall foliage. I giggle when thousands of colorful butterflies cross our path. Taking in a deep breath, I enjoy the aroma of the newly blossomed flowers that surrounds us. It's beautiful here and I'm happy just being with my friends.

Takoda takes my hand, which always makes me smile. I look up at him and we engulf ourselves within the love we share. It is then that the treetops explode in tall red and yellow flames. The world suddenly stops around us and all is quiet. I glance over to where the deer were just grazing and frown. The field is now empty. Before I can sort things out, Takoda scoops me into his arms. He's running under the blazing trees. I scream as the flaming leaves fall. The burning embers scorch my arms. My internal alarm never had time to sound. Too much happened too fast. Deep inside, my heart pounds. I'm too confused to be afraid and I'm too afraid to think.

Water splashes against my face as Takoda jumps into the small pond. My feet sink into the murky bottom, and I breathe in a small sigh of relief. The cool water is soothing my burnt skin. Several frightened students huddle with us in the murky water. Clean streaks from tears stain their now dirty cheeks. They're just as afraid as I am.

Why is it so darn quiet?

Takoda's mouth moves as if he's speaking. He's pointing to my arms and legs. I lean over and gasp. My arms are swollen and covered in bright pink blotches. My jeans are singed and burnt in some spots. I still cannot hear a word anyone is saying. I winch as pain prickles throughout my body. A Swetaachata girl grabs a handful of mud and spreads the slimy mixture over my burns. The pain disappears. She's saying something because I can see her lips moving. I nod.

"I do not know why but it helps." *Is she whispering?* I can barely make out what she's saying by reading her lips.

"The train!" Someone screams out. I heard it that time.

A loud screeching is coming from near the gazebo. I heard that sound too. A man is pointing toward a far mountain. He's flailing his arms around. His wide eyes show the terror he's feeling. As he lowers his head and covers his eyes, flames shoot up from the distant tree-ridden ravine.

Oh no. Did the just train explode?

The hills all around us erupt in flames and the dark smoke spreads through the sky. Patrol officers are now directing students to the shelters. They look just as frightened as the rest of us.

With the heat searing over our heads, we stand helpless in the murky water. My eyes burn as I try to see through the dense smoke. Squatting into the water to protect ourselves, a mountain ridge behind the school suddenly explodes. Rocks and hot ash crash down around us. More people scream.

"Beams!" a young man yells. "The beams have returned!" I heard his cries but just barely. It almost sounds as if I have a bucket crammed over my head.

"Run for the shelter!" Another person yells.

Takoda grabs my arm. We half walk, half crawl from the muddy water. Running away from the burning buildings, we aim to where the deer were once grazing. There's no time to talk or ask questions. Others are following us and they're just as panicky and terrified. My lungs ache with each breath. The hot ash is darkening the skies and reminding me of a volcanic explosion. However, this planet doesn't have any volcanoes.

"Quickly!" someone screams.

"Hurry!" another voice says.

"This way!" A female voice this time.

"Everyone inside!" A high-pitched male voice.

The ground hardens beneath my feet. No longer am I running on the soft grass. We're now on solid concrete.

Did we make it to safety?

As my eyes adjust to the darkness, my mind slowly clears. Then, my heart sinks. Weeping students, sitting along the walls, are seriously hurt. People wearing white smocks are tending to them the best they can. One patrol officer asks Takoda if I need any medical attention. I shake my head. The mud seems to have stopped the hot ash from doing any serious damage. I'm more worried about everyone else and for our families at home. The librarian, leaning against a wall, smiles as we make eye contact. Just a few days ago, she helped us check out some books on the council.

A Patrol officer brushes past, pulling me from my thoughts. "What's going on?" I ask.

"Beams!" he yells and points to the sky.

"The Tarkadians," I whisper, grabbing onto Takoda's arm. "The Tarkadians have returned?"

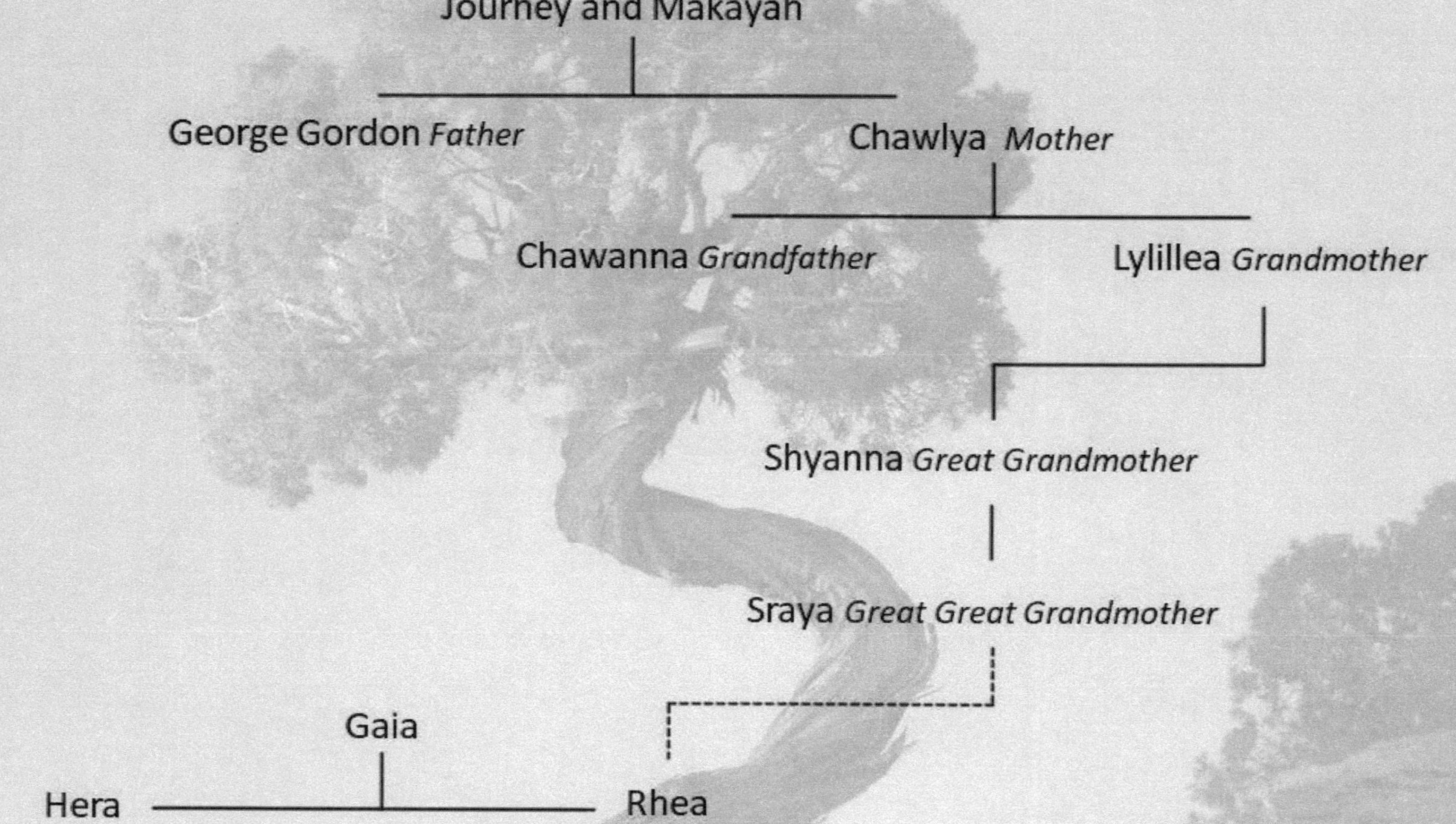

Journey and Makayah
George Gordon Father
Chawlya Mother
Chawanna Grandfather
Lylillea Grandmother
Shyanna Great Grandmother
Sraya Great Great Grandmother
Gaia
Hera
Rhea

Journey and Makayah
Chawlya *Mother*
George Gordon *Father*
Cecilia Aryee Plantaino *Grandmother*
Kachada *Grandfather / White Man*
Aponivi *Great Grandmother / Where The Wind Blows*
AHOTEb *Great Grandfather / Restless One*
Masauwu / *Skeleton Man*
Mongwau *Great Great Grandmother Mother / Owl*
Qaletaqa *Great Great Grandfather / Guardian of the People*
Tawa – *The Sun Spirit*
Unknown Lineage

Gaia
|
Rhea
|
Rheallia
Liauba
Ubeara
Reara
Syeara
Sraya
Shyanna
Lylillea
Chawlya
Journey & Makayah

Journey's lineage is long and complicated. Her ancestors govern through a matrilineal idealism, where the fathers are of no consequence and are often not included in the ancestral chart. Listed here are the mothers from Journey and Makayah up through Gaia.

Journey's travels continue . . .

MIRRORS Book 2 of Journey's Travels

Mirrors examines how history tends to repeat itself. Journey studies the past to determine the future as she helps to fight off the Tarkadians. A race with the goal of annihilation.

(Anticipated Release Summer 2021)

DIMENSIONS Book 3 of Journey's Travels

Dimensions requires Journey to dissect her soul and her reality to scrutinize the Wanderers and their heritage. As she reshapes her broken people, she must rebuild her relationship with her estranged family.

(Anticipated Release Summer 2022)

DUPLICITY Book 4 of Journey's Travels

Duplicity follows Journey and Takoda as they settle into their married life. Journey's learning how to be a good wife and mother while serving in her position for the new Council. Unfortunately, her trials and tribulations do not end there. Journey's world explodes when an intergalactic war erupts with a race that is more treacherous and evil than the Tarkadians.

(Anticipated Release Summer 2023)

CONSENSUS Book 5 of Journey's Travels

Consensus provides insight into how people recuperate after a war. When they attempt to regain power, Journey's ancestors turn Journey's first-born child against her. While investigating mysterious murders and evil sacrifices, Journey must make harsh decisions that will forever change her life and mold her soul.

(Anticipated Release Summer 2024)

Lynn Yvonne Moon is an award-winning, bestselling author whose many accolades include the prestigious *Dante Rossetti Award* and the *Independent Publisher Book Award*. She is a two-time winner of the *Moonbeam Children's Book Award* and is a five-star recipient of Reader's Favorite. Lynn resides in Virginia Beach, Virginia with her family.